INVASION!

THE Warhammer World is a grim and war-torn land, where men stand shoulder-to-shoulder against the twisted forces of Chaos, the brutal greenskins and the fearsome undead. These are dark times, of mighty heroes and foul villains, when the rivers run red with blood and the screams of men rent the air. Let the skies darken, let battle be joined – to war!

Invasion! is an exciting collection of Warhammer short stories which take the reader from the shores of Naggaroth, the Land of Chill, to the dark forests that lie at the heart of the Empire. With exclusive new stories by best-loved authors Nathan Long, Mike Lee, Steven Savile and many more, these tales will thrill and entertain.

INVASION!

Edited by Marc Gascoigne & Christian Dunn

A Black Library Publication

First published in Great Britain in 2007 by
BL Publishing,
Games Workshop Ltd.,
Willow Road, Nottingham,
NG7 2WS, UK

10 9 8 7 6 5 4 3 2 1

Cover illustration by David Gallagher.

A CIP record for this book is available from the British Library.

ISBN 13: 978 1 84416 480 6
ISBN 10: 1 84416 480 2

Distributed in the US by Simon & Schuster
1230 Avenue of the Americas, New York, NY 10020.

See the Black Library on the Internet at
www.blacklibrary.com

Find out more about Games Workshop
and the world of Warhammer at
www.games-workshop.com

CONTENTS

THIS IS A DARK age, a bloody age, an age of daemons and of sorcery. It is an age of battle and death, and of the world's ending. Amidst all of the fire, flame and fury it is a time, too, of mighty heroes, of bold deeds and great courage.

AT THE HEART of the Old World sprawls the Empire, the largest and most powerful of the human realms. Known for its engineers, sorcerers, traders and soldiers, it is a land of great mountains, mighty rivers, dark forests and vast cities. And from his throne in Altdorf reigns the Emperor Karl-Franz, sacred descendent of the founder of these lands, Sigmar, and wielder of his magical warhammer.

BUT THESE ARE far from civilised times. Across the length and breadth of the Old World, from the knightly palaces of Bretonnia to ice-bound Kislev in the far north, come rumblings of war. In the towering World's Edge Mountains, the orc tribes are gathering for another assault. Bandits and renegades harry the wild southern lands of the Border Princes. There are rumours of rat-things, the skaven, emerging from the sewers and swamps across the land. And from the northern wildernesses there is the ever-present threat of Chaos, of daemons and beastmen corrupted by the foul powers of the Dark Gods. As the time of battle draws ever near, the Empire needs heroes like never before.

NONE SO BLIND
by Nathan Long

IT HAD BEEN a great and terrible day. Great because Alith Anar stood once again on the shores of Naggaroth, his destined home, the true home of his people, the land that was, by right, his to rule, and his blood sang with the joy of it. Great because the handful of Asur and Nagarythe that had landed on the rocky beach below the Blood Cliffs – the first fighting force to reach the Witch King's domain since the beginning of the long war – had this morning won an almost impossible victory against a force four times their size. Terrible because the victory had come at a dreadful cost. Terrible because it seemed that, having come so far, they might, with their target not more than a few hours' march away, sail home again with nothing accomplished.

Alith Anar stood in the brazier-lit interior of Eltharion's tent listening to the great Swordmaster's stifled moans as an assassin's poison tore at his insides. Eltharion's blind eyes were hidden, as always, by a tied red scarf, but pain showed in every line of his face.

Belannaer, the venerable Loremaster of Hoeth, one of the greatest sorcerers of Ulthuan, knelt over the fallen hero, whispering spells of strength and healing, as elf field surgeons practised more mundane remedies.

Alith Anar knew that he and Eltharion should be grateful to Belannaer, for without his timely arrival with two companies of Lothern Sea Guard at his back, the day could have gone very differently indeed. But he could muster no love for the Loremaster, for it was he who was urging retreat when their dagger was but an inch from Malekith's throat.

'I beg you, Eltharion,' said Belannaer as he finished his incantation, 'return to Ulthuan. You are too stricken to continue.'

'Then say your spells again,' rasped Eltharion, 'for I will not leave here without facing Malekith, no matter what my strength.'

'Even knowing you cannot hope to prevail?'

'If you would aid me instead of badgering me, I might yet do so.'

Belannaer sighed and stood, looking down at the elf who had once been his student. 'I chased you from Ulthuan to dissuade you from this folly, not to aid you in it. It is too great a risk: the odds too slim, the cost too high. Already you have pushed your luck beyond reason. It amazes me that you have won this far.'

It amazed Alith Anar too, truth be told. The venture had had the whiff of noble folly about it from the beginning, when Eltharion, refused ships and support by the Phoenix King, had come to ruined Anlec and knelt before the shattered throne of Nagarythe, asking like the humblest supplicant for Alith Anar's help to strike at Malekith in the heart of his land.

Eltharion had not knelt in vain. Malekith's death was Alith Anar's most treasured dream. With Malekith dead, Naggaroth would shatter into warring shards as the

Witch King's generals slaughtered each other for the chance to sit on the barbed throne. How easy then for the true king of Naggaroth to sweep them away with his army of avenging shadows and take his rightful place on the throne. At long last would the war between Ulthuan and Naggaroth be ended, and the two families of the Asur reunited. At long last the vagabond sons of Nagarythe would be able to call some place home, and Alith Anar could allow himself to rest.

With these visions glittering before his eyes, Alith Anar had granted Eltharion's every boon: a company of Shadow Warriors to act as scouts for Eltharion's Swordmasters, a ship to carry them, and Alith Anar himself to guide them to the Witch King's doorstep.

They had sailed just before mid-summer. Alith Anar, who had slipped in and out of Naggaroth almost half as many times as the stories said he had, led them the long way around Karond Nar and through the Witch's Knives, a route he had used without detection many times before. From there they had quickly crossed the Sea of Chill, so as to avoid the druchii's shipping lanes, then hugged the east and south coasts of the Sea of Malice all the way to the Blood Cliffs, less than two days' march from Naggarond.

The first boats had grounded on the shore of the hidden cove a few hours after a moonless midnight, and within an hour all had disembarked: a hundred Hoeth Swordmasters in shining ithilmar mail, a hundred grey-cloaked Nagarythe skirmishers in cloaks like shadows. They had broken their fast on the beach, and then started single file up the narrow, winding path that scaled the sandy cliffs.

A red dawn had been bleeding over the jagged peaks of the distant Iron Mountains when the last Swordmasters topped the cliff and took their places in the order of march. But there would be no marching, for though

Alith Anar could have sworn that never in their journey had they been close enough to any druchii settlement to be observed, glinting spear tips and martial banners had emerged from the blood tinged morning mist, and hovering above them like a piece of night that refused to cede to the dawn, an enormous black dragon and its rider – Malekith.

It was the strangest battle of Alith Anar's life, for, on both sides, the threat most feared fought the least, while the most hidden threat did the most to turn the tide. On the druchii side, Malekith's dragon, which could have won the battle with one strafing breath, never attacked, only circled above, leaving Eltharion to call in vain for the Witch King to dismount and face him. On the high elves' side, Eltharion slew not one druchii. Although the grim-visaged Har Ganeth Executioners closed with Eltharion's Swordmasters, they gave the blind champion a wide berth. While all around him Swordmasters and Shadow Warriors fought Malekith's Dark Riders and his spear companies, Eltharion stood stymied in an open circle with no one to fight.

Then Eltharion fell.

Looking up from killing a Naggarond spear captain, Alith Anar saw the Swordmaster collapsing before a black-clad druchii. Anar roared and charged as the druchii raised his curved blade for the kill, then cut him down as he turned to defend himself. A dagger fell from the assassin's hand. It was crusted with black venom.

Things looked grim. Eltharion's collapse heartened the dark elves, and they redoubled their attack, pushing the raiders back to the cliff, but just as it seemed the high elves would be driven over the edge, up the winding path from the beach charged Belannaer and two hundred Lothern Sea Guards, trumpets blaring and blue and white uniforms blazing in the sun.

It was the strangest moment of a strange day, for it was impossible that the Sea Guard were there. It had taken nearly two weeks for Alith Anar's ship to travel from Ulthuan. Any ship following them would have been seen days ago, and Anar's sailors had seen nothing. Yet here they were.

The Sea Guard punched into the flank of the druchii spears and routed them, then closed with the Executioners. Malekith had had enough. The retreat was sounded and the druchii fell back. Anar shouted to his Shadows to chase them down, but the Sea Guards' trumpet called 'hold ground' and the charge faltered, allowing the druchii to withdraw. It was then that Alith Anar's relief at Belannaer's timely rescue turned to anger at his untimely interference.

It was sunset, and his anger had not subsided. It seemed Belannaer had chased them all the way from Ulthuan just to wag his finger at Eltharion!

'You have forgotten the most basic lessons of the Swordmaster's art,' Belannaer was saying. His voice quavered with exhaustion, for the explanation for the miraculous appearance of the Sea Guard was that the Loremaster had used his magic to hide the ship from mortal eyes. He had been chanting a spell of concealment unceasingly since their ship entered the Sea of Chill, and it had enervated him. 'A blow struck in anger as often strikes the attacker. You come here seeking vengeance, not tactical advantage, and you are nearly killed for it.'

'Do you say killing Malekith would not give Ulthuan an advantage?' snarled Alith Anar. 'It would be the end for the druchii.'

'If you could accomplish it,' said Belannaer, turning, 'but you cannot. Your presence is known. Your goal is known. Malekith has a thousand troops in Naggarond, and thousands more within five days' march. He rides a dragon that could turn your entire force to ash in one pass if he so wished. I know not why he has failed to strike with all his might, but while you have been given this reprieve, use it! Return to Ulthuan and use this impossible victory to win support for a real invasion. Do not waste the small advantage you have achieved by snatching futilely at the impossible.'

'No,' croaked Eltharion, struggling to sit up, 'we have achieved nothing.' He levered himself out of the cot, feebly pushing his physicians away. 'We did not sail from Ulthuan to kill a few Executioners, and I will not return until we have won a *real* advantage.' He glared at Belannaer. 'Anar's Shadows say that Malekith and his troops have fallen back to a watch tower not three hours march from here. Even if Malekith eludes me again, with the Sea Guard bolstering us, we can at least destroy the tower.'

'The Sea Guard are not yours to command,' said Belannaer, 'and I will not join you in your folly.'

Eltharion growled. 'Then I will not command them, only ask them.' He turned and lurched unsteadily through the flap of the tent.

'Brothers!' called Eltharion, his voice hoarse, as he limped into the late afternoon sun and faced the companies of Swordmasters, Sea Guard and Shadow Warriors that were making camp in the field above the cliff. 'I come before you to ask you your will.'

Belannaer and Alith Anar remained in the shadow of the Swordmaster's tent and watched as the troops stopped their labours and turned to listen.

'Belannaer has urged me to count today as a victory,' Eltharion continued, 'and to return to Ulthuan with my head high. He says that there is safety behind us, and only death before us. In this he is right. The chances of any of us surviving if we press on are slim indeed.' He coughed and drew a ragged breath, then lifted his blind eyes again. 'But what of your wives and daughters and sons in Ulthuan? Will they be safe if we choose safety? No! They will be dead unless we choose death! If we return home, if we save ourselves and leave him alive, Malekith will come again, as certain as winter, and we will fight this battle on our own shores.' He spread his arms. 'Sons of Nagarythe, do you wish to see your lands laid waste again? Your women at the mercy of your savage cousins? Brothers of Hoeth, do you relish defending fair Saphery from Morathi's hags? Do you wish to see your kin poisoned in mind and spirit? Elves of Lothern, will you wait until the Cursed One again knocks upon the Phoenix Gate before you take up arms against him?'

A rousing chorus of 'no' rose from the ranks, and Alith Anar smiled. Who would have thought the dour Swordmaster such a fine speechmaker? Belannaer's knuckles were white on his gilded staff. He looked as if he wanted to hit Eltharion over the head with it.

'Or will you follow me now! Here!' cried Eltharion, his voice cracking with strain. 'And strike down the Witch King on his very doorstep, where only our lives are at stake?'

The elf troops thrust their swords and spears in the air and roared their approval, the Sea Guard of Lothern loudest of all.

Eltharion turned to Belannaer with a crooked smile. 'You may give your orders now, Loremaster.'

ALITH ANAR SHOULD have been with his skirmishers, starting the attack by setting fire to druchii tents and raining arrows on their occupants as they ran out to escape the flames. But he wanted to see Malekith die, so he had joined Eltharion in the second wave, charging into the burning camp and chopping down unprepared druchii right and left. While the Swordmasters and the Sea Guard pressed their enemies back on all sides, Eltharion and

Alith Anar, and a handful of picked Hoethi made directly
for Malekith's tent. The only signs that the assassin's poison still flowed through the blind champion's veins were
his clenched teeth and an occasional angry hiss.

Belannaer ran with them, cursing as he fought.
Though he had been furious with Eltharion for under-
mining his authority with the Sea Guard, and had
wanted nothing further to do with the raid, in the end he
had decided that he could not abandon his troops, even
to folly.

Through the smoke, Alith Anar could hear druchii captains calling to their troops to form up. Horns blew ragged
rallies. To his left, two Executioners fought back to back in
a ring of Lothern spears. To his right, a druchii general fired
a repeating crossbow at a Swordmaster. The angry roar of
Malekith's dragon could be heard somewhere ahead of
them. Anar cut down a druchii with a spear and leapt his
corpse, trying to stay abreast of Eltharion, who moved like
a white ghost; a ghost with a killing touch, for wherever he
passed, dark elves fell, blood spraying from cuts so swift
that Alith Anar never saw when they had been struck.

At last Eltharion's company saw Malekith's lavish pavilion emerging from a veil of trailing smoke: a tent like a
palace, with wings and cupolas, all of violet silk as dark as
their owner's heart. Four guards in dragonscale mail protected the entrance, but they were dead by Eltharion's
sword before they could call their challenge. Eltharion
stepped over their bodies into the brazier-lit vastness of the
interior, Belannaer and Alith Anar at his sides.

The central tent was palatial indeed. Thick carpets hid the
ground, tapestries depicting excruciating pleasures hung
before the black canvas walls, tables overflowed with food
and drink, naked slaves cowered in the shadows and hid
behind the curtains that led to the other rooms, and in the
centre stood an ebony throne, carved with dragons and
harpies. It was empty.

Eltharion raised his chin, like a wolf sniffing the wind. 'He is not here.' He turned in a circle. 'Coward!' he cried. 'Did I cut you so deeply that you fear to face me again?' He hacked down tapestries and sliced open door curtains. 'Come out, craven! Is this the bravery of the druchii? Is the spirit of the warrior that they hold so...?'

He stopped and looked up. The thunder of enormous wings filled the air. A powerful downdraft buffeted the tent's silk roof, making it billow and snap. Alith Anar froze, expecting the walls to burst into flames around them. Eltharion didn't seem to care. He raced outside, sword pointing at the sky. 'Coward! Come back and face me!'

Belannaer and Alith Anar stepped out after him, just in time to see a massive black shape bank around the curve of the stone watchtower, before disappearing into the night. After a moment Eltharion lowered his sword and sheathed it, his face cold and still. 'We continue to Naggarond.'

'No, MY LORD,' said Belannaer, a short while later, 'you must not persist in this folly.'

The druchii had been routed, retreating in disarray towards Naggarond, leaving their dead behind. The Shadow Warriors busied themselves smashing the tower's signal lamps and digging out the earth under the east wall so that it would topple like a tree. The rest of the Ulthuan force were seeing to their dead and wounded and, much to Belannaer's dismay, preparing to march again.

'Can you not see that this is some ruse of Malekith's?' persisted Belannaer as Eltharion stared sightlessly into the night. 'We have won no victories. We have been allowed to succeed. Twice the Witch King might have set his dragon upon us and ended this adventure in an instant, and he did not. Why? Because he wants us to come further in. He has some use for us.'

'Use me?' scoffed Eltharion. 'Let him try. I am a tool that turns in the hand. We march.'

'Did you lie then?' asked Belannaer. 'Did you not say you would be satisfied with the destruction of the tower?'

'I would have, had I killed Malekith. But he ran, so we march.'

'*You* may march. I will return to the ships, and this time I will not let you sway me from ordering my troops away. I will play Malekith's game no longer.' He started down the slope towards the Sea Guard who were forming up, their wounded on litters behind them.

Eltharion's fists clenched. He growled. Alith Anar wasn't sure if from anger or pain. Anar watched Belannaer go with mixed feelings. He hated him for a being naysayer and a nag, and for taking away half their fighting force when they most needed it, but at the same time the old Loremaster was right. The high elves should not have won the two battles they had fought this day. Malekith's dragon could have burned them all to cinders and turned the tide in both. Why had the Witch King stayed his hand? What devious plan was he concocting?

Belannaer had almost reached the bottom of the slope when Eltharion called after him. 'Loremaster, wait. I have reconsidered.'

Belannaer turned, a suspicious frown on his brow. 'Reconsidered?'

'Yes.' Eltharion started down the slope. 'You are right. We are toyed with. We cannot hope to succeed. As much as I wish to kill Malekith, I cannot force him to face me.'

Belannaer looked relieved. 'You see it at last.'

Eltharion turned to Alith Anar. 'Instruct your warriors to take the armour, cloaks and helms of the fallen druchii. My Swordmasters will do the same. We will at least have trophies of this brave venture to show those who dare doubt us that we truly made it to this fell shore.'

Alith Anar tried to hide the disappointment in his voice. 'As you wish, Swordmaster.' Though he knew it was the wiser course, he was crushed. Eltharion's fiery righteousness had made victory seem inevitable. There was nothing his rage couldn't conquer. No wall was high enough, and no army strong enough to stand in his way. To hear the Swordmaster speaking reason was strangely heartbreaking.

Belannaer took Eltharion's hand. 'Thank you, old friend. I am glad to see that vengeance has not clouded your wisdom after all.'

'Come away, my lords,' said a dirt-covered shadow captain. 'The tower is about to collapse.'

THE CLIFFS WERE an hour away and dawn still invisible beneath the thick roof of the forest through which the soldiers of Ulthuan trudged, when Liss, Alith Anar's chief scout, emerged from the shadows and gave her report. All was quiet.

As she faded away again, Eltharion fell into step beside the King of Shadows. 'We are unobserved, then?'

'Aye, Swordmaster,' said Alith Anar. 'No scouts observe us. No harpies circle above us. The way ahead is clear.'

'Good.' Eltharion nodded curtly. 'Then call a halt. We have come far enough.'

'Far enough for what?' asked Belannaer, turning. Eltharion paid him no mind. 'Alith Anar, instruct your Shadows to don the druchii cloaks and armour. My Swordmasters will do the same. We will wait here until nightfall, and then approach Naggarond as a returning company of druchii.'

Alith Anar's heart leapt. The Swordmaster had not given up after all!

Belannaer was less pleased. 'Another deceit!' he cried. 'Would you lie to your oldest friend?'

Eltharion ignored the interruption. 'Loremaster, you and the Sea Guard will return to the ships as you have wished all along. You will sail them out to sea, making it seem that we are in full retreat. Return tomorrow at

dawn. If we are not on the beach within an hour, return
to Ulthuan and tell them we died bravely.'

'I will tell them you died foolishly!' said Belannaer. 'By
Aenarion's sword, your rage blinds you more fully than
the wounds Malekith gave you ever did!'

Eltharion drew himself up. 'You were no part of this
venture until you thrust yourself into it. Those of us who
conceived it knew from the beginning that we would die
here. If you have no wish to help us, then go. Take your
ship and leave ours, but do not try to hinder me again.
Malekith will die by my hand before I leave this shore.'

Belannaer glared at Eltharion for a long moment, fury
in his ancient eyes. Then he turned to Alenael, captain of
the Sea Guard. 'Take the Guard to the ships and sail them
both out to sea, making it seem that we are in full retreat.
You will return tomorrow at dawn. If we are not on the
beach within an hour, return to Ulthuan and tell them...
tell them that Belannaer was the greatest fool of all.'

WHATEVER BELANNAER'S MISGIVINGS, having agreed to
come, he did all he could to ensure that the raid succeeded. While the companies of Swordmasters and
Shadow Warriors slept and prepared their disguises, he
murmured a constant incantation to ward off unwanted
attention.

It was clear that his efforts, coming so soon after performing the same service all the way across the Seas of
Chill and Malice, wore on him. His face was drawn, his
movements those of a sleepwalker. One of the four Sea
Guard who had remained behind as his retinue stayed at
his elbow at all times, keeping him steady.

Yet Belannaer continued his litany into the night as the
Swordmasters and Shadow Warriors, dressed in the
peaked helms and black scale *dalakoi* of druchii city
guard, moved swiftly through the woods towards
Naggarond. The Loremaster brought up the rear on a

captured druchii warhorse, while Eltharion, his bandaged eyes hidden behind the visor of a druchii helm, limped stoically at the head of the column.

Alith Anar walked beside him, his thoughts pulling his heart this way and that. He was glad that Eltharion had not given up, and the Swordmaster's cunning pleased him. He too had often used misdirection in his war against Naggaroth. Had he not danced with Morathi in the Witch King's fortress disguised as a druchii reaver? Had he not stolen the Stone of Midnight from her treasury? But there was a difference between his previous exploits and this one. His infiltrations had been entirely solo, not because he didn't want to share the glory, but because he knew that what he did was mad, and he didn't want to be responsible for the death of any but himself.

Eltharion, on the other hand, brought a hundred elves along with him to his ruin. It was true they had gone willingly, prepared to die in order to slay the Witch King, but Alith Anar was no longer certain that killing Malekith was possible; not here, not now. And yet Eltharion persisted, apparently without any plan but to fight through every obstacle. He seemed more intent on smashing himself against the walls of Naggarond than actually accomplishing what they had come to do.

So Anar's heart and mind fought. His heart wanted nothing more than to follow the hero of the Dragon Gate to glory and victory. His mind knew that Belannaer was right, and that they should be returning to the ships and sailing back to Ulthuan. Despite this certainty, he marched on, letting inaction lead him ever closer to inevitable destruction.

Shortly before nightfall the forest ended, and the elves marched through the open lands that surrounded Naggarond. The fortress city's towers jutted up before the distant peaks of the Iron Mountains like obsidian daggers. A chill ran down Alith Anar's spine at the sight. They were so few, against the greatest city of Naggaroth. It was insane. Yet still he marched on.

They encountered no troops, and saw no druchii except for whip-wielding overseers in the furrowed fields to either side of the road, herding their human field slaves back to their barracks after a day's labour. They paid them no heed.

A few hours later, as night fell, the forward scouts came back to the main force, carrying a barely conscious Swordmaster. He had been horribly tortured, his sword arm mutilated with surgical precision. They had found him lying beside the road, nearly dead from loss of blood.

Eltharion halted the column and knelt beside the elf. Belannaer and Alith Anar joined him.

'How did you come here, Swordmaster?' asked Eltharion.

'My lord,' said the elf weakly, 'I was captured by a druchii, at the watch tower, a general. He took me to Naggarond. His torturers tried to wrest our plans from me but... but, Asuryan be thanked, I resisted, and later slew my tormentors and escaped.'

'Escaped Naggarond?' Eltharion raised an eyebrow.

'Aye, lord,' gasped the elf, 'and with news you must hear.'

'Speak then.'

The young Swordmaster drew a feeble breath. 'While at their mercy I heard the general speak to a lieutenant. He asked after the defence of a sally port known as the Brass Portal, on the east side of the city. He said it was the weakest point in Naggarond's defences and wanted to be sure it was well guarded. His lieutenant assured him it would be.'

Eltharion frowned. Alith Anar exchanged a glance with Belannaer.

'Thank you, Swordmaster,' said Eltharion. 'This is valuable information.'

Eltharion stood as physicians tended to the elf, and moved away with Alith Anar and Belannaer. 'This is a trap,' he said.

'Indeed, Swordmaster,' said Alith Anar. 'No elf so wounded could escape the fortress city undetected. He was allowed to leave, so that he might speak his tale. Be certain, if we attack this portal, they will be waiting for us.'

'Then we must find another way,' said Eltharion. He turned to Belannaer. 'Loremaster, perhaps your art?'

Belannaer shook his head. 'There would be no swifter way to draw Malekith's attention, and, were I to try, I might not have the strength to protect us, or take us away after the deed is done.'

'My lord, I have it!' said Alith Anar, interrupting. He smiled, at ease at last, for in an instant he had found a way to satisfy both heart and mind, if only Eltharion would agree.

'Speak then,' said Eltharion.

'We will attack this Brass Portal,' said Alith Anar, 'just as they wish, and when they spring their ambush, we will fall back in confusion and return to the coast, defeated.'

'Defeated,' said Eltharion, flat.

Alith Anar nodded. 'That is how it will appear. The druchii will see Eltharion and Alith Anar and Belannaer repulsed from their walls and think we have lost heart. In reality, we will have dressed our best captains in our armour while we and a small picked squad slip into the city at another point, dressed as druchii.'

Belannaer frowned, and then shrugged. 'It is still folly, but it holds at least some chance of success. A small force might slip unnoticed through the city where a larger force would fight every step of the way, and they will not be searching for us if they think we have retreated.'

And, thought Alith Anar, the majority of their troops will have been spared the certain doom that waited for Eltharion, Belannaer and himself.

'But *is* there another way in?' asked Eltharion.

'Aye, swordmaster,' said Alith Anar. 'I have used it once before. It is easy for one elf, but impossible for an army. A few might just manage it.'

A FEW HOURS later, while the high elf raiders hammered in vain upon the Brass Portal, a slave barge spun lazily down the canal that connected Naggarond to its mines in the foothills. The barge did not answer the challenges from the guards of the wharf, nor did it stop at their orders. Only when it ground against the submerged chains stretched before the portcullis that guarded the port did it halt, bumping them in the sluggish current.

The guards on the gate towers called down, and then murmured in confusion as they saw that its crew was nowhere to be seen. A squad of harbour guards rowed out to investigate, covering the barge with their crossbows as the portcullis was raised.

The last thing Alith Anar heard before he allowed the weight of the druchii armour he carried to pull him under the water behind the barge, were the baffled voices of the guards as they searched the barge and found no enemies on board. With his companions swimming behind, he kicked under the barge and into the port, a satisfied smile on his lips.

THE THING HE had not taken into account, thought Alith Anar as he clenched his chattering teeth, was that even in high summer, Naggaroth was a cold, windy place, and the gusts that moaned through the maze of Naggarond's stone streets were colder than the breath of an ice wyrm, at least it felt that way to elves dressed in damp clothes and wet armour.

The high elves marched openly through the city, Alith Anar dressed as a captain of the city guard, Eltharion and Belannaer in visored helmets as his sergeants, and their retinues – four Swordmasters each for Eltharion and

Belannaer, and four Shadow Warriors for Alith Anar – dressed as their guard company, all carrying druchii spears, swords and crossbows.

The streets had so far been empty but for the occasional patrol, which they had avoided. The houses of the city were dark and shuttered. It seemed Malekith had ordered Naggarond to lock down in anticipation of the high elves' attack. An over-reaction, Alith Anar thought, in light of how few the invaders were.

As they crossed a broad square, Alith Anar looked with distaste at the huge fountain in its centre. A monolithic statue of Khaine rose from the pool, slitting the throat of Caledor, the Phoenix King. Red liquid poured continuously from Caledor's throat and splashed into the pool, and from the thick, coppery reek of it, Alith Anar was certain that it was real blood.

Beside him, Belannaer stopped, staring above the grisly fountain. 'Look,' he said.

Alith Anar followed the Loremaster's gaze. Malekith's tower rose in the distance, and at its top, silhouetted against sickly green Morrslieb, the Witch King's dragon stretched and flapped its wings like an unsettled crow.

'Is there trouble?' asked Eltharion.

Belannaer shook his head. 'No, but we know that Malekith is at home. His dragon roosts upon his tower.'

'Anything to report, captain?' asked a female voice to their left.

Alith Anar whipped around, his heart banging. Eltharion, Belannaer and their retinues went on guard. Coming from a side street, as silent as cats, was a squad of masked druchii, twelve warriors led by three women, one with the silver hadrilkar of a captain. Alith Anar stiffened as he took in the druchii's elaborate armour and identical, daemon-faced masks. These were Immortals, Malekith's fabled personal guard, elite warriors and witches charged with the defence of the Witch King and his fortress.

He willed his heart to slow, and saluted, trying to put the proper druchii sneer into his voice. 'All quiet but for the wind, lady.'

The masked witch nodded, and her squad turned down the street from which the high elves had just come. 'Carry on.'

Alith Anar let out a breath and motioned the others on. He couldn't believe their luck. Their disguises must have been better than he thought.

'Captain?' came the witch's voice again.

Alith Anar stopped and turned.

The witch was bending over dark spots on the plaza's flagstones: a trail of wet footprints. She looked up. 'Have you been swimming?'

Belannaer was first to react, with Eltharion only an eye blink after. While Alith Anar was still struggling to think of some story, Belannaer sang out an arcane phrase and the air around the two groups was suddenly close and dead, as if they were in a small room instead of an open square. At the same time, Eltharion sprang for the witches, drawing his two-handed Hoethi blade from his back.

The Immortals were just as fast. The warriors surged forward to protect the witches as the masked women hissed wards and counter spells. Two warriors fell instantly to Eltharion's shining sword. The others closed around him.

Alith Anar charged in with the Swordmasters. His Shadow Warriors needed no orders to do their part. Even as Alith Anar crossed swords with one of the towering Immortals, a crossbow bolt sprouted from the druchii's neck, having found a tiny gap between his bevor and daemonic mask. The thrum and thud of loosed bolts was all around.

Alith Anar kicked the dying druchii aside and thrust at another. The Immortal's riposte was so fast that it hit Anar before his hand could move to parry, a screeching scrape across his hadrilkar collar. He shivered. Had he been wearing his usual skirmish kit, the blade would have pierced his throat. He backed off and took up a more cautious stance. To his left, a Swordmaster fell sideways, his head rolling off his shoulders and thudding to the ground.

Eltharion whirled within a circle of Immortals, his stolen black armour making him a blurred shadow, out of which shot white lightning that struck sparks and sprayed blood wherever it touched. One Immortal fell, and then another.

'On the witches,' croaked Belannaer, behind them. 'I cannot keep them penned for long.'

The Shadows turned their crossbows on the witches. The results were disastrous. Their bolts glanced off the air around the masked women and flew instead at the Swordmasters. One gasped as a shaft pierced his leg. His druchii opponent cut him down.

Eltharion strove towards the witches, fighting off five Immortals at once, but though they could not touch him, neither could he advance. His Swordmasters ranked up beside him, pressing hard.

The witches rasped as they tried to mouth their spells, fighting to draw upon their dark energies within Belannaer's sphere of confinement. With a supreme effort, the witch captain spat out a torrent of syllables, and the Loremaster staggered, grunting.

'Go! Fly!' she shrieked at one of her sisters. 'To Malekith!'

With a word, the witch rose off the ground like a dandelion seed. Belannaer recovered, and his sphere snapped closed again, but too late. The witch floated up into the night sky.

'Stop her!' hissed the sorcerer, fighting desperately to keep the others contained.

Alith Anar disengaged and leapt up onto the knee of the statue of Khaine, then to its shoulder. He drew the

Moonbow and aimed at the witch floating over the
rooftops at the edge of the square. He flexed the ithilmar-
cored bow to its limit, tracking her, and then let fly. The
black arrow vanished in the darkness, but Anar was
rewarded a second later with a harsh cry, and then two
thuds as the witch dropped to a sharp peaked roof, and
slid off to smash against the street.

Alith Anar looked down and discovered that the battle
was over. The witch captain was crumpling before
Eltharion, her head split, her silver daemon mask falling
away in two perfect halves. The other Immortals lay
sprawled at Eltharion's feet like discarded black cloaks.

But there were too many Swordmasters among the dead:
three of Eltharion's four, and one of Belannaer's. Liss, Alith
Anar's most trusted scout, was dead too, frozen to death by
some witchery. Icicles grew from her eyes and mouth like
glass daggers.

Not one of the survivors was unwounded. Eltharion had
a gash on his left leg. Belannaer had to be helped to his
feet by his guards. He looked as fragile as old parchment.

'Swiftly,' said Eltharion. 'Hide the bodies in the fountain.'

Alith Anar and the others hurriedly lowered the bodies
of foe and friend alike into the bubbling red pool. Anar
shivered as he let go of Liss's wrists and watched her ice-
violated face disappear beneath the blood. It felt wrong, as
if they were performing some dark sacrifice to Khaine.

As they resumed their journey towards Malekith's tower,
Belannaer spoke up. He was moving more slowly than
ever, and wheezing with every step. 'Do not rely on me further for sorcerous assistance,' he said. 'If I am to whisk us
away after you dispatch Malekith, I must conserve my
strength. Indeed, I pray I still have enough.'

'THIS IS WORSE than the assassin's poison,' said Eltharion,
cringing.

He, Alith Anar, Belannaer and their surviving guards watched from a dark archway as a long column of druchii warriors passed them, marching towards Malekith's fortress, singing bloodthirsty parodies of old Ulthuan victory songs.

'Truly,' said Belannaer, leaning wearily against the wall, 'I have heard dwarfs sing better.'

The druchii strode past proudly, some limping, some carrying their comrades, but all with chins held high. 'You'd think they had defeated all of Ulthuan,' Alith Anar growled, 'not chased off two hundred unsupported elves. But this may provide an opportunity.'

He looked at his companions, and then nodded. 'We are all convincingly wounded. Loremaster, if you would consent to being carried on crossed spears, I believe we will pass muster. Only one thing more is necessary to complete the masquerade. We must sing.'

Eltharion and Belannaer groaned.

ALITH ANAR'S THROAT was raw and his nerves frayed by the time they reached the barracks, but the ruse had worked. They were inside Malekith's fortress. As they had marched through the gates and under the thick black walls, carrying Belannaer on crossed spears between them, Anar had felt as if every eye was upon him, that he and his companions stuck out like dragons in a sheep pen. But, to his great relief, guards had not called for them to stop, alarms had not sounded, and Morathi had not appeared and blasted them into dust.

From the shadow of a temple of Khaine, the high elves watched Malekith's tower, the tallest in all Naggarond, and as wide as a castle keep at its base. It was connected by only a single enclosed corridor to the sprawling palace where his courtiers lived and where he conducted affairs of state, and had its own private entrances and defences. A tall stone wall surrounded it, with one main gate facing east, and two smaller gates north and south. The tower had three corresponding entrances, the main doors, and two smaller entries that led to a stables and a garden respectively. All were guarded. Alith Anar had sent his Shadows to reconnoitre and they had reported that a company of Black Guard watched each door, with crossbow guards on balconies above them.

'This will require some subtlety,' said Alith Anar, looking thoughtfully from gate to gate and up and down the tower. The gates were open at least, with guards going in and out, but they would close at the first sign of trouble, and the tower doors appeared to be locked tight. 'A distraction, perhaps. A fire? A feint?'

'The time for subtlety is past,' said Eltharion. He stepped from the temple's shadow and strode towards the main gate.

Alith Anar cursed.

'Eltharion!' hissed Belannaer. 'Stop! The doors are locked!'

It was too late. The guards at the gate were turning to see who approached.

'Asuryan take him!' said Alith Anar. 'Fall in!'

Anar and the others hurried after Eltharion, forming up behind him as if they were his retinue. We will die here, Anar thought, without ever entering the tower. No sword would cut through those iron-banded doors, not even one wielded by as great a hero as Eltharion.

The captain of the guard raised his hand as they neared. 'Halt, captain. What is your business?'

Eltharion stopped before him, and then reached up and removed his druchii helm, letting his white hair fall around his shoulders and revealing the red scarf that hid his eyes. 'I am Eltharion of Yvresse, and I come to kill Malekith the Cursed.'

The guards gasped and stepped back, astounded, and in that moment they died. In one smooth movement, Eltharion dropped the helm, drew his double-handed blade from his back and swept it in a wide arc. It cut down four druchii, slicing through their black armour as if it were candle wax.

Belannaer and Alith Anar and their retinues fell upon the others as Eltharion sprinted forward. The guards died screaming for the gates to be closed, but Eltharion was already through, and Alith Anar and the others were right on his heels.

They sprinted for the main doors. Forty heavily-armoured, full Black Guard blocked their way, elite warriors armed with cruel, hook-backed halberds. The guards above the door fired down with repeater cross-bows. Eltharion knocked bolts out of the air with his sword, and Belannaer did his best to turn aside the rest, but too many got through. A Shadow Warrior stumbled and fell. A Swordmaster vomited blood around the shaft of a bolt that had found his mouth. Only three remained alive.

'Into the melee,' called Alith Anar to his last two Shadows, 'or they will pick you off.'

The Black Guards set their halberds to receive the high elves' meagre charge. Eltharion leapt over them like a gazelle and dropped in their midst. Halberd heads and severed arms spun through the air behind his blurring blade. Those in the front rank turned their heads, amazed, and in that moment of distraction, Alith Anar and his companions hit them, cutting them down before they could recover. Belannaer drew his sword, but stayed back, too weary to fight.

Alas, the shock of Eltharion's attack did not last long. The Black Guard were hardened warriors. They quickly surrounded the high elves, and Belannaer found that he must fight after all. Eltharion fared well

enough, moving like flowing silk through the Guard
and leaving falling bodies and sprays of red in his
wake, but the others did not have his skill or strength.
Belannaer might have been one of the greatest swords
of Hoeth, but he was too tired to do more than defend
himself. Alith Anar faced a bristling thicket of halberds and found that his sword wouldn't reach
beyond their slashing hooks and stabbing blades. In
desperation he took up a fallen halberd and flailed
inexpertly with it. He did little damage, but at least it
kept the druchii a little further away.

The three Swordmasters managed better, their long
swords chopping through the shafts of the halberds
and finding the arms and knees of their opponents,
but this was the wrong sort of fight for the Shadow
Warriors, and to Alith Anar's grief and fury he saw his
last two faithful Nagarythe fall with throats cut and
chests split. It was all for naught. There were too many
guards, and more were coming. Eltharion's mad raid
would end here in pointless slaughter.

A black form flashed above the melee. Alith Anar
thought for an instant that it was Malekith's dragon,
diving to incinerate them. But no, it was Eltharion. He
had leapt over the heads of the Guard and caught hold
of the baroque ornamentation that bordered the enormous doors. The druchii shouted and surged after him
as he swarmed up the wall and onto the balcony. The
surprised crossbow squadron died before the
onslaught of his gleaming blade like shadows before
the sun, and then he was gone, through the balcony
door and into the tower.

Alith Anar stared, and almost took a halberd
through the heart for it. By Asuryan, he thought, his
mind reeling as he returned his attention to the fight,
the revenge-mad lunatic had abandoned them, left
them to die while he went in search of Malekith. The

blind Swordmaster's companions had been nothing to him but another way to distract his enemies. The arrogance of it! The cold-heartedness! The…

With a muffled rattle of chains and gears, the great doors swung open. Eltharion charged out through the widening gap, slashing at the backs of the Black Guard.

'Hurry!' he called. 'To me!'

Alith Anar, Belannaer and the three Swordmasters surged forward with renewed energy as Eltharion kept the door clear. Alith Anar scolded himself for his unworthy thoughts. The blind elf might be mad, but perhaps not as callous as he had painted him.

With a last push, Alith Anar and the Swordmasters fought through to Eltharion, then ran through the door with the Black Guard behind them. Eltharion spun to the side, and with a single blow slashed through the chain that operated the door mechanism. The doors boomed shut with a rushing clatter, crushing several druchii between them.

Eltharion, Alith Anar, Belannaer and the Swordmasters quickly slew the few Black Guards who had made it through, but even as the guards died, they heard the tower's north and south doors opening, and the thunder of running boots.

'To the stairs!' said Eltharion, leading the way to the basalt spiral that twisted up into the cross-vaulted ceiling as the boot steps rang closer. Belannaer hobbled after the others as fast as he could, leaning upon his staff as if it was a crutch. Blood seeped from gashes in his khaitan.

Before they had climbed thirty steps, a black tide of druchii flooded into the entry hall from the north and south archways. They saw the high elves on the stairs and surged after them, bellowing.

'Faster,' said Eltharion, 'or they will overwhelm us.'

'I cannot,' said Belannaer. 'I am at the end of my strength.'

'Then I will carry you,' said Eltharion.

The Black Guard were at the base of the stairs and swarming up.

'Then how will you fight those we will meet above?' asked Belannaer, shaking his head. 'No. I will stop them.'

The Loremaster faced down the stair and raised his staff. The Black Guard swarmed towards him like a glittering black centipede. Belannaer took a deep breath, then called out an ear-splitting phrase and struck the butt of his staff sharply on the step before him.

With a deafening crack, the spiral stairs below the wizard shattered into a thousand pieces. The druchii upon them fell screaming in a shower of basalt boulders that smashed upon the floor in a billowing cloud of black dust.

Belannaer stepped delicately back from what was now the stairway's last step, forty feet above the floor, then swayed and nearly fell. One of his Swordmasters caught his arm.

'Well done, master,' said Eltharion, as the companions turned and continued up the stairs.

'No,' said Belannaer, glaring wearily at Eltharion, 'poorly done, for I now have no strength to carry us away.'

BY THE TIME they reached Malekith's throne room, only Eltharion, Belannaer and Alith Anar were left alive, for though Belannaer had neatly cut off pursuit from below, the upper floors of the tower had been defended by a host of Black Guards, Immortals and diabolical traps. The last three Swordmasters had died one by one, their corpses left to lie beside the druchii they had killed as Eltharion pressed remorselessly on.

At last they came to the throne room's iron doors, Eltharion striding tall and proud, and Belannaer barely conscious, his arm draped over Alith Anar's shoulder. The halberds of the two throne room guards shook as they lowered them at Eltharion. Alith Anar could well understand their fear, for Eltharion looked more daemon than elf as he approached them. His stolen black armour was crimson with the blood of a hundred druchii, and his white face was streaked with gore.

'For Malekith!' cried the first guard as he charged.

'For the Witch King!' cried the other.

Those were their last words.

Eltharion stepped over their bodies and thrust open the iron doors. Three highborn druchii generals in elaborate black armour whipped around as they entered, and drew their weapons.

Alith Anar surveyed the room quickly, looking for hidden assailants. It was octagonal, and smaller than he expected, but no less grand. Stone dragons lined the walls, all bowing towards the raised throne that dominated the far wall. Green witch light glowed from tall braziers, but their light was dim by comparison to the terrible white glare of the pulsing, boulder-sized crystal that hung in an iron cage from a heavy chain in the centre of the room. The light stung the eyes like poison, and Alith Anar could not shake the feeling that the crystal was looking at him.

There was no one but the generals in the room. The Barbed Throne was empty.

Eltharion sensed it. 'Where is Malekith?' he demanded.

The three highborn exchanged glances. One was a grizzled veteran, horribly scarred on the left side of his face, who carried two short swords in the fashion of the warriors of old Nagarythe. The second was high-browed and sneering, with a nose like a hawk's beak. He held a delicate, deadly duelling sword. The third

was bald, and gripped the curved sword of a Cold One
cavalry officer.

'So much for your grand plan,' the bald one said,
glaring at the scarred veteran.

'We can still make something of this,' the veteran
replied. 'If we kill Eltharion when the Witch King ran
from him, who will they follow then?'

The hawk-nosed one shrugged. 'Why not,' he said. 'It
will be a cleaner death than Malekith will give us.'

'For Naggaroth!' roared the scarred one.

'For Naggaroth!' echoed the others.

They charged as one.

Alith Anar pushed Belannaer unceremoniously away
and leapt with Eltharion to meet them. He closed with
Hawk-nose, exchanging thrusts and parries. Eltharion
flowed right, slipping between the veteran and the
bald one and ducking their swings, his white sword
trailing behind him. It seemed almost an accident that
its keen edge caressed the bald one's neck in passing,
a chance collision.

A red line appeared on the bald one's throat,
between visor and bevor. His eyes went wide. He
clutched at his neck instinctively. Red mist sprayed
between his fingers and he crumpled, choking on his
own blood.

Alith Anar beat aside Hawk-nose's sword and
lunged, only to find that the lighter blade had slith-
ered back into guard and was aiming at his neck. He
twisted away at the last possible second and stumbled
past the highborn, off balance.

Hawk-nose smiled as he turned and pressed his
advantage. 'So, they are not all wizards of the blade.'

Anar backed and parried desperately, finding it
almost impossible to follow the highborn's flickering
sword. It appeared that Eltharion had found a worthy
opponent as well. Remarkably, the scarred general had

not died in the first pass, and was in fact holding his own.

The hawk-nosed druchii slipped on his bald comrade's blood. An opening! Alith Anar feinted and lunged. The highborn turned like a dancer, letting Anar's sword stab harmlessly past him, and then slashed down. Anar ducked and veered. A deafening clang rang in his ears and his head was knocked sideways. His stolen druchii helm bounced noisily across the marble floor. He spun and returned to guard, his black hair spilling down his back.

The highborn sneered. 'Nagarythe, eh? A traitor to your own kind.'

'It is you who are traitor to me,' said Alith Anar, 'the True King of Naggaroth.'

For a moment the highborn didn't understand. Then his eyes glowed. 'Blessed murderer!' he said. 'The White Sword and the King of Shadows in one blow? We will be heroes!'

He sprang forward, avoiding Alith Anar's sword with ease and lunging for his heart. But in his eagerness to kill the holder of the Shadow Crown, he neglected to see that Alith Anar had drawn a dagger with his off hand. Anar parried with it and thrust up between them with his sword. The tip stabbed through the underside of the druchii's jaw and into his brain. He fell against Alith Anar's chest, eyes dimming, and slid to the floor.

Alith Anar freed his sword and turned to assist Eltharion, but there was no need. Eltharion stood with his arm at full extension, his sword buried in the scarred general's chest up to the quillions.

The scarred general stared at him as he slid slowly backward off the blade. 'Well struck, Swordmaster,' he rasped, blood bubbling from his lips. 'May you do the same to Malekith one day.'

'Today,' said Eltharion.

The general dropped from the sword and sprawled, slack limbed, across the black marble floor. Eltharion cleaned his blade with a fold of his khaitan and turned in a slow circle, ears cocked and chin lifted, hunting for sign of Malekith.

'*Well struck indeed,*' said a voice like iron on stone.

The high elves looked up, for the voice seemed to come from above them, but all they could see was the eye-blistering light of the caged crystal.

'*I owe you a debt, Swordmaster,*' said the voice again, and Alith Anar was certain this time that it came from the crystal. It seemed to ring from it like an echo from a cave.

'Malekith!' hissed Eltharion.

'*You have done me three good turns this day,*' continued the voice, ignoring him. '*You have exposed traitors in my court. You have disposed of them for me, and you have trapped yourself. The death you have so eagerly sought approaches, Swordmaster. May it be all you hoped for. Farewell.*'

'Malekith!' shouted Eltharion. 'Show yourself!'

The stone did not answer.

With a curse, Eltharion raised his sword and made to leap up and strike the stone.

'Eltharion! No!' cried Belannaer from where he leaned against a pillar. 'It would destroy us all.'

Eltharion stayed his hand. 'Destroy us?'

Belannaer stood. 'It is the Ainur Tel, the Eye of Fate, an ancient and powerful scrying stone. With it, one can see through the eyes of another, no matter the distance, and twist his mind, even destroy it if one has will enough. It is a thing of pure Chaos, taken from the Wastes in the days when the world was young, and were you to strike it, it would explode and the dread energy within it would kill us all. Indeed, it would murder the whole city, and poison this place for generations to come.' He shuddered. 'It is a terrible thing.'

'The whole city,' echoed Eltharion.

There was a rumble of swiftly approaching boots outside the throne room. The Black Guard had apparently found a way past the broken stairs. Alith Anar ran to the iron doors and locked them, setting the bolts and bars, and not a moment too soon. Boots and raised voices sounded right outside, and the doors flexed inward. Alith Anar hurried back to Eltharion and Belannaer.

Eltharion's face remained raised to the Ainur Tel, his expression inscrutable.

'Come, Eltharion,' said Belannaer, looking uneasily at the door. 'If you still mean to find Malekith, we must...'

'The Eye of Fate,' interrupted Eltharion, 'it is well named, for it is fate that I find it here. It is a gift from Khaine, a glorious gift. With it I will kill not only Malekith, but Naggarond itself. The war will be ended.'

He turned eagerly to Belannaer and Alith Anar. 'Come, assist me. We must all strike together, so that we assure its destruction. With one blow we can end the power of the druchii for once and all.'

Alith Anar stared at him, open mouthed.

Belannaer looked too shocked to speak.

'Quickly!' snapped Eltharion, impatient. 'They will soon be through the door. We will die regardless, but this way it need not be in vain. It will be the greatest sacrifice in the history of Ulthuan. Though we perish, our kin will forever more be free of the menace of Naggaroth.'

Belannaer finally found his voice. 'No, Eltharion, you must not do this. What you propose is evil. You will kill thousands of innocent slaves and corrupt this land for generations to come. You will make this place a festering wasteland of Chaos energy. It will breed more evil than you destroy.'

'Evil in Naggaroth does not concern me,' said Eltharion, 'so long as it stays in Naggaroth.'

Alith Anar jerked as if slapped. 'My lord,' he said, stiffly, raising his voice over the pounding from outside the doors. 'My lord, I have followed you from Anlec and put my warriors at your disposal, because you said that your goal was the death of Malekith. We vowed to die if it meant his distraction, and I am still willing, but you will remember that I am the True King of Naggaroth. This is the home of my people. It has always been our plan to return here once Malekith and his ilk have been defeated. I would not have my home poisoned.'

Eltharion looked about to speak, but Alith Anar pressed on. 'Why not use the Eye to target Malekith? Surely the hate we two have for him would be enough to destroy his mind.'

'It is not enough,' said Eltharion. He pointed at the dead generals on the floor. 'Look at the filth we have just despatched, all plotting for the Witch King's throne. There are a thousand Malekiths here, an entire race of them. Were we to kill only him, another would take his place, just as devious and bent on our destruction as the last. No, they must be wiped from the face of the earth, all of them. Any evil, any sacrifice, is worth the death of their vile breed. If innocents must die, if children must die, if I must poison Naggaroth for a thousand generations, so be it. At least Ulthuan will be safe, and I will be avenged.'

Alith Anar stood straight, his eyes blazing. 'Ulthuan might indeed be safe from Naggaroth,' he snarled, 'but it will have created a new enemy in Anlec.'

'What?' cried Eltharion, levelling his sword at Alith Anar's chest. 'Do you turn traitor? Does Nagarythe reveal its true colours at last? Only druchii by another name?'

'Lords!' called Belannaer. 'Control yourselves.'

Alith Anar slapped the tip of Eltharion's sword away. 'Is that how you think of us? Black hair does not presume a black heart, my lord, nor white hair a pure one. You look more suited to that throne than I at the moment.'

Eltharion went rigid. 'What did you say?' He returned his sword point to Alith Anar's breastplate.

'My lords,' Belannaer said again, hobbling forward in an attempt to get between them.

The oak bars locking the throne room doors were splintering.

'I said,' spat Anar, 'that it is well you mean to kill yourself when you kill Malekith, else you would take his place ere long.'

'Infamy!' cried Eltharion, thrusting forward.

The tip of his blade skidded across Alith Anar's black armour and plunged into the gap twixt chest and shoulder piece, gashing him horribly under the arm. He cried out and clutched at the wound. Blood pumped through his fingers.

'Anar!' cried Belannaer.

The True King of Naggaroth staggered and fell against a pillar. 'Well struck, Swordmaster,' he mumbled, and slid to the floor.

Eltharion stepped back, staring sightlessly at his fallen companion. He dropped his sword with a clang. 'What have I done?' He fell to his knees beside him. 'Asuryan's mercy, what have I done? What madness came over me?' His long fingers began unlacing Anar's pauldron with a dexterity a sighted elf might have envied. 'My friend, forgive me. Belannaer is right. I have been blind. For the first time in my life I have been truly blind, and worse, I struck him who would have removed the caul from my eyes.' He tore his black silk khaitan into strips and began wrapping Alith Anar's wound. 'We must get you away.'

Alith Anar looked up at him. 'You no longer wish to kill Malekith?' he asked weakly.

'He will not face me, and I haven't the power to force him. I should have seen this from the battle on the cliffs. I am blind. Blind!'

He raised his head, apparently becoming aware of their situation for the first time. The iron doors were bulging in. The three companions would be overwhelmed in moments. Eltharion cursed. 'My blindness has trapped us here. We cannot fight through the whole city, and Belannaer is too weak from protecting us from my follies to spirit us away.' He took up his sword and faced the door. 'Forgive me again, friends. I will die defending you, but there is no honour in it, for it was I who endangered you in the first place.'

'No,' croaked Belannaer, 'I will find the strength.' He pulled himself to his feet with his staff. 'Take up Alith Anar and prepare yourselves.' He smiled grimly. 'If we die, it is only a different death.'

Murmuring in an ancient tongue, he gripped Eltharion's shoulder as the Swordmaster lifted Alith Anar into his arms. He raised his staff, trembling with fatigue. The winds of magic buffeted him cruelly as he opened up to them. His frail voice lifted in a high quaver and the amber globe at the tip of the staff glowed brighter and brighter.

With a crack like a cannon firing, the bars on the throne room doors split at last, and a phalanx of Black Guard poured into the room, howling for high elf blood.

Belannaer swept his staff in a circle and cried a final syllable. The throne room exploded with golden light that knocked the druchii back to the walls. When the light faded, Eltharion, Alith Anar and Belannaer were nowhere to be seen.

Beneath Morrslieb's sickly light, Alith Anar's sleek cutter and the Sea Guard's sturdy warship sailed north and east across the Sea of Malice.

Alith Anar lay in a narrow cupboard bed in the captain's quarters of the Lothern ship and eyed Eltharion with concern. The Swordmaster sat slumped upon the long bench under the stern window, staring blindly out into the night. His left leg stuck straight out before him, splinted and stiff. Belannaer lay in another built-in bed on the starboard bulkhead, his eyes closed, as still and unresponsive as he had been since their escape.

The Loremaster's spell had worked, but not well. The golden fire of the staff had whirled them out of the tower in a confusion of wind and motion, and then winked out like a snuffed candle some two hundred feet above the waters of the cove of the Blood Cliffs. When the Sea Guard and the Nagarythe had fished them, unconscious, out of the water, Alith Anar had a broken arm in addition to the wound Eltharion had given him, Eltharion had a broken leg, Belannaer's staff was snapped and its amber globe shattered, and the Loremaster had not regained consciousness.

'Why could I not see?' asked the Swordmaster for the hundredth time that day. 'My lust for vengeance did more than blind me, it corrupted me. I so wanted revenge on Malekith that I nearly became him. I was willing to sacrifice my friends, my honour, and the present and future of an entire city, to kill one man. How could I have so completely lost my way? By Isha,' he cried, turning towards Alith Anar, 'had you not worn that breastplate, I would have killed you!'

'It was the Eye,' said Anar. 'Its emanations maddened us both. Do not torture yourself so.'

'Aye, perhaps,' said Eltharion, 'but the Eye came at the end. What explains the rest?' He turned back to the dark window, his face disappearing in shadow. 'What explains the rest?'

PREMONITION
by Chris Wraight

SUMMONED BY THE commotion above her, Athien climbed from her cabin and on to the heavily pitching deck. The air was clear and cold, spray flying into the faces of the elf crew as they steered the mighty Hawk Ship *Riallanthros* through a powerful swell. Telaris caught sight of her from the prow, and a grin broke across his normally severe face. He had the haughty, graceful looks of all of his kind, a true son of Ulthuan, but today they were illuminated with an open pleasure.

'Cousin!' he cried, his long hair whipping across his brow. 'You should see this.'

Athien made her way to the high prow unsteadily. Ahead of them the ocean swept away in contours of choppy brilliance, the waves crested with diamond bright foam. Telaris kissed her in greeting and passed her his bronze bound spyglass, the sun glinting sharply off the polished crystal lenses.

'Take a look,' he said.

She held it to her eye, sweeping across the horizon, and there it was: a low smudge of green against a piled mass of white cloud. Land, after so many days. She felt her heart leap with joy.

'How long?' she asked, her voice giving away her yearning.

Telaris laughed, and took back the spyglass.

'A while yet,' he said. 'I need to find the river, the passage to the heart of the hidden land. But my hopes are high. All being well, we'll be raising our tents before the week's end.'

Athien's eyes were bright.

'I long for it,' she breathed. '*Elthin Arven*, the endless forest beyond the seas, to see it as it really is...'

Athien looked up to see Telaris regarding her with fondness. But there was something else too: that faint trace of reserve. She knew he doubted the wisdom of bringing her on the expedition. She also knew he regarded her as a dreamer, a book lover and a gatherer of dangerous fancies. If it hadn't been for old Ferien and his endless insistence, he'd never have agreed to take her along.

'We'll be there soon enough,' Telaris said, his mind moving back to the burden of command. 'Stay at the prow for as long as you wish. The land will soon be visible even without the glass.'

He left her alone, the sun, spray and salt set against her face. She settled into a comfortable position, enjoying the sure surge of the *Riallanthros* as she ploughed her way through the sea. Telaris could be a pompous ass at times, she thought. Not that she could entirely blame him: she was young, a mere child by the reckoning of her people, cloistered in the narrow halls of Tor Yvresse her whole life. She was hardly the great warrior or mage who would be useful on a daring expedition to the hidden reaches of Eästernesse, the vast land of which the Asur knew so little. But she had hidden talents. Her archery was far better than Telaris realised, and Ferien hadn't spoken on her account for nothing.

'You see things deeply,' he had told her as they sat in his chamber discussing Telaris's plans. 'It'll do him good to have you along. He might just learn a thing or two.'

She recalled the words with pleasure. Most of the time, it was hard to feel anything other than superfluous amongst Telaris's grave, competent companions. They tolerated her presence for the sake of their commander, but she knew that sooner or later she would have to find some useful role to play on the expedition. There was little enough space on the ship for all the stores they needed, let alone wide-eyed passengers with more curiosity than sense.

THEY BEAT THEIR way east for the next few days, and the weather changed from fair to stormy. A difficult passage around a jagged headland, iron grey in the driving rain, was the worst of it. Telaris drove the ship and crew hard, anxious to find the passage he had been promised, doubtful of his charts and half-reliable testimonies. None of the Asur had ever sailed so far to found a colony. Maybe it was the rumours of a subtle change in the far north of the world that prevented them, whispers of a distant terror growing across the savage plains of ice. But the glittering halls of the princes were thirsty for knowledge of the distant places of lore and legend, and also for the spoils of conquest. The rewards for courage were high, as were the penalties for defeat. At times Athien thought Telaris wore the strain of it on his face. She knew he would rather die than fail.

They sailed more easily once the storms had passed, skirting close to the tree-lined shore, the eaves of the limitless forests gloomy and mysterious. Athien found herself gazing at them for long periods. The twisted branches seemed like the tendrils of some vast, ancient being, all-knowing, all-powerful, suspicious of interlopers and hostile. When night came, a shudder would pass along her spine as the *Riallanthros*, rocking gently on the calm water amidst the deep dark, strayed too close to the shadow-clad shallows. When her unease rose too sharply she would bring out the amulet her mother had given her on leaving, a golden spiral around an amethyst core. It reminded her of the pleasures of home, of all the beauty of Tor Yvresse. Even in the weakest light a fire seemed to kindle in its heart. It was not magical, nor particularly valuable, but she cherished it, and it banished the mysterious foreboding of the trees.

Telaris shared none of her flights of imagination, and delighted in the progress of the ship. His first triumph was the discovery of the predicted estuary running south from the coast. His second, a few days later, was arriving at its confluence with two other broad, fast flowing rivers, each capable of accommodating the draught of even the heaviest warship. In the distant south-west a range of mountains reared their heads skywards. There were strange outcrops of weather-worn rock scattered amidst the grasping branches, the stone a striking white in the direct light of the afternoon sun. Telaris nodded with approval when he saw them.

'A good site,' he mused. 'See how the rivers converge? This place must be at the head of a wider network. These tributaries are mighty indeed.'

'We disembark, then?' asked Athien, the familiar unease coming over her again. There was something about the place that she didn't like, but it was hard to say what, since it looked more or less the same as the other miles and miles of forest they had passed by.

Telaris nodded, consulting an ancient looking chart as he did so.

'The accounts of this region are vague. We must go with the evidence of our senses. I can see the potential here. A stronghold in such a place could govern the land about it for many leagues. Then there is the trade. Think of it, cousin; one day, Asuryan willing, we'll be the masters of a city here, beholden to no one but ourselves, princes of all within our considerable gaze.'

Athien failed to smile. Her heart was still heavy with misgivings.

'Well,' said Telaris, frowning, 'if you're going to sulk you can go below. I don't want anyone getting under our feet.'

Within the hour, Athien saw what he meant. The ship's boats were lowered swiftly, and under Telaris's direction the crew rowed back and forth between the *Riallanthros* and the shore until the sun was low in the sky, carrying piles of stores, barrels, planks, weapons, tools, crates and cages full of bleating, clucking and snorting animals, and a thousand other necessary items.

By nightfall the camp had been put in some kind of order, the tents distributed around a blazing fire and stony faced sentries standing guard under the branches of the nearest trees. Asrel, the young mage Telaris had chosen to lend magical support to the expedition, led a simple ceremony of thanksgiving, his clear voice ringing as prayers to Isha, Kurnous and Asuryan were recited. Then, as dusk fell, the fires were stoked and the feast was laid. They ate with relish, songs and laughter rising high into the cool air. Athien's mood improved with the wine. As the night deepened and the party began to drift to sleep, Telaris got up and wandered down to the river's edge, the dark water suffused with the ivory light of the moon. Athien joined him, and together they surveyed the peaceful scene.

'This is magical, is it not?' he asked quietly, his eyes alive with pleasure.

'It is, cousin,' she said. 'I'm glad you brought me here. I won't forget it.'

Telaris looked down at her, and laughed. He ruffled her hair affectionately as he used to when they were children.

'Good,' he said. 'I feel sure great things will happen to us here.'

* * *

THE SUBSEQUENT DAYS were full of activity. The ancient trees around the site were felled and stakes were raised along the perimeter of the planned colony. Tents were replaced by wooden frames, and plots for crops marked out. The burgundy and gold standard of Telaris's family was hoisted over the makeshift camp: a sea serpent coiled around a spear, crowned with the rune Menlui, the sign of water. Soon the place began to resemble a proper settlement rather than a resting place for brigands.

Athien, as was her wont, took to walking into the forest with her scraps of parchment, recording anything of interest she found. She gradually ventured further from the compound, pocketing strange plants and tracking elusive animals far into the interior of their labyrinthine domain. She knew Telaris was uneasy with her travelling far in such unknown, uncharted country, but there was too much to do for him to spare her an escort, or for him to spend all his time checking on her. Besides, she was no fool. Despite what he thought of her she was more than capable with a bow, and took a full quiver with her on every outing. Her returning gifts of fresh game, sharply shot in the dim light of the thick forest, were appreciated.

Her forays into the wild provoked discord nonetheless, particularly with Telaris. One evening Athien stumbled back to the camp after a whole day trekking through the wildwood to the north, her hair dishevelled and her clothes caked with mud, just as the fire was being kindled. He was angry, his eyes rimmed with red. He looked exhausted.

'Where have you been?' he asked quietly, his voice thick with irritation.

Athien looked back evenly. 'Exploring, as I came here to do.'

'You shouldn't venture so far, not without telling me where you're going.'

'You can't...' began Athien, wearily preparing herself to test wills against her cousin, but she was halted.

An unearthly screeching noise filled the air. The whole company stopped what they were doing. The wailing rose and fell, echoing strangely on the chill breeze. It stopped. Then, just on the edge of hearing, another voice rose, apparently in answer. Telaris listened intently. After a moment, the night reverted to its normal condition with the creaking of the trees, and the gentle slapping of the river against the new wooden jetty. The workers stood immobile for a few moments, before gradually resuming their tasks.

'There are things out there we know nothing of, Athien,' said Telaris at last, wearily, his voice full of care. 'I can't command you, but stay close to the camp for the sake of your parents, who entrusted you to my care.'

Athien's fight had left her. Numbly, she nodded, and went to the fire to get warm. Telaris stalked off to assist with the construction of the half-completed watchtower. Moodily, Athien poked the burning branches with her boot.

The next day she stayed inside the compound, helping to weave rush mats for the interior of the wooden huts being raised all around her. She laughed and joked with her companions as she did so, but her spirits were low. Already the memory of the night noises had faded, and under the sun the forest once more seemed a place of wonder and mystery. By the end of the week, her confidence further bolstered by the new, sturdy walls raised around the community, she was ready to creep off at dawn to explore once more. She went quietly, collecting a hunting dagger in addition to her favoured bow, avoiding the disapproving stares of the guards as she went.

As the light strengthened and no retrieval party came after her, she relaxed. The forest was cool, the mists of the night lingering around the boles of the giant trees.

The canopy was alive with the noises of birds, the earth
under her feet black and moist. There was a joy in being
under an unfamiliar sky, and this strange new world had
a unique beauty, a savage, feral quality, which drew her
ever further in. She wandered far, barely noticing the
direction she took. The shadows of the forest began to
close in around her. In the deeps of the valleys the air
became heavy and thick, filled with clouds of tiny
insects. Athien found herself pushing hard against tangles of briars to make her way, and her hands and face
quickly bore the lattice of a thousand tiny scratches.

Then she heard it: a sudden flurry of leaves falling and
a shuffling of feet. Her heart leapt, her hand reaching for
the dagger concealed within her clothing. She drew it
quickly. She remembered the strange noises of the night.
Telaris was right; it was foolish to stray too far. Trying to
gauge how far she'd travelled, she turned and began to
walk back the way she had come. Every so often she
would pause and listen. It wasn't just her imagination;
there was a presence in the trees, one that stopped when
she did, and moved when she moved. However hard she
screwed her eyes against the jumble of foliage, she could
make out no sign of her pursuer. She picked up her pace,
marching briskly back along the paths she had ambled
down minutes earlier. Even as her feet crunched through
the leaf litter, even as her mind told her to concentrate,
she couldn't help but notice the sounds around her.
Something was travelling with her, something unseen.

She turned her head quickly, trying to see where the
noise was coming from. It was all around her now. She
started to run, scrabbling at the creepers draped in her
path like animal traps. Fumbling and crashing through
the undergrowth, and with a sudden pang of fear, she
realised she might be heading deeper into the forest.
Then she saw the river, just ahead. Relieved, she made to
call out for Telaris, just as her feet got caught in the

undergrowth, sending her crashing through the brambles to the floor. Winded, she lifted herself from the
earth on to all-fours, leaves and twigs falling from her.
She looked up, straight into the gaze of two brown eyes.

Her heart stopped.

The eyes gazed back, unblinking. They were a few
paces away, screened by the leaves. She could just make
out a face: heavy features, dark, filthy, obscured by shadows. Long, straggling hair framed it. Was it even a
person? It was surely no animal. It didn't move. Athien
gradually became aware of her body again. Her breathing restarted, her heart beating hard in her chest once
more. Slowly, gingerly, ready to bolt at any moment, she
climbed to her feet. As she did so, the branches shook
with a sudden flurry and the face disappeared.

'No!' cried Athien, without thinking.

It was gone. She fumbled around for a few moments,
but it was no use. Clearly, whatever it was could stay
hidden if it wanted to. She brushed herself down and
tried to calm her breathing. She needed to get back to
the camp, however cold a welcome she was likely to get
from Telaris. Having got her bearings once more, she
travelled quickly, and before long the compound was in
front of her. As she passed under the newly completed
watchtower, she realised she had dropped the dagger.
She looked over her shoulder, back the way she had
come. The forest gazed back at her with a malign indif-
ference. She shuddered, and went inside. It could stay
there.

Telaris was waiting, his face a mask of suppressed
anger. But when he saw her disarranged state, his expression mellowed a little.

'What happened?' he asked.

Athien shook her head.

'I don't know,' she said. 'There's something in the forest. I saw it. It saw me. We're not alone.'

As if on command, the weird screeching noise started again from the trees. It was closer. By daylight, the effect was even more chilling. All the workers put down their tools and listened. The answering cries were closer too, and there were more of them. One sounded like the bellowing of a great bull, distorted and corrupted. After what seemed a long time, the calls ceased, the dying echoes fading into the silent walls of the valley.

Telaris looked haggard.

'Keep working!' he yelled at his companions. Slowly, they picked up their tools.

'Can we go back to the ship, cousin?' asked Athien weakly. 'There's something wrong with this place. I can feel it. We'd be safer on the water.'

Telaris shook his head.

'All the stores have been landed,' he said. 'We've finished the wall. You're safe here. We can't give up after a few animal noises. We'll stick it out.'

He turned to her with a bleak expression.

'We've sharpened the swords, though. Get one, and learn how to use it, and don't leave the compound again.'

FOR TWO MORE days, the noises increased, especially at night. Athien slept fitfully, her dreams of the eyes in the leaves broken by howls and bellowing from the hills around the camp. Even the guards, their grey eyes used to the rigours of war, fingered their spears fitfully as they paced the walls of the stockade. Telaris ordered the animals to be brought inside the walls, and the boats were drawn up from the river's edge.

On the third night, the forest around them was ringed with tiny lights. Walking on the ramparts under the stars, Athien went up to one of the guards, his long face sheathed in a close fitting helm.

'What are they?' she whispered, peering out into the gloom at the twinkling points.

'Eyes, my lady,' said the guard, a grim tone to his voice. 'There are things waiting under the trees. I should stay by the fire.'

Athien gave him a horrified look, before rushing down to Telaris's quarters, pushing her way roughly past his attendants.

'They're here,' she blurted. 'What are we going to do?'

Telaris looked careworn.

'You think I don't know that?' he asked wearily. 'Don't concern yourself. Perhaps the creature you disturbed in the forest has come back to find you.'

He gave a wintry smile. Athien hesitated. The brown eyes that haunted her dreams had little in common with the glistening, bestial orbs waiting in the night. Before she could reply, the master of the garrison entered, bowing brusquely.

'We're ready, my lord.'

Telaris nodded.

'Stay here, Athien,' he said, sharply. 'Now you'll see what we're going to do.'

Then he was gone. Athien rushed after him. The warriors of the company were assembled before the gates. Blades were drawn in the blood-red light of the fire. Archers had been stationed on the walls, the mage Asrel amongst them, his fingers crackling with energy. Telaris looked around, and raised his long sword in the air.

'Brothers, now is the time to cleanse this place! No sheltering behind these walls of wood. Follow me, and drive the foul beasts back into the hills!'

The company around him gave a roar of approval, and the gates were cranked open. Beyond, the shadows were alive with howls and unnatural movement. Asrel threw a swirling ball of blue light into the night air, its explosion illuminating the clearing with a blinding luminescence.

The warriors charged from the compound, a hail of arrows preceding them from the walls. Barks and screams emerged from the trees. As the unnatural light faded Athien made out the scurrying and limping of dark forms. She raced up a ladder to the ramparts to get a better view.

It was hard to see clearly what was going on. Telaris was at the forefront of the attack, his sword whirling. There were monstrous forms in the shadows, some horned, and all cloven hoofed, their warped and distended faces mad with fury. The warriors were amongst them, their blades flashing in the dark. Asrel cast targeted bolts of preternatural energy wherever the beasts clustered, scattering the grotesque creatures as they tried to rally. Athien saw a young straw-haired lad, as meek as milk during the voyage, tear into a huge bear-like beast with knives in both hands, bloodlust high in both. A tall spearman was borne down by a grotesque mule-headed figure. A troupe of swordsmen cut the legs from a great centaur-like monstrosity, its eyes flaming and its axe swinging even as it was hacked apart. She felt a sudden rush of fury.

'Asuryan!' she cried, seizing a sword clumsily and plunging down the stairs to the open gates below. But she was too late. She arrived to see the last of the living beasts staggering back into the depths of the trees. The ground was heavy and sodden with blood. Some of the warriors made to pursue their quarry, but Telaris called them back.

'We can't follow them,' he said, leaning heavily against the gore streaked trunk of a tree. 'They'll gather again in the deep forest. But at least we've taught them our swords are sharp. Perhaps that'll be the last we see of them.'

Athien looked around. Amidst the foul stench of the beasts' carcasses, the bodies of her kin lay immobile in the grime. Many of those who walked did so with a limp, or cradled a broken wrist or forearm. Ashamed of her failure to join them, she felt a fresh surge of anger. But this was no time for self-indulgence: Telaris was exhausted and the warband was aimless. Collecting herself, she turned to the battered warriors.

'Brothers, let us gather the dead and see to the wounded. We must close the gate and stoke the fire before the beasts know our weakness.'

With a heavy heart she turned to the task ahead, and those around her did likewise. Her fear had turned to sickness, her joy extinguished.

IF TELARIS HAD truly believed the beasts would leave them alone, he was wrong. The next night they were back, and then the next, their serried eyes glinting in the darkness. Over and again he led his swordsmen into the night, driving the creatures from the stockade and back into the trees, the tireless Asrel casting spell after spell in their support. Athien at last had a role to play, standing on the ramparts with her bow prepared, firing arrows at the hearts of the foul invaders, each one sent with hate over the slender walls of the colony. The happy glint of wonder in her eyes was long gone and she burned with a zeal that surprised her. Never again did she ask to retreat to the ship, still moored in the middle of the great river. This was their land, purchased with blood, and no stinking beast of the wilds would drive them from it.

As the moon sank towards the earth on the third night of fighting, the attackers were once more banished from the compound's edge, again leaving the bodies of defenders behind them in the saturated earth. When all was done to succour the wounded, Athien sought out Telaris. He lay, weary as death, on his couch.

'We're killing three of them for every wound they cause us,' he said, a coarse pride in his voice, 'but is it enough?'

Athien laid a cooling hand on his brow.

'It is,' she said, smiling. 'We can hold, as long as the walls do. They must lose heart in time, but we'll never lose heart in you.'

Telaris gave a weak smile, and slipped into an exhausted sleep. Athien stayed beside him for a moment before feeling the dead weight of fatigue slide over her too. Pulling a blanket around her shoulders, she fell back into her chair, her eyes closing.

And then it happened: the warning horn, the shouts from the compound, the clash of steel and bronze. They were back. Athien started from her slumber and looked to Telaris. He was awake in an instant, his face pale, his eyes alive. He flung off his blanket and tore out of the chamber, his body suddenly animated and alive. Athien followed him, wiping her eyes and fumbling for a bow.

'Sword kin! To me!' roared Telaris, the guards on his heels as he sped across the compound, hurriedly pulling on their helms and reaching for their weapons. As he gained the gates there was a crack, a roar from outside, and the hideous sound that Athien had feared for two days: the sigh of wooden stakes keeling over under pressure. As if in a dream, she saw the posts lurch crazily, and then topple. Beyond, all was madness: horns, hooves, fangs, leaping flames, and tattered banners swaying to the rhythm of drums. There was screaming and a frenzy of bloodlust, and the beastmen erupted into the stockade in a single wave. Telaris did not falter, plunging into the horde like a spear-tip into water, slashing a swathe either side of him as he went. His bodyguard was with him, their bright helms and swords flashing in the lurid red night. A vast, bull-headed monster crashed its way through two swordsmen. Telaris swung towards it, ducking under a ferocious swipe to plunge a dagger deep into its barrel-wide midriff. A malformed goat-like freak leapt over the falling bull's shoulders, cut down by a brace of arrows in its throat, and swept under the hooves of the onrushing herd.

Athien felt her heart beating heavily, her palms slick with sweat as she scrabbled for arrows to join the defence. Her fear ran strong, there were so many of them. If Telaris could hold the line... but then a shiver seemed to pass through the ranks of frenzied Chaos spawn. They fell back, making a corridor between their number. Telaris cried aloud, exhorting his companions onward. But then his voice died in his throat. A pair of twisted horns rose against the flames, monstrous in size and girth. Something was striding through the press of beasts, something terrible. It came forward, and all were frozen before its advance. A baleful flickering illuminated the object of the beastmen's awe and fear: a grin, a wicked grin with lines of knife sharp teeth ranged across a sickening, long, horse face. Its shoulders were broad and bunched, its fur-clad legs long and cloven hoofed. Clad in bloodstained rags, it carried a scythe in its brutal arms. Athien understood the reason for its appearance. The pretence was over. The colony's doom was sealed.

She shot a panicked glance towards Telaris, her cry of warning lost as the beastmen took up their maddening yelping once more. He was pale, drained, his face streaked with blood. But he stood his ground, and his eyes yet burned with the stubborn fire she knew so well. He would wait for his doom and meet it, and there was no power in the world strong enough to deflect that. The beast approached, and its shadow fell across him. The scythe swung.

'For Isha and Kurnous!' cried Telaris, bringing his sword to meet the blow, and the metal clashed in a shower of sparks.

As if released from a spell, the beastmen charged in around their leader with a horrifying roar, the defenders surging to meet them. Steel clashed on steel, the night air ringing with cries of defiance, madness and agony. Asrel, looking exhausted from his earlier exertions, had joined the fray, his eyes glinting savagely, strands of lurid energy streaming from his fingertips as he attempted to pick out the beastlord amongst the confusion. Telaris danced around his opponent, trusting to speed rather than bulk. The monster lunged after him time and again, each blow missing by a hand's breadth. Telaris's strokes were cleaner. He blooded the beast twice. Athien roused herself, cursing her slowness. She ran up the remaining ladder and curled her leg around the rungs to make a platform. Pulling the string tight, she let fly the first of her arrows. It flew spinning deep into the morass of fur and horns. A strangled yell told her it had found its target, and she smiled grimly. Two more followed. Others joined her on the walls, and the air filled with the whine of yew and sinew.

But the numbers were too great. The flaxen-haired youth was brought down at last, two tusked horrors dragging him into the mud. Even as he stabbed at them in defiance, his struggle ended with a sickening crunch of bone. The guards were driven back from the watchtower and towards the fire, their white cloaks and silver mail bloodied, sullied and ruptured. The bolts of magic from the ramparts ceased, Asrel's bloodied figure at last overwhelmed by the endless forms swarming up the wooden walls. Telaris fought on, desperately rallying his troops around him, fighting furiously against the towering lord of the beasts. As if defying the pull of the earth, his sword still thrust in glittering arcs, and his body still rose into the air to meet the curve of the scythe. But he had to fall back as his companions were cut down around him. The arrows flew, but it was not enough. With a gurgled roar of triumph, its back bristling with feathered shafts, the beastlord raised the scythe one more time. Telaris was off-balance. Athien felt the scream of warning clog in her

throat. The blade fell. He crumpled into the gore trod-
den earth.

Athien cried out, tears of rage stinging her eyes. A wave
of grief and horror passed through her. The beastlord
raised its obscene arms to the night and bellowed to the
stars. She drew a sword from beside her, a madness rising. Death was certain for all of them, but there was still
vengeance. With a prayer to Khaine, her first, she made
to leap into the slaughter below.

But then, confusion. There was something else in the
compound. A ripple of indecision passed through the
ranks of the braying horde. Their champion hesitated,
and then turned, his roars silenced. The surviving
defenders felt it, and raised their swords once more. Her
own blade in hand, Athien halted, a flicker of desperate
hope kindling. There were obscure forms, dozens of
them, in the shadows. They were at the back of the
beasts, hacking with axes, plunging into the heart of the
marauding mass.

'Sword kin!' she cried, collecting her wits. 'With me,
for Telaris and Ulthuan!'

Battered they may have been, but the elf defenders rose
up as one. The beasts were suddenly consumed with
doubt. From the edge of her vision, Athien saw their lord
stagger and fall, the axes rising over his prone body.
There were figures all around them, leaping from the
darkness, clad in rags, their shaggy hair streaming in the
firelight like flails. Athien charged into the fray, filled
with a sudden, savage elation, her sword ringing as it fell
against the filth and horror before it. She was no sword-
maiden, and her unpracticed blows were wild, but the
blood of Isha and Kurnous ran in her veins and the look
in her eyes would have set back her old tutors in Yvresse
if they could have seen it. Swords and axes rose in unison, and the thick blood of the beasts ran freely with that
of the fallen defenders. The twisted horrors scattered

against the furious assault, creeping and yelping as they sought refuge beyond the gates. But they were caught between two foes, and the blades pursued them with bitter intent. The butchery began.

MUCH LATER, SWEAT-STREAKED and weary, Athien leaned on her sword. The sky was grey in the east, the fire a smoking pile of angry embers. She looked around. With a pang of grief, she saw how many had died. If it had not been for their strange allies, none would be alive to bury them. Now they were slipping back into the trees, merging into the land like spectres, all but one. He stood before her, his brown eyes as steady as before, his tanned skin stained with blood. He was not as tall as her, but was broader, and had a calm solidity.

There were no words they could exchange, but when Athien looked into his eyes once more she saw the intelligence there. They were not animals, then, not like the rabble they had driven back into the shadows.

He put his hand out. It cradled her dagger. She nodded, and took it back. The gesture demanded a response; her mind searched for one. With a lurch of reluctance, she reached for her amulet, unclasped the chain, and gave it to him in turn. It seemed the proper thing. He bowed, accepted it, and turned it over in his hands, regarding it with a steady, attentive gaze. Even in the weak light, its amethyst heart was ablaze.

Then he came closer. She could smell his strong odour, the scent of the forest. Once more she found herself transfixed by his gaze. She didn't pull away this time, but returned it. He was trying to tell her something, something about the place. His eyes left hers, and he looked around, to the rocky outcrops, the river and the clearing in the trees. Slowly, she began to grasp the sense of it: the land, they wanted it. These strange newcomers were the true invaders. Telaris had seen it. A stronghold in such a place could govern the land around it for many leagues, he'd said. And they knew it too.

But could such... savages really raise their own settlement here? She felt her mind exploring the strands of possibility. *You see things deeply*, Ferien had said. And now she sensed, albeit as a mere glimpse reflected in the brown eyes before her, the destiny of the strangers, their strength and their resolve. She knew that more of them were coming. If they could see off the beastmen, they were neither as weak nor as backward as they first appeared. She looked back at the figure before her, and smiled resignedly. His impassive gaze seemed to promise so much. She wanted to talk to him, advise him, teach him, but there were no words.

She heard her name being called, apparently from far away. It was Telaris. Hope leapt in her, and she made to run back to the compound. She turned as she did so, but the strange figure was already loping off into the trees. He was gone in a moment. Athien paused, her mind in two places, but it was no good, she couldn't follow him. She hurried instead inside the ruined walls, the compound busy with the guards tending to the wounded and dousing the few remaining fires. Telaris lay against the shell of the watchtower, propped against the charred wood. An ugly gash traversed his forehead. His shirt was brown with his own blood. Athien rushed to his side, clasping his hand to her cheek.

'I thought you were dead, cousin,' she whispered, the tears rising in her at last.

Telaris winced.

'I too, for a time,' he croaked, 'but I'm told we had allies in the forest. You should have wandered around up there more often.'

Athien laughed, her eyes moist, the relief and the lingering grief taking their toll. Telaris looked around the ruined camp and sighed deeply.

'Well, we've survived,' he said grimly. 'Once the dead are buried, we can rebuild the wall. I feel sure the worst is over.'

Athien shook her head, stroking Telaris's hand tenderly.

'No, cousin,' she said softly, 'this place is not for us. We're not the only invaders here. You've seen the others. I don't know where they're from, and they may appear weak now, but I've looked into their eyes. I've seen their intention, and their intention is to rule.'

Telaris shook his head.

'The savages?' he asked weakly. 'I cannot believe it. We have a task to perform: to found a city, a colony for the glory of Asuryan. I won't return before I accomplish it.'

'The task will be fulfilled,' said Athien, with a sad certainty. 'There will be a white-walled city here, and no doubt a mighty realm around it. Ships will ply the waterways, and the forests will give way to roads and fields, just as they do in Ulthuan. But we won't build it. They will. Search your heart and you will know the truth of it.'

Telaris met her gaze for a moment, the flame of defiance in his face. Then it faded. He looked around: the walls were torn open, the dead lying where they had fallen. The sea serpent banner fluttered weakly from its splintered staff. Those that still walked did so with effort. The colony was rent apart, its spirit dissipated. His eyes lowered.

'When the camp is in order,' he said, his voice strained, 'we'll begin to load the ship.'

He looked broken. Athien stroked his cheek lightly, knowing how deeply Telaris felt the pain of defeat. But he would recover, and there were pressing tasks ahead for all of them. She rose, and began to direct the treatment of the wounded.

As she went, she knew she was being watched. Somewhere, high in the hills above the river, brown eyes were regarding her, brown fingers clutching an amulet tightly, its artistry far beyond his people's skill or knowledge, for now. She paused for a moment, looking around at the tree covered hills. The fast rising sun had gilded the branches with a skein of gold, the river glowing a deep green under the overhanging boughs. For all the terrors within, it was still a paradise.

Make good use of it, she thought to herself, as if addressing her unseen observer.

Then she turned, and walked down the path to the ship.

PURIFICATION
by Robert E. Vardeman

THEODRIC FAHRENGELD HESITATED, cocked his head to one side and listened hard. He was being stalked. The roar of the Howling River behind him drowned out the small clicking sounds of toenails against rock, almost. He looked up into the foothills of the World's Edge Mountains, hunting for movement, the glint of setting sunlight on steel, anything. It was the deep whiff he took of the razor cold air that alerted him to his foe. With a swift movement, he drew his sword, swung around and stared into the skaven's squinting, blood-shot eyes. Theodric's first savage slash cut off a hand holding a dagger. Blood spurted outwards over him in a sticky red fountain. Locked in a furious rage, he slashed, and took off an extended arm clutching a sharp edged sword.

The skaven he faced snarled, showed broken yellow teeth and waved bloody stumps at him. This time Theodric planted his feet, took his sword hilt firmly in both hands and directed the blunted, battle-nicked blade at the ratman's scrawny throat. The impact of steel against spine knocked Theodric back a step, and only partially decapitated his mortal enemy.

It took a second cut to completely part head from body. The scrawny rat carcass quivered and kicked in its death throes.

For a moment all Theodric could do was pant harshly and stare at the corpse. Then pain clawed at his brain, and his eye burned with hellish fury. He clapped a hand over his right eye and tried to dig it out to give release from the intense pain.

No, do not. You must put out the food.

The voice in his head vibrated, and threatened to knock loose what little sanity he had left. He had no choice but to obey. Blinking furiously, he opened both eyes and stared. His vision was slightly blurred in his right eye because of the daemonic maggot burrowing inside it.

Now, came the command he could not resist. *You will not fail me. I let you kill that one because you have not completed what I need done.*

'I hate you!' Theodric tried to draw his knife and plunge it into his own heart, through the armhole in his chainmail. Better to die a coward on his own blade than to betray his city, his beloved wife Signy and his two daughters, Kara hardly five and Gretchen scant weeks past three. If he did as the maggot ordered, they would die along with his city and his honour. Thedoric wore the burden heavily because he was the captain of the guard, entrusted with protecting Hochwald from its enemies, not betraying it.

His hand shook as he pulled the blade closer to his flesh, but every thought he had, every move he made, was studied closely by the damnable maggot that had insinuated itself into his eye. Ottiwell, Hochwald's sorcerer, had cried out one morning eight days ago that witchsight burned his brain. Something new and terrible

had come to bedevil the city. No patrol of callow youth
would suffice to meet this danger outside the city walls.
On a patrol with his four most trusted veteran soldiers,
Theodric had come upon a sorcerer busying himself with
arcane doings. He knew immediately that this was the
source of Ottiwell's anguish. His skin had crawled and
he felt immediately nauseous.

When the shrivelled man crouching in the centre of
the sandy spit looked up, Theodric knew fear. The eyes
fixed on his were filled with more hate than he believed
existed in the world.

He did not remember giving the order to attack, but
his men had surged forward, into spells cast by that sorcerer of Nurgle, Lord of Pestilence. A cry had ripped from
the lips of Norbert, to Theodric's right, as an inky veil
was cast forth and descended on him, slashing deep,
bloody channels in his flesh. The instant a strand of that
horror net touched his handsome face, necrosis began.
The flesh decayed into stringy, grey gobbets until only
stark white skull bone showed. Burnick, to his left had
fared no better. A greasy snake had whipped along the
ground at the vile sorcerer's conjuring. Its mouth had
opened impossibly wide and Burnick had been sucked
within, swallowed whole. Theodric had not heard the
man's death cries; he had felt them deep in his soul.
Within seconds, only viscous brown sputum with the
aspect of sewage leaked from the snake's fanged mouth.
Theodric had slashed viciously, severing the snake's
head.

Ankle-deep in filth as the magical snake fell apart,
Theodric had watched helplessly as Arienn and Willem
died together from the sorcerer's next casting. Their bel-
lies bulged, then exploded. Only their armour held them
together long enough for their bodies to collapse. Then
their guts oozed forth in an obscene tide of gore and
entrails.

Although it was steel against sorcery, Theodric had set upon the man, now weakened from casting such horrific spells in his own defence. The accursed sorcerer of Nurgle defended himself well with first dagger and then spell. The four with Theodric had been slain; they were the lucky ones.

Before the minion of Nurgle had at last perished under Theodric's relentless blade, he had cast a final spell, sending a sorcerous worm into the soldier's mouth. Theodric had tried to spit it out, cut it out, and drive it from him with a firebrand. To no avail. It had slowly bored upwards through the roof of his mouth and had lodged in his right eye. What daemonic instructions or perilous mission it had been entrusted with mattered less to Theodric than the agony he bore, in body and mind, if he tried to disobey the maggot. It saw what he saw and knew what he intended. It read his mind and fought constantly to control his actions. If cajoling failed, it resorted to soul-slaying pain.

Theodric failed to kill himself. Instead, he dropped his dagger and opened a sealed jar, as ordered. He began spreading the foul meat along the protective wall on Hochwald's north-east corner where no guard patrolled. The Howling River rushed past the north side of the walled city, affording only a narrow path between unscalable wall and treacherous flowing water.

No man could attack from that vantage, but the skaven were not men. If drawn to this spot, they could clamber up the east wall in numbers great enough to overwhelm the city watch. Before Ottiwell's insect-destroying spell had been laid, years of insect borne diseases had reduced the ranks of fighting men inside the walls, forcing the diminished guard to stare out over plains to the south and farmlands to the west where other, human armies were most likely to attack. Northern water and eastern foothills were only occasionally under scrutiny. Therein lay the maggot's plan. Lure the skaven from their underground lair to the city's weak point.

The daemonic worm had learned of this failing in Hochwald's defence from Theodric, reading his mind, forcing him to think of ways to defeat his own people. He closed his right eye and stared hard at the fallen dagger, but he knew he could never kill himself. The worm knew his intention at the same instant he did and countered him every time.

As he scattered the rotted entrails, he heard the chittering of skaven scouts in the nearby eastern hills. He was betraying his city, his family and his clan. The ratmen's attack would succeed, because Theodric could do naught but obey the Nurgle-sent worm in his eye.

With a disgusted heave, he threw the rest of the meat away from the guard wall into a pool carved into the riverbank. His sword slid smoothly from its scabbard when he saw two skaven already on the odorous trail into the heart of the city that he was honour bound to protect.

No, let them...

Theodric forced away the command by will alone. A berserk rage seized him, wresting control from the daemon maggot. He was blind in his right eye, but he cared nothing. Fury such as he had never experienced, even in the heat of battle at Middenheim, possessed him totally. Sword swinging, he thundered forward. He heard distant echoes in his brain telling him to stop, but the rage overwhelmed his senses.

Theodric's blade slashed a bright, deadly arc and cut deeply into a skaven warrior's torso. Foul blood spurted, and the ratman let out an ear splitting screech. Theodric put his foot against the skaven's thin armour and tough body, and kicked hard, freeing his blade from its leather armour sheath so that he could twist around and gut another of the huge rats.

He got in one last swipe at a third ratman, now far past danger from his blade, before his rage faded and the maggot regained control. The skaven scout vanished eastward into the hills. Theodric dropped to his knees and lowered his defiled blade as he waited for death.

It did not come. A sense of triumph filled him, but it was not his triumph.

I have impressed on the ratman's mind that a religious artefact, a claw from their great Lord Skrolk, is being desecrated within the city. Nothing will stop the ratmen from climbing the city walls!

Theodric sobbed heavily. He had failed. The daemonic maggot had won. Within days the skaven horde would surge forwards and overwhelm his city.

'Go away,' Theodric called. He had seen Signy, dressed in the fine quilted coat he had given her on his promotion to city captain, coming up the winding path, but had hoped she would not discover him. She was almost as good a tracker as he was, and was focused on finding him. He hunkered down in the rocky depression and clung to his sword. He worried that the daemon worm in his eye would find a use for her. Theodric was tired to the bone from fighting the worm these past three days. It waited for something, and the man feared that he knew what. The skaven were gathering in a cavern that opened above Hochwald. With the lies the maggot had forced into the ferocious brain of their scout, the entire skaven clan would attack an unsuspecting city.

'I will not. Theo, come out here.' Signy stamped her tiny foot and put her balled fists on her hips. She might have been ordering their small daughters about, instead of her husband and captain of the city guard. 'Everyone in the city thinks you are dead. I knew you weren't.'

'Why not?'

'I... I didn't *feel* it,' she said. 'Now come out where I can see you.' She gasped and took an involuntary step back when she saw him.

'Go away. Hurry. You have to warn everyone in the city that the skaven are going to attack.'

'Skaven? They're nothing but tales to frighten the children.' She took a deep whiff of him and almost gagged. Once, he had cut a heroic figure in his uniform. Not now. His sallet was dented and the insignia of his rank had been torn free. His demeanour matched the aspect of his tattered, filthy long coat. 'I fear for you, Theo. Please, come back with me.'

'I carry their scent,' Theodric said, holding up his arms. He was still drenched in their vile blood. The worm refused to allow him to cleanse himself. His chainmail rattled and clanked with his every movement as the rings rotated, scrubbing themselves of rust and blood, but his flesh still chafed from contact with the skaven blood.

'I...' Signy hesitated. She stared hard at him and saw the truth on his face. 'They *are* real?'

'That is what Ottiwell's witchsight revealed.'

'Come back, then, Theo. You can rally the guard. They are in such disarray with you gone, my dear.'

'Horst is not much of a commander,' he said. His chief lieutenant was a political appointment, although Horst sometimes showed flashes of skill in combat. But as a leader, he left much to be desired.

'Come along. We can bathe you and–'

'No!'

She stared at him with her sky bright eyes. Her mouth opened and then clamped shut. Signy started to speak again and then she began to shake all over.

'No, no, stop, stop!' Theodric hammered at his head with his fist, trying to deter the daemon worm. Madness threatened him, but it would be preferable to allowing the maggot to influence Signy.

She is mine now, the maggot said smugly. *She will obey me.*

'Not when she's out of your sight. I'll cut my own hamstrings so I can't follow.'

The worm did not respond. There was no need. Theodric knew he would be unable to injure himself to such an extent before Nurgle's worm stopped him.

'Who are you talking to?' Signy was pale and her voice was strained, but she seemed unaware that she had experienced a seizure.

'Run, Signy, return to the city and warn them the skaven are preparing to attack on the eastern salient. Even Horst can mount a decent defence given enough time.'

'I... what am I supposed to tell them?' Confusion warped her lovely face as she struggled to remember what he had told her.

'The skaven: the ratmen are going to attack.'

'What?'

She is unable to warn them. I have ordered her to forget. The worm laughed harshly. The sound echoed within Theodric's head until he wanted to scream in agony.

'What of Blackwind?'

'Our raven? He is above somewhere.' Signy put her fingers into her mouth and let loose a shrill whistle. From high above came a black speck that grew in size with frightening speed. At the last possible instant, a huge raven thrust out its wings, braked and landed lightly on the padded shoulder of her heavy coat.

'Skaven are going to attack,' Theodric said quickly. 'Warn the guard in my name.'

It will do no good, the maggot said. *The raven is quite intelligent and its split tongue gives it the power of speech, but it cannot warn the city, either.*

'Damn you, damn you,' Theodric cried, falling to his knees. He looked up at his wife and the bird fluttering to maintain its balance on her shoulder. He had hoped the worm would not realise the raven's speech ability, but then the magical worm knew whatever he did. How could he outsmart himself?

You cannot, the maggot gloated. *Nurgle will be served. Your city and all within it will die. The skaven will gnaw the bones of your family.*

'Leave, go back to Hochwald,' Theodric said. That was not what he wanted to tell Signy. He wanted her to gather their daughters and flee the city before the skaven destroyed it. The worm would not allow him to give her such a warning. But a thought came to him that had been crouching at the fringes of his imagination. The worm could not enter Hochwald by itself.

Ottiwell! The entire city was under the sorcerer's protective spell. After being overrun by locusts that threatened to devour their grain, Ottiwell had cast a sheltering spell that drove out all insects. The spell must still be in full force, otherwise the maggot would allow Theodric to enter, and there the worm would complete whatever Nurgle spawned plot it had been entrusted with.

'Goodbye, Theo,' Signy said. She reached up to Blackwind, transferring the raven from her shoulder to her left wrist as if it were a gyrfalcon preparing to take flight after pigeons.

He tried to beg her to take her regards to Ottiwell. With his witchsight, the sorcerer might sense the foul stench of Nurgle's magicks on her and respond. But words would not come to his lips, thanks to the daemonic presence in his eye. Theodric watched her leave, knowing she was magically bound never to speak of the warning, and had no reason to seek out Ottiwell. Hochwald would perish and, along with the city, so would his family. The man cried openly, to the maggot's great pleasure.

* * *

HE COULD NOT count their numbers. The skaven scampered through the cavern in the foothills above Hochwald, hidden in shadows, caused by sunlight angling inward from outside, but revealing themselves by their stench. Theodric stood a little straighter and wondered if dying at the gnarled hand of a skaven warrior would be possible. Drop his sword just a bit from en garde, let a high-line blade thrust end his life. That would relieve him of the guilt he felt for luring the skaven to his city, showing them how to breach the defences and – his heart almost exploded from hammering so hard – the inevitable death of his family.

I will not let them harm you, the maggot said. *They are simple-minded and easily controlled.*

'Then you don't need me. Let me die.'

I want you to suffer.

Theodric knew there was more reason than this for the daemonic worm keeping him alive. No matter how much magic had been infused into the worm by the well-slain sorcerer, it could never move as quickly as a man strode. Theodric could travel thirty miles a day, if necessary. A worm, even a daemonic one, might wriggle only thirty feet. The only consolation he had was in forcing the worm to summon the skaven army, because Ottiwell's ward spell prevented insects and their ilk, including maggots and worms, from entering Hochwald.

Stop thinking that, the maggot ordered sharply. *You will never attempt to enter Hochwald.*

'The spell would kill you, wouldn't it?'

You will die, too.

Theodric said nothing. He wished he was at the front gate of his city so he could rush forward until the sorcerer's ward spell drove the maggot from his head. What did it matter if he died? Had he not tried to kill himself rather than suffer the shame his actions brought down on him?

You will live to see the skaven ripping the flesh off your daughters' living bodies, the daemon worm crowed.

Theodric's hand shook as he gripped his sword hilt. He looked into the dimly lit cavern filled with skaven and wondered if even a fully armed and warned army could turn them when they attacked. They were so numerous that it hardly seemed likely.

They need prodding, the maggot said. *They assemble but do not venture forth.*

Theodric stumbled when he was forced to turn and walk away from the cavern mouth. The steep slope took its toll on him physically. He had not eaten well since the worm had invaded his eye; it had not allowed it. Theodric trudged along, an unwilling participant in whatever new scheme the worm had concocted. Once free of the cave, he was directed towards the spot where he had killed Nurgle's sorcerer. Hope was born again. There might be something hidden among the dead mage's belongings that would be useful.

You do not know the spells, the daemon worm said coldly. *You will find the pit holding the warpstone.*

'I can't handle that. It will kill me. The smallest touch will drive me insane!'

How strong is the will to live in you feeble humans, the worm observed. *Do you want to die? Then why do you balk at touching warpstone?*

Theodric could not answer. All his life he had feared magical things. Although Ottiwell protected Hochwald and even used his magical skills, giving hope with the occasional healing, Theodric wanted as little to do with the Dark Powers as possible. If a man should die, let it be in battle, swinging a sword. An arrow or crossbow bolt through the heart was a better death than rotting from some vile spell. He had no idea what might happen if he touched the warpstone, but it had to be horrific.

'What do you plan to do with the warpstone?' It hardly seemed fair that the daemon worm could read his thoughts, but he had no idea what the maggot planned. This thought caused him to laugh harshly. Nothing had been fair since he had slain Nurgle's minion.

The skaven need to be given an incentive to attack Hochwald, the worm said. *This will provide it.*

'Will it kill them?'

Theodric believed he had got a whiff of the maggot's plan. The skaven were fierce fighters but lacked direction. Tossing warpstone into their midst would focus them on Hochwald in ways that a few pounds of rotten entrails and a couple of magically implanted suggestions never could.

They will fight to retrieve their artefact.

'Their hero's nonexistent claw,' Theodric said. 'Why do you want Hochwald destroyed? Because of Ottiwell's spell? All you need to do is avoid the city.' Even as he spoke he knew the maggot had been conjured into existence after its master had come to the walls. Whatever necessity there had once been for destroying Hochwald had died with Nurgle's sorcerer. Something more was at play.

I am as much a pawn as you are, the maggot said in a surprising revelation. *Now dig. Dig!*

Theodric stumbled forward and fell to his knees. He saw where something had been hidden under a huge stack of rocks. Throwing back the smaller ones left a trio of immense rocks that he could hardly reach around, much less move. The worm kept him hard at work, trying different tactics to move the boulders. He finally got a long branch, found a fulcrum for the lever and used that to budge one rock. The instant the stone rolled away, Theodric dropped the branch and threw up his hands to cover his eyes.

Look into the face of hell, the worm said.

The radiant power of the skull-sized warpstone was immediately evident. Theodric clamped his left eye closed, but from his right where the maggot resided leapt a lambent green luminescence that enfolded the warpstone and dimmed its raw power.

Wrap the warpstone in cloth, ordered the maggot.

With a heavy heart, Theodric did as he was ordered. The worm used its power over him only twice to send lightning bolts of pain down into his groin to ensure his obedience. The heavy lump of warpstone secured in the dead sorcerer's cloak, Theodric slung it over his shoulder and began the hike back to the cavern where the skaven were assembled.

The world shifted endlessly around him as he walked. Theodric swallowed hard and tried to keep his balance.

Do not fail me, warned the worm. *The warpstone works on your senses. Keep walking. Get to the skaven army and throw the warpstone into their midst!*

Theodric knew what the result would be. The ratmen would go berserk. The snapping, snarling tide would flood out of the cave and down the slopes to Hochwald. Without an adequate guard on the east wall, the skaven could clamber up and into the city. The walls that had protected those within so ably, and for so long, would turn into a prison. The skaven would slaughter them no matter how hard they fought.

Hurry! I grow impatient for this to be over.

'Why?' asked Theodric. 'What is within Hochwald that incites you so?'

He swung the warpstone around, pulling it up higher so that it bumped into his head. As it touched Theodric's skull, the maggot reacted. Theodric felt an excitement more than sexual, more than physical, more than spiritual. In that instant, the worm leaked a small thought that Theodric intercepted.

He caught his breath. A silk-thread case of eggs lay within Hochwald, unaffected by Ottiwell's ward spell because they were still dormant. Should the protoworms be fertilised, if Ottiwell's spell was lifted, they would hatch and swarm throughout the city. Once each worm found a human host, they would spread throughout the Badlands to the south, to Tilea, north to the Empire. Theodric stumbled and staggered as the daemon worm revelled in the power of the warpstone.

To cover the zephyr of thought he had inadvertently shared, Theodric swung the cloak with the warpstone wrapped within above his head. Like a hammer thrower, he heaved with all the power in his back, sending the cloak with its load high into the air. For a brief instant, it blazed brighter than the sun. Or was that the worm within his eye reacting to the warpstone? Blinded, he let out a scream and stumbled backwards as the warpstone smashed into the ground and exploded in a radiant cloud of dust. Each particle blazed like a new sun and twisted sinuously before fading, only to be replaced by yet another fragment.

Away, away, attack the human city!

Sightless, repelled by the feel of skaven pressing against him as they rushed through the cavern mouth towards Hochwald, Theodric cowered down. He had not realised he had come exactly to the spot the maggot wanted; his sense of time was twisted and wrong. Theodric clung to the hilt of his sword although he could not see. He thought to draw it and simply swing wildly, but the press of ratmen shifted too dramatically. At first they had rushed from the cave towards his city, but now they surged back. Theodric opened his eyes, but he remained blind.

To the city! The daemonic maggot tried to rally the skaven and keep them moving, but the warpstone had done more than whip them to frenzied activity. It had confused them as much as it had Theodric.

Blinking hard, he caught vague images and finally regained his sight. The worm had been agitated by the warpstone and still fought to control not only its own turbulent thoughts but also the skaven.

Theodric pressed back against a rock and saw that only a few skaven ventured out to attack against Hochwald. But this hesitation would be short-lived when the maggot regained its senses. He dug his toes in and ran as hard as he could. As he passed each ratman he took a swipe with his sword. Sometimes he struck, other times he did not, but the closer he got to Hochwald the more he realised the worm was reasserting its power over him. The respite granted by the warpstone faded.

Stop. Do not attack the ratmen. Let them find their way to the walls of your city. They will dine on human flesh tonight!

Theodric fell to his knees, sobbing in anger and frustration. The worm had regained its control over him. His sword clattered to the ground. All around, he heard the excited chittering of the rats as the daemonic maggot urged them onwards. Theodric looked up at a distant sound, scanning the sky until he saw a tiny black speck. He watched, uncomprehending. Then he understood.

The worm understood the danger at the same instant; too late.

Theodric's raven, Blackwind, dived like a feathered arrow, beak outstretched. Theodric screamed as the bird hit him in full dive and knocked him backwards. Then he gave voice to true pain as Blackwind pecked at his right eye. The sharp beak tip tapped first against his forehead, causing a tiny fountain of blood to flow down and blind the maggot-infested eye. Blackwind sank talons into Theodric's neck to steady itself. It found its true target and drove downward, beak severing first his eyelid and then the sensitive flesh holding the eye. A wet popping sound was followed by a jolt of pain that seized Theodric and caused his entire body to go rigid. The rictus quickly passed, and he twitched feebly. He wiped blood and the remains of his sundered eye socket away to see the raven raise its head, open its beak and then swallow his eye, whole, with the daemon worm inside it.

'Blackwind,' he gasped out. Theodric pressed his hand to his empty eye socket. 'Thank you.' The raven turned its head to one side, looked at him knowingly, then launched into the air. In seconds the bird had vanished.

Theodric squared his shoulders, took one last look into the cloudless sky and knew he had lost a companion and true friend. If the bird's sacrifice was not to be forfeit, Theodric had to reach Hochwald and rally the guard. Even Horst would have to see the menace facing the city when the first wave of skaven swarmed from the foothills out of their underground lair.

His body exhausted, Theodric moved by force of will. Picturing Signy and his daughters helped. The need to make up for his lapse of honour in rousing the skaven, though it had been at the maggot's command, drove him even harder. After what seemed an eternity, he stumbled towards the roar of the river and finally saw the stone walls and main gate of his city.

'Alert!' he cried. 'Alert the guard. Attack! The city is under attack!'

'That you, cap'n?' A youngling, hardly sixteen summers past, peered nearsightedly at him from a watchtower.

'Skaven,' he gasped out. 'There's an army of skaven on my heels. We must repel them. They'll attack along the east wall.'

'But we don't have no guards there,' the young man said, confused.

'Open the gate. Let me in. That's an order, soldier.'

Theodric was glad to see that some measure of discipline still held. The youngling scampered down to open the gate personally.

'We thought you was dead. Ain't seen you in weeks, Cap'n Fahrengeld.'

'Ring the alarm bell, and send word immediately to Ottiwell. There're enemy spells involved.'

Theodric was barely strong enough to swing the heavy gate closed behind him, but he succeeded. Then he made certain the locking bar fell into place. The skaven would not attack this point at first, but when their assault on the east wall failed, they would try other routes to gain entry. The maggot had instilled the false message in enough of them, and had spurred them on with the warpstone.

The bell clanged loudly and echoed throughout Hochwald, calling out the soldiers and alerting the populace.

'Who ordered the alarm?' Horst pushed his way from his command post near the gate and then stopped and stared, open mouth. 'Is it you, captain? Truly you?'

'Reinforce the east wall immediately. Then double the guard. Get enough arms and arrows there for a long fight. And Ottiwell, summon the sorcerer right away.'

'It *is* you! Under all that blood and dirt, it *is* you!' crowed Horst. He grabbed Theodric by the shoulders and pulled him around to be certain of his identity. 'No one else would have such presence to command–'

'Obey!' Theodric braced himself on the curving wall of the staircase spiralling up to the walkways. He was pleased to see Horst coming to heel without more of his endless yammering.

'Right away, captain!' Horst cried. He spun and bellowed, 'A hundred of the guard to the east wall.' He glanced over his shoulder at his commander and then changed the order. 'Two hundred! Two hundred guardsmen to the eastern battlements!'

Theodric clapped Horst on the shoulder, more to support himself than to assure the man he had done well.

'Go,' Theodric gasped. 'Take charge until I get there. It will be the fight of our lives!' He saw Horst blanch and then nod once. 'Courage,' Theodric said. This simple order stiffened Horst's backbone and sent the officer rushing off, bellowing for guardsmen to supply those on the wall and reinforce their line, should it be necessary. Theodric hoped it would be enough. He knew the danger they faced. Horst did not.

Legs swollen and arms like lead, Theodric made his way to the top of the guard wall. He reached up and put his hand over the empty eye socket that still oozed blood. His depth perception was gone. In the distance everything looked equally far away. That would not matter. He gripped the hilt of his sword and began walking around to get to the east wall.

He saw a ripple of dread pass through the guards who had already responded to Horst's command. Theodric knew what caused their uneasiness.

'Archers, fire!' he bellowed. 'Not a single ratman is to reach the top. Slay them with arrows, then use your swords. When they are even closer, use your daggers! None shall enter my city!'

Seeing their captain buoyed their spirits and lent accuracy to their arrows. By the time Theodric reached the wall and peered down, a pile of dead skaven had provided a stepping stone for hundreds more. The ratmen died by tens and hundreds, and still they came.

Theodric lopped off the snout of the first rat warrior to reach the top of the wall. It squealed in pain and rage, and tumbled backwards into its fellows. Arrows whistled past Theodric's ears, and his world filled with an unending stream of flashing swords and dying skaven. He tried not to dwell on the huge numbers of his own men who perished at the blades and teeth of the skaven.

When he was sure he could no longer fight, he fought another minute, and then another few seconds. Then he cried out encouragement, hoarsely, until he could no longer hear his own voice. The stench of spilled blood and fear quietly faded as Theodric passed into unconsciousness.

He dreamed. It had to be a dream because it was so pleasant.

'My love,' Signy said and kissed him.

'My love,' he replied. Dead arms resurrected to embrace her. Then he realised this was no dream. His eye opened and fixed on his wife's lovely face only inches from his. 'You're alive?'

'Of course I am, and so are you.'

'Kara and Gretchen?'

'Safe. Everyone's safe because of you. The skaven have been defeated.'

'Run off, not defeated,' he said grimly. He used Signy as a crutch to stand. He sloshed about in ankle-deep blood as he moved along the parapet. His men cheered him, and he acknowledged them as best he could.

'Let's get you to a chirurgeon,' Signy said, steering him from the scene of the battle.

Theodric marvelled that the rats had been turned, but at such a huge cost! A hundred or more of his soldiers had died. He caught his breath. The youngling who had admitted him to the city and raised the alarm at his order had died and been partially gnawed.

'You are a hero of Hochwald,' came a deeply resonant voice.

Theodric turned his head and had trouble focusing. Having only one eye would require practice in seeing. He managed to work through the welter of colours in Ottiwell's robes, the purples and greens mingling with splotches of yellow and red.

'Ottiwell,' he said, head bowing to the deformed sorcerer. 'I want to commend you on your purification spell. It kept Nurgle's worm from the city.' He caught his breath as he remembered. 'There's an egg sac somewhere. I must–'

'It has been discovered and burned,' Ottiwell assured him.

Theodric looked at the sorcerer and for the first time, a smile came to his lips. 'Our master gives us all hope.'

'The forces of corruption have been routed,' Ottiwell said. 'That which was, is no more. The Lord of Change has prevailed!'

A joyous cry went up behind them, and from on high came a loud screech. Theodric canted his head to one side and saw Blackwind wheeling around above them. He held out his arm. The raven spiralled down and then suddenly veered away. Ottiwell's ward spell kept all insects at bay, including Nurgle's worm, resting in Blackwind's gut. Theodric mourned for the loss of the raven even as he rejoiced at all who had been saved.

'I would see our children,' he said.

Signy helped him down the stone steps and into a city honouring his valour.

SANCTITY
by Nick Kyme

DAWN LIGHT CREPT over the horizon as the wagon emerged from the gathering mist, heading for Hochenheim. The driver urged on the beast pulling the huge wagon, and the creature's heaving flanks were lathered in feverish sweat. Behind it, the forest was a dense black line. Drakwald they called it: a place of shadows, fraught with dark imaginings. Yarik knew it well.

From his position in the watchtower, he watched the wagon intently as it got closer to the village gates. Years ago, Yarik had worked as a road warden for Baron Krugedorf. During his tenure guarding the highways of the land Yarik had seen it all. Never, though, had he witnessed a wagon travelling alone in this part of the forest. On the edge of the Drakwald forest, even the villages required defences. Hochenheim itself was surrounded by a solid wooden stockade, with two watchtowers and a stout gate, bolted shut at night. Yet this wagon appeared to be without protection; he couldn't see a single outrider.

Grimacing, Yarik got to his feet.

'Wait here,' he growled to Falker. The young Middenlander, cradling a loaded crossbow, nodded obediently.

A speck of flame flared in the half-light as Yarik drew deeply on his pipe. Below him, Hochenheim was waking. Fires were being stoked to ward off a chill morning, a frail old woman was wringing out clothes before attaching them to a line, and the resonant din of a smithy at his anvil emanated from an unseen forge.

Trudging down the wooden steps of the tower, Yarik saw the gates were opening, as they did every day at dawn. As he reached the village entrance, he tried to rub the arthritis out of his hands, remembering wistfully the lost strength of former days, and went to greet the wagon.

'Ho there,' Yarik called, showing his palm in a gesture for the driver to stop at the open gateway.

The wagon looked even more massive up close. Six stout, iron-shod wheels accommodated its weight, and leather flaps covered both sides. The horse pulling it wore a sacking hood over its head, coarse slits in it serving as eyeholes. It was incredible that one beast could bear such a burden.

Yarik gripped the pommel of his sheathed sword as he went to speak to the driver. He moved to pat the beast's flank, but recoiled when it turned sharply with a muted snarl. The wagonner laid a hand on the horse's rump, soothing the creature's belligerence. He held the reins nonchalantly as he leant back, a bizarre, patchwork coat flapping down over his body. Long, black hair shrouded most of his face, and he wore a thin, curled moustache with a tightly cropped spike of beard. Yarik judged men by their eyes, but this fellow's were difficult to discern, obscured by a tall, wide-brimmed hat.

'State your business,' Yarik barked, his breath misting the cold morning air.

'Greetings noble lord,' uttered the driver silkily. 'I am Zanikoff,' he declared, 'and my business, put simply...' he said, leaping from his seat and landing with a flourish, as a bunch of paper flowers appeared in his hand, '...is entertainment,' Zanikoff concluded, with a devilish smile. A flick of the wrist and the flowers vanished.

Yarik was taken aback by the sudden display and half-drew his sword. 'We don't harbour sorcerers here,' he told the stranger.

Behind him, a crowd had gathered.

'I do not intend to bewitch you,' said Zanikoff plaintively, 'merely beguile you with trickery and show.' He moved beyond the gates and towards the crowd. The flowers reappeared in his other hand. 'It's just sleight of hand,' he explained, with a wink, and put his finger to his lips.

Zanikoff turned his attention to the mystified onlookers. He produced a long cane from one of his coat sleeves and walked over to them, singling out a village maiden. He bowed, and gave her the tattered paper flowers. Blushing, the maiden took them.

'Milady,' Zanikoff purred, before twirling to face a young boy, watching the impromptu pantomime open-mouthed. The boy's eyes sparkled at three silver coins that had appeared in Zanikoff's splayed fingers. Juggling them effortlessly, he threw the coins high into the air. The boy tried to follow, but lost them in the light.

'I know what you're thinking,' Zanikoff said, leaning in towards the boy. 'Where are they?' he whispered. Reaching behind the boy's ear, his hand emerged holding a silver coin. 'Here, all the time,' he said, flicking the coin to the boy, who snatched it eagerly.

'Ladies and gentlemen,' Zanikoff continued, walking back to the wagon, which had made its way through the gates and into the square, Yarik starting at its sudden appearance. 'I am Zanikoff,' he said, doffing his hat with a mock courtly bow, 'and may I present for your edification, your delectation and delight, your sheer, pure and unadulterated gratification…' Zanikoff took a deep breath, observing the befuddled faces with veiled amusement, '…the Carnival of Mystery!' He smacked the side of the wagon with his cane and the leather flap covering it rolled away to reveal a garish banner beneath. Two theatrical masks – one happy, the other sad – were described upon it, surrounded by a myriad of colourful images. Amazing beasts, jugglers, sword swallowers, fire-eaters, clowns and acrobats all vied for the crowd's attention. 'Carnival of Mystery' was etched above and below in faded archaic script, and read by the few literate onlookers. The banner was well worn and cracked in places, but still it drew excited gasps.

'What do you want here?' asked Yarik.

Zanikoff swaggered towards the old soldier theatrically.

'Why, that is simple,' he said, eyes widening with glee, 'to perform.' He rapped three more times on the wagon and the back fell open. A menagerie of gaudy characters issued forth. Fire-eaters painted in bizarre tattoos were joined by brutish strongmen, jesters and jugglers, while musicians played out merry tunes on drums and pipes, wearing fantastical costumes, their faces concealed by decadent masks.

'Plays and pantomime is what we offer,' Zanikoff informed the awestruck Hochenheimers, 'great tales of valour,' he said deeply, puffing up his chest, 'tragedy,' he added with a sorrowful frown, 'and comedy!' he concluded raucously, a jester slipping onto his arse to the collective laughter of the entire village.

'Meagre tribute is all we ask,' Zanikoff said, growing serious, shifting his attention back to Yarik. 'To bestow such gifts of mirth and merriment, we crave a simple indulgence.'

Yarik looked back at him nonplussed.

'A stage,' said Zanikoff, a wide grin spreading across his handsome features.

A RAISED WOODEN platform in the village square, usually used for storing sacks of grain, was cleared quickly and turned into a makeshift stage. A vast array of backdrops and pantomime furnishings dressed it. The fixtures looked old and slightly tarnished, but the bedazzled villagers of Hochenheim paid these details no heed. A great apple tree overshadowed the stage. It was the biggest in all of Hochenheim and a symbol of the village, its abundant blossoms full of the promise of spring.

Yarik sat on a barrel, away from the thronging crowd that cooed and called, and laughed at the antics of the Carnival of Mystery. Smoking his pipe, he noticed Alderman Greims, and even Mayor Hansat, entranced by the troupe of masked players. Yarik was secretly impressed by their realistic costumes, turning them into maidens, monsters and mythic heroes.

Other entertainments were going on around the main stage, too: a jester performed tumbling tricks and a ventriloquist with a hand puppet regaled a group of children with his talents. It appeared as if they were moving away from the main crowd. The puppet was a bedraggled looking thing, a mangy dog with one eye, but the engrossed youngsters seemed oblivious.

There was no sign of Zanikoff. After introducing the various festivities, he had vanished. Yarik didn't trust him and wanted to know where he was. He swept his gaze across the crowd and thought he saw something in the shadow of the village tavern, the Black Bear. The wagon Zanikoff and his troupe had arrived in was stationed there, along with the hooded steed. As Yarik got up, he didn't relish reacquainting himself with that beast.

Negotiating the crowd, he headed for the wagon. The noise was almost deafening, such were the raucous cheers and thunderous laughter. But Yarik kept his eyes on the tight alley next to the Black Bear and the thing in the shadows that had caught his attention. For a moment, out of the corner of his eye, he thought he saw a lone young girl following the puppeteer further away from the stage, but he soon lost sight of her, more intent on his investigations.

As he got closer, Yarik saw Zanikoff. He was hefting something heavy into the wagon and after a moment inside, emerged unburdened. Yarik's suspicions grew and for a moment he thought about seeking out Falker; he hadn't seen the young Middenlander for hours.

Yarik pressed on, unperturbed, but by the time he reached the Black Bear, Zanikoff had gone. The wagon door was open, so, giving the horse a wide berth, he worked his way around the wagon. Darkness persisted within. He drew his dagger and took a tentative step up inside.

The wagon's interior was vast; it seemed far larger inside than outside. Yarik willed his eyes to adjust quicker to the dark and his beating heart not to thump so loudly. Taking another step, Yarik realised there was something at the back of the wagon, something big. He swore he could hear it breathing, and a horrible stink assailed his nostrils. Another horse? It would explain how the animal he had seen could carry such a burden if it were shared. As Yarik got closer, he discerned a mis-shapen silhouette, too large and grotesque to be a horse. His days as a road warden, and all the things he had seen dwelling in the deepest bowels of the Drakwald, returned to him and suddenly he knew what this thing was.

'By the gods,' he breathed, reaching slowly for his sword and backing away.

'My noble lord Yarik,' said Zanikoff from behind him.

Yarik turned quickly to find the carnival master blocking his path, his long, sleek silhouette described by the
light at the wagon door as he stood just outside.

Yarik's mind and body screamed at him to flee, but
somehow, through sheer force of will, he compelled himself to stay. To flee now would mean death, he was certain
of that.

Behind him, there was the faint rattling of chains as the
creature shifted. Yarik started to slide out his sword.

'Would you like to peek?' Zanikoff intoned playfully.

Yarik shook his head weakly, mouthing the words he
was desperate to articulate. The drone of the crowd was
distant now, as if heard from underwater. 'No?' Zanikoff
answered for him. 'Tell me,' he said, 'do you know what
curiosity did to the cat?'

Yarik couldn't speak, his mouth sketching words noise-
lessly. He couldn't even shake his head. Hot breath
lapped at his neck; the nauseating stench of decay came
with it, making him retch and it took all of his resolve not
to vomit. Warm piss trickled down his leg and tears filled
his eyes, as all those years of hunting and fighting in the
dark, all that fortitude and bravery, were stripped away.

'I thought not,' Zanikoff said, stepping back from the
wagon's entrance. 'Let me educate you.' The door
slammed shut and Yarik was trapped.

Outside, Zanikoff watched with some satisfaction as
the wagon rocked violently back and forth, the cries of
the ex-road warden quickly muted, much like his fellow
soldier's had been. Molmoth was ever ravenous, his
appetite seldom sated for long.

In the distance, a mother cried out for her child, but the
roaring crowd, oblivious in adulation, smothered her
desperate call.

Zanikoff smiled, watching as the players sprang
through the village, spreading their gifts. The seeds had

been sown and soon, very soon, the harvest would begin.

THE BEATING OF *drums was like thunder across the open plain. Atop a craggy rise a force of knights knelt in prayer, their silver armour gleaming, framed against a blackening horizon. They surrounded a great stone temple with two doves flying above it, despite the approaching storm. A priestess stood at the centre of the penitent warriors, a sword at her side, a book in her hand. She looked down at the foot of the great rise where their enemies gathered, eager for slaughter.*

To the west, there massed a mighty horde, thousands strong, black banners fluttering. Armoured warriors, faces obscured by metal, stood side-by-side with loping daemons. Whelp masters held snarling hounds as they strained at the leash, while above the sound of drums was joined by the beating of wings. A champion of the dark gods waited amongst them, riding a huge and fearsome steed. His armour was the colour of night and the slits in his helm flared with flame-red malevolence.

From the east came rotting warriors encased in husks of rusted armour, their tarnished blades held aloft in tribute. Daemons: horned, cyclopean creatures riddled with decay, capered with them. Their silent lord sat upon an emaciated steed. A ragged hood concealed his face, and pustule ravaged, bone-thin hands clutched a pitted scythe.

At some unseen command, the armies of darkness charged, zealous fury lending them vigour. The knights rose as one to meet them. The priestess raised her sword, tears streaming down her face.

Fury charged the air and the smell of steel filled it. The sound of the charging legions resonated throughout the hillside and then, at last, as the three armies met, a great peal of thunder roiled across the heavens and lightning tore down with all the anger of the gods.

* * *

'WAKE UP.'
  Steel crashed.
  'Mikael…'
  Blood ran like rain.
  'Wake up.'
  Lightning flashed.
  'Mikael!'
Mikael awoke, gasping for breath, as strong hands
shook him. Cold pricked at his sweat soaked face. His
heart beat with the sound of remembered thunder.
Instinctively, he reached for his sword. He found the
templar blade readily, felt the skull-shaped pommel.

'Easy son,' said a giant man clad in thick, black armour,
wrought with sigils of death and mortality. They were the
symbols of their god, Morr. It was Halbranc, his brother-
at-arms.

'You slept like the dead,' he said, voice deep and resonant. He crouched over the young knight, a broad smile
cracking his battle-scarred face.

Mikael looked around, trying to get his bearings. He
was surrounded by trees. A light snow, drifting in a fitful winter breeze, laid a white veneer over their camp.
The others were already up it seemed; the previous
night's fire a blackened scar on the forest floor. Mikael
hugged his black cloak around him. He'd stripped off
his black armour. It lay cradled in a blanket. Recall
rushed back.

They'd been in the Drakwald for three days, hunting
in the shadows and the dark. They'd left their horses at
the Road Warden's Rest, a fortified coaching inn several
miles back, as the forest was too thick and too dangerous for steeds to venture into. They'd been searching
blindly for a renegade, with no guarantee of success, a
warlock of the Cult of the Burning Hand.

Halbranc stood up. His formidable presence cast a
long shadow; he was every inch the avenging knight of

Morr. The hilt of his zweihander protruded from beneath his cloak and was strapped to his back. Snow fell upon his bald pate, but his chiselled features betrayed no discomfort.

'Strap on your armour,' he said, passing Mikael a breastplate with a gauntleted hand. 'Valen has found the renegade's trail.'

'YOU ARE CERTAIN it is Kleiten?' asked Reiner, without emotion. He stood over the young templar scout, one hand resting on the pommel of his blade.

'I cannot be sure,' Valen answered his captain, 'but something has come this way recently and the earth is scorched, yet there are no signs of burnt kindling.'

Reiner turned to Sigson; his cold blue eyes held a question.

'The cult has been known to use the wind of Aqshy in its magics,' said the warrior priest, drawing his cloak tight to his body as he suppressed a shiver.

Reiner held Sigson's gaze, unmoving.

'Kleiten is a fire wizard,' Sigson elaborated, wiping an encrusted veneer of frost from his grey spike of beard.

'Your knowledge of the arcane is… unsettling,' said Reiner with some consideration. He turned back to Valen, who was already on his feet. His twin brother, Vaust was alongside him.

'Find what's keeping Halbranc,' said Reiner. 'We follow the trail.'

Vaust nodded, hurrying back to the nearby campsite to find Reiner's second in command. The fact they were so close only made it all the more galling that they'd missed the renegade's trail earlier. Vaust had only just set off when Halbranc and Mikael emerged into the clearing where their comrades congregated.

'Where is Köller?' Reiner asked. He was the only knight still not present.

'Here,' a low voice answered. Köller emerged from the shadows, regarding his fellow knights with hooded eyes.

Death was no stranger to any of those who came into the service of Morr. Every man in that clearing had a story of loss. Most kept such tragedies to themselves and Köller was no exception, but he bore a particularly terrible burden, and one that never seemed to lift.

Reiner's look was reproachful.

'I'm sorry,' Köller said. 'I was searching for further signs.'

'This is the Drakwald,' Reiner reminded him. 'We stay together.' The captain turned to Valen. 'Lead the way,' he ordered icily, with a final piercing look at Mikael.

The youthful knight couldn't hold his gaze and was glad when Reiner stalked off after the scout.

'I doubt he feels it,' Halbranc whispered to Mikael as they trudged after the others.

'Feels what?'

'The cold,' Halbranc said, a broad smile splitting his craggy features.

'I wonder if he "feels" at all.'

Halbranc laughed, slapping Mikael on the back, sending shudders through his armour.

'Come on,' he urged.

It happened quickly. One moment they were following Valen as he stalked the renegade's trail, the next Köller had started off alone, running as if all the hellish daemons of Chaos were after him.

Reiner had immediately signalled the rest of the knights to pursue.

Mikael was close behind the fleeing knight, hot breath misting in the air as he exerted himself.

'Köller!' a voice echoed from the gloom. 'Köller, where are you going?'

It was Vaust, at Mikael's heels.

Köller paused to wave them on and then continued.

'Köll–' Vaust's shout was arrested by a giant hand covering his mouth.

'Quiet, you fool,' Halbranc hissed in his ear. 'You'll have every denizen of the Drakwald upon us.'

Mikael saw his captain, several feet across from him; slashes of black between the stout trunks of trees as he followed silently and stealthily after Köller. Mikael wasn't sure whether his captain wanted to catch him to prevent mishap or to put him to the sword for his erratic behaviour. Reiner's stony demeanour made it impossible to tell.

They were gaining. Ahead, the forest had thickened and Köller was finding it hard going. Valen headed the chasing pack. He made good headway, despite the weight of his armour and the snow underfoot.

Halbranc was not so adept. He slipped, barging through the clawing bracken, and was lost from sight. Sigson was nowhere to be seen.

Mikael managed to stick close to Valen. He was an Ostermarker by birth. A childhood spent in the deep forests of that province had taught him much about traversing them. His was a childhood tainted by tragedy. Thoughts sprang unbidden into Mikael's mind: the flash of the dagger, a cry in the dark, the creaking of the rope.

Searing pain brought Mikael back, a sharp branch slashing open his cheek as he ran past it. None of them were wearing their helmets: they dulled awareness. To be so disadvantaged in a forest, the Drakwald of all places, was unwise. Mikael's blood felt hot as it ran down his face. He wiped it away, instead focusing on getting to Köller. The Drakwald was no place for a mindless chase into shadows.

Köller stopped abruptly as if whatever had been compelling him had gone.

Valen reached him first, followed by Mikael a few moments later.

'Köller, what happened?' Valen asked.

The rest of the company caught up, Vaust then Reiner. A battered Halbranc brought up the rear with Sigson, the old priest bent over and gasping for breath.

Köller turned to face Valen.

'A woman,' he gasped, 'she wanted me… to follow.'

Mikael had seen nothing. There were no tracks in the snow and no broken branches. He noticed a dark glance pass between Reiner and Sigson. Both men knew of the unseen dangers of the Drakwald, of the phantoms of those long dead, calling others to join them in damnation, of strange magics that possessed men and enslaved them.

'What is that?' Valen asked suddenly, pointing through a gap in the trees.

Mikael followed his gaze.

Beyond the tree line, a light invaded the forest shadow, and a few hundred feet beyond stood a walled settlement. A simple road led up to it, emerging from another part of the Drakwald.

'It's a village,' said Mikael.

Two DILAPIDATED WATCHTOWERS stood at the village's entrance, an ironbound gate hanging limply on a rusted hinge between them. A wooden stockade wall surrounded the village and, getting closer, the knights saw that the wall was cracked, age-worn timber yielding to the ravages of time.

Passing through the yawning gateway they saw a line of frost-caked clothes, eroded by decay, swinging in the breeze. Chimneys were dormant, emaciated animals wandered aimlessly, and a great tree stood withered and forlorn, wasted apples clinging to skeletal branches. Silence reigned; the village was empty, ghost-like.

'What happened here?' asked Mikael. It reminded him of home, back in Ostermark. He found the thought saddening.

'I see no signs of a battle,' growled Halbranc.

'Let us find out,' said Reiner. 'Knights, draw swords,' he ordered and they drew as one, a chorus of scraping steel.

The captain signalled the knights to split into groups. Reiner moved up the village square with Valen and Vaust, and Halbranc accompanied Köller who ranged right, while Mikael and Sigson went left.

AFTER SEARCHING SEVERAL hovels without success, Mikael came to a blacksmith's forge. Peering tentatively inside, he saw that tools were left out. A horseshoe sat upon the anvil, pinched between a pair of rusted metal tongs. A lantern swung noisily on a chain set into the roof.

'It's as if this place has been abandoned for years,' he muttered to himself.

'You're bleeding, Mikael,' said Sigson, noticing the cut on Mikael's cheek.

'It's nothing,' he said absently, wiping away the blood and crouching down, as he noticed something in the frosty earth at his feet.

'What is it?' asked Sigson, joining him.

'I'm not sure.' Mikael brushed the snow away carefully with his hand, revealing something large and flat. 'Looks like a sign,' he said.

'Dropped by the smithy, perhaps,' Sigson wondered. 'What does it say?'

Mikael swept away the grime and filth, using his dagger to chip away at the rusted metal.

'Hochenheim.'

There was a distant cry, Köller's voice preventing further exploration. The knight and the priest got up and dashed outside.

Halbranc was running after Köller with the other knights in tow.

'I saw her,' cried Köller, 'the woman, she is here,' he said, disappearing from view behind a dishevelled tavern.

THEY FOUND KÖLLER standing before a tombstone, a mass of other graves arrayed around him in a garden of Morr.

Mikael saw Reiner mutter a prayer to the death-god, before entering.

'She was here,' said Köller.

Mikael looked down at the grave which was marked by a nondescript and unadorned headstone.

Reiner stalked away with a meaningful glance at Sigson who nodded, and went to Köller. Mikael couldn't hear what the priest was saying, but his tone was soothing.

'What is happening?' Köller cried out. 'I swear I saw...' The young knight paused, looking out beyond the cemetery.

Mikael followed his gaze to a steep hillside.

At first he saw the shadows at the crest of the hill; then he heard cries and the clash of steel.

WITH THE WINTER sun almost faded behind them, the templars of Morr reached the top of the hillside, where they saw a large stone temple. Outside it, a battle raged.

Mikael made out a horde of misshapen creatures in the twilight. They surrounded a band of knights, who were backing off towards the temple. One knight was torn down by a claw-handed freak, his torso severed in two, turning the snow crimson.

'Mutants,' Halbranc hissed.

'Sigson, who are these men?' asked Reiner, his eyes never leaving the brutal combat.

'They bear the livery of the Baron of Krugedorf, it's a town in this province,' Sigson replied, discerning the design on the knights' tabards. The warrior priest was learned not just in matters of his faith, his knowledge extended far beyond that purview, a valuable asset the knights often called upon.

Mikael went over to the warrior priest, slipping on the snow. He crashed into the ground, reopening the cut in his cheek. Blood dripped down onto the snow, blossoming readily. He saw a piece of cloth sticking out of the snow, and, picking it up, used it to stem the bleeding.

At the temple, another knight was dragged, screaming, to his death.

'We must aid them!' Vaust hissed urgently.

Reiner had seen enough.

'Such abominations must not be allowed to endure,' he growled, donning his helmet and sliding the skull faceplate down as he got to his feet.

The other knights followed suit, each drawing down the death masks that were part of their helmets, a symbol of their intent to do battle. Mikael quickly tucked the cloth beneath his armoured greave before pulling down his own faceplate.

'Knights! To arms!' Reiner bellowed, drawing his sword.

Charging over the rise, the knights struck the mutant horde with righteous fury.

Valen and Vaust waded in silently. Vaust hacked the leg off one creature, its features obliterated by boils. Valen impaled another, his blade sinking into the distended maw of a half man, half beast.

Halbranc carved a red ruin in the diseased throng, opening up a massively bloated monster with his zweihander, maggot-ridden entrails sloughing from the ragged tear in its belly.

Sigson cut down a horned mutant before reaching into his robes and pulling out a glass vial of shimmering liquid.

'I cast thee back into the void,' he intoned, hurling the holy water at the bloated creature's disgorged intestines. The stink of burning viscera tainted the breeze.

A goat-headed man brayed its defiance at Mikael. The templar roared, cutting the beast's head from its shoulders, black blood fountaining.

Reiner was deadly.

'I am Morr's instrument, through me is his will enacted,' he uttered, tearing into the abominations with ruthless efficiency.

Köller though, was unstoppable.

Misshapen limbs and grotesque heads fell like macabre rain upon the ground as he carved through the horde like a butcher.

Recognising allies when they saw them, the Krugedorf knights rallied and redoubled their efforts.

'Knights of Morr, to me!' Reiner cried, seeking to break through the back of the encircling creatures.

The templars of Morr followed dutifully, smashing a hole in the mutants' death pincer.

'Look,' cried one of the Krugedorf knights.

A veritable sea of boil ridden, plague ravaged wretches erupted over the rise.

Hacking down a cloven-hoofed monstrosity, Mikael noticed another group watching them, far behind the onrushing horde. At the centre was a thin figure, his long coat flapping in the breeze. It might have been his imagination, but Mikael swore he saw it bow towards the knights.

'We cannot overcome such odds,' said Sigson, gutting a beast on his blade.

'Your priest is right,' said a Krugedorf knight. Mikael assumed it was their leader. His face, hidden behind his blood spattered helmet, was unreadable. 'I have men in the temple,' he added, cutting down another mutant, 'we can regroup there.'

'Agreed,' said Reiner, felling another as he backed away from the reinforcements.

The knights of Krugedorf and Morr raced the short distance to the temple and hurled themselves through the entrance, slamming shut the door immediately after them.

Mikael looked back to see two armour-clad warriors, with swords drawn.

'They are allies,' the Krugedorf leader told them, 'knights of Morr. Quickly,' he added urgently, his voice dull and resonant inside his helmet, 'we must barricade the entrances.'

Halbranc needed little encouragement. Hefting a massive wooden bench up over his head, he slammed it down against the door. Reiner dragged over another, ramming it against a window, a Krugedorf knight bracing it with a massive wrought iron candlestick. Mikael and another Krugedorfer heaved a statue of some long-forgotten saint across the final window.

The tide of mutants crashed against the temple. The door shuddered as the debased creatures hammered on it with unholy vigour, massing like diseased surf. Claws and pockmarked talons reached in through gaps in the barricades, only to be cut off. Others were impaled as the knights thrust their blades through the openings in desperation, rewarded with disembodied mutant screams. At last, amidst shouting and crashing steel, the barrage stopped. Dust motes drifted silently from the ceiling. After a few moments, Valen peered through an opening in one of the barricades.

'They have gone,' he said quietly.

'For now,' said the Krugedorf leader, removing his helmet. Long blond hair fell down onto his shoulders as a handsome face was revealed in the light of a flickering torch ensconced on one of the walls.

The knights stood in a small entrance chamber at the back of which was a gateless arch that led into a long chapel, full of overturned pews. Strangely, this place, although dusty and ancient, bore no signs of the blight that had afflicted the rest of Hochenheim.

'You think they will return?' asked Mikael of the blond-haired noble.

'They will return,' a deep voice said from the shadows. Another knight stepped forward, his ornate helmet covering the upper half of his face. He wore a black beard, and a mace hung at his hip, slick with blood.

'I am Heinrich of Krugedorf,' the blond-haired knight interjected, extending a gauntleted hand towards Reiner.

'Reiner,' the captain growled warily, shaking Heinrich's hand as he lifted the death mask and removed his helmet, 'servant of Morr,' he added. The others followed his example and introduced themselves to the strangers.

Heinrich gestured to his warriors.

'Goiter,' he said. The dark-bearded knight remained unmoved. 'Kurn,' he continued. Kurn, sticking to the shadows, was broad, and taller even than Halbranc. He wore a full-faced helmet, a mighty zweihander at his side, and gave a mute greeting. 'Mordan.' A youthful, wiry-looking knight, with a number of small daggers up his right arm nodded. His left arm was harnessed in a sling. 'And Veiter,' Heinrich concluded.

The last knight smiled and bowed slightly, twin short swords sheathed at his hips. His hair was the colour of sackcloth, his eyes suspicious and alert.

The Krugedorfers were unshaven and drawn. Clearly they too had been on the road, and they each bore the crest of what Mikael assumed must be the Baron of Krugedorf: a red shield with a bearded stag at opposite diagonals, doubtless some reference to the hunting heritage of their lord.

'What is your purpose here?' asked Reiner.

'We come on an errand from our liege-lord, the baron,' said Heinrich. 'We are to salvage the relics of this temple and take them to a place of safety,' he explained.

'Then let us help you. We can reclaim them together,' said Reiner matter-of-factly, 'and leave this damned place.' He turned to Halbranc. 'Fortify the entrance,' he ordered, 'Mikael and Sigson with me, the rest, assist Halbranc.'

'I'm afraid it isn't quite that simple,' warned Heinrich.

Reiner turned to face him. His expression demanded explanations.

'BEYOND THIS DOOR lies the relic chamber,' Heinrich informed them.

Reiner, Sigson and Mikael, together with Heinrich and Kurn, stood in a long, narrow corridor at the foot of a set of stone steps. The stairway had led them to these catacombs from a trapdoor in the chapel and now they faced a single, stone door.

'I warn you,' Heinrich intoned darkly, 'there is peril beyond it. Steel yourselves.'

'Knights of Morr fear not the darkness,' Reiner told him with the utmost certainty.

Mikael felt his heart beating.

Heinrich motioned to Kurn, and the silent giant gripped the great iron manacle of the door and heaved with all his considerable might. As the door ground open, noisily kicking up grit and dust, Mikael gripped his sword. There was a long, wide room beyond it, flickering torches illuminating the threshold. Further in, there was only darkness.

'I see little peril here,' Sigson remarked, driven by curiosity as he stepped beyond the shallow cordon of light.

'Wait!' Heinrich warned.

'There is noth–' he said, and then cried out as a long cut appeared on his arm.

Heinrich hauled him back into the light.

Mikael muttered a prayer to Morr as a shimmering, ethereal blade materialised in the darkness. A hand coalesced around it, then an arm, and then a torso, until the spectre was revealed. Hollow, sunken eyes, ragged robes and skeletal limbs marked this thing as a wight, one of the unquiet dead.

More phantoms appeared alongside, their faces pitiless and cold. In their unearthly lustre they revealed the ancient bones of priests and other relics. But it was the woman, kneeling in silent vigil, dressed in dishevelled robes, who got the knights' attention. She was flesh and blood. Her hair was lank, her face wizened and encrusted with filth. She chanted wordlessly. Behind her was a second, much smaller, chamber, delineated by a wide arch. Set in the back wall was a large circular window coated in dust so thick it blocked out the light.

Looking at her, Mikael felt an overwhelming sense of sadness.

'There,' Heinrich intoned quietly, interrupting Mikael's thoughts, 'you see the witch?'

Reiner nodded sternly.

'We found her hiding in this place, doubtless seeking refuge from those who might put her to the torch,' he spat.

Reiner's jaw locked.

'Before we could slay her, she summoned these… spirits,' Heinrich continued. 'We have been unable to approach her since. As those who follow the Lord of Death and Dreams, do you think you can lay these ghosts to rest?'

Reiner looked to Sigson, who held onto his arm, his expression pained.

'It will take time,' the warrior priest told them.

* * *

NIGHT, IT SEEMED, came all too swiftly, but there had been no more attacks on the temple. The knights worked quickly, bolstering the barricades and lighting the remaining torches in the chapel. The mutants knew they were there, no sense in trying to hide their presence and the heat was welcome respite against the cold.

Mikael stared into the flames, hugging his arms around his body as he sat on one of the wooden pews, the wrathful wind providing a moaning chorus to his thoughts.

'Sigson has yet to return,' Halbranc said. Mikael wasn't even aware he was next to him and started at the big man's sudden presence.

'Easy,' he said, 'it's just me, lad.' He handed Mikael a slice of salted pork, but the young knight refused it.

'This silence unnerves me,' Mikael admitted. 'I have no care for it,' he added, looking around the room.

Valen and Vaust talked quietly amongst themselves as they ate, making the most of the opportunity before the fighting started again. Köller lay on the floor, his cloak wrapped tight around him, shivering in his sleep. Reiner had stayed with Sigson.

Mikael knew the captain didn't trust the Krugedorf knights. His gaze fell to them next, regarding the knights of Morr beneath the glow of torchlight, the faint hubbub of whispers barely audible. But then Reiner trusted no one, not even his own men.

'Don't dwell on it,' Halbranc advised. 'Here,' he said, producing a small silver flask from beneath his cloak, 'take a swig of this; it'll warm your blood.'

Mikael shook his head.

'If Reiner saw that…' he began.

'I dare say he would not approve,' Halbranc agreed, 'but then our fearless captain approves of very little,' he said, taking a belt of liquor from the flask, grimacing as it scorched his throat.

'You don't know what you're missing,' he said afterwards.

Mikael smiled; the ephemeral expression fading as he looked into Halbranc's eyes. He knew very little of the man's history, save that he was once a mercenary and had fought across much of the Empire and beyond. There was a sadness in him, one that he could not shake, only dull with alcohol. He'd heard him at night, crying in his sleep at dark dreams that Mikael could only guess at. Halbranc would never admit to the hidden pain in his soul, but he knew that Mikael was aware of it.

'How are there so many of them?' Mikael asked, finding the abrupt silence uncomfortable.

'Them?' Halbranc asked, concealing the flask beneath his cloak.

'The mutants.'

'What do you think happened to all the villagers?' asked Halbranc grimly, getting to his feet. 'We fought them today.'

'By the breath of Morr,' Mikael said, at last understanding.

'Do not think on it,' Halbranc told him sternly. 'Get some sleep,' he added, his face softening. 'We don't know when we might get another opportunity.'

'Don't worry,' he said, 'I'll keep a watch. Don't feel much like sleeping, anyway.'

Mikael watched Halbranc go to stand at the barricade, peering out into the night. He sank back against the pew. It was hard and unyielding, but he was exhausted, the cold and his dark thoughts sapping his endurance. Reluctantly, he fell into a fitful sleep.

THE FOREST ROSE *up around him, thick branches tugging at his clothes, briars scraping exposed flesh. There was a dagger in his hand. It was stained with blood. He was running; a shadow figure a few paces ahead. He almost reached it when*

*he saw a mighty bearded stag looking at him from a sun dap-
pled clearing. A second, identical beast emerged from the
forest beside it.*

*The two creatures charged each other, locking antlers
fiercely. He watched, horrified as the antlers started to merge
together in a terrible union, the stags becoming one hideous,
mutated beast.*

*Four baleful eyes stared back at him from a single head as
the abomination burst into bright red flame.*

MIKAEL AWOKE TO desperate cries and rushing feet. He
saw Vaust, struggling to hold back the wooden bench at
the window. Valen lay on the floor beneath him, clutching his shoulder. Halbranc was running to him, Heinrich
not far behind.

Goiter dragged Köller up, muttering a curse.

Kurn's armoured bulk was pressed against the door,
while Mordan and Veiter hefted another bench between
them to seal the second window, which gaped open, the
statue in rubble beneath.

Mikael caught a glimpse of Reiner in the corner of his
eye, appearing from the trapdoor. There was no sign of
Sigson. He must still be in the relic room. Getting to his
feet, Mikael ran towards Vaust. Then the temple door
exploded.

Halbranc and Heinrich were thrown to the ground.
Kurn bore the brunt of the blast, engulfed in a splinter
storm of broken wood and iron. Incredibly, he stayed
upright.

Flames lapped at the edges of the shattered door, the
twisted iron jutting out like broken limbs. Smoke issued
through the huge gap, shifting figures visible through it.
The stench was unmistakeable: blackpowder.

The mutants howled as they emerged through the haze
and into the temple. Kurn swept his blade in a punish-
ing arc, but missed as a creature dressed like a macabre

jester thwarted his aim. It rode around on a skeletal hob-byhorse with a cadaverous head. It smashed the massive Krugedorf knight to the ground with a huge, unwieldy mace.

Mikael charged at the grotesque jester, but his path was blocked by two girls holding hands. He wavered for a moment, his blade stayed by their apparent inno-cence. Then he saw their hands, fused together in a gelatinous mass of flesh and knew they were not chil-dren. Snarling viciously, revealing deadly fangs, they sprang on top of Mikael. The templar dropped his sword, desperately trying to fend off the weird sisters as they clawed and bit.

He felt their weight lifting and vaguely saw the hideous twins flailing off into the dark. Halbranc stood before him.

'Pick up your swor–' he began, but was smashed aside, a hugely obese woman crushing him into the wall with her bulk.

Reiner raced to Halbranc's aid, blade in hand, but was confronted by a diminutive, sallow-skinned freak, mouth sewn shut crudely with thick, black thread. In one hand it clutched a rusted dagger; on the other was the puppet of a mangy dog. The mute shook the puppet free, revealing a small, daemon-like creature, instead of a hand.

'Die!' the daemon-hand hissed, its voice bubbling like melting flesh.

Reiner roared, cutting the daemon thing off at the wrist and sending it flying. The mute scampered after it, ducking and weaving under the blades of the other knights as it went.

At the wall, Halbranc was slowly being smothered. Mikael and Reiner plunged their swords into the hideous woman crushing him. The creature laughed, black ooze running down the knights' blades, corroding the metal. They dropped their weapons as the caustic blood devoured them.

Mikael was reaching for another blade, when a long shadow fell across him. He turned quickly, short sword in hand and found himself gazing up at an incredibly tall, thin man, a strange, almost infantile head on his shoulders. It swung a massive glaive at the templar, who leapt to avoid it, chunks of flagstone debris erupting in his wake. He sprang up to face it, abhorred as the creature's head detached from its body and with a horrifying screech launched itself at the temple roof, thin, spidery legs punching from the cranium and gaining purchase in solid stone. The spider-thing chittered as it came towards him, the headless freak still swinging the glaive. There was the flash of silver and the spider-thing fell, a dagger protruding from its forehead. Both the stickman and the spider-thing retreated.

Mikael turned to see Mordan, another dagger in his hand, about to throw it when he was split in two, a grotesquely muscled freak with a tiny hooded head, cutting him down with an axe.

Mikael lost the creature amidst the chaos, his attention arrested by Halbranc's muffled cries as he was still pinned by the obese woman.

Reiner had shaken off another mutant and was moving in, when Heinrich appeared beside them, hefting a torch from the wall and ramming the fiery brand into the obese freak's wound. Its jaw distended horribly to reveal the half-digested corpse of a Krugedorf knight, slain in the first battle, as it recoiled from the fire, shuffling away into the shadows.

Gasping for breath, Halbranc slumped to his knees, his zweihander clattering to the ground.

Around them, the smoke was clearing, the freaks defeated, but Mordan was dead and Valen badly wounded.

Mikael regarded the carnage, the corpses of slain villagers, afflicted by the plague, were everywhere, but of
the macabre circus freaks, there was no sign.

'I brought down at least one,' growled Goiter, apparently reading Mikael's mind as he wiped the gore from
his mace.

'I too felled one of them that could not have lived,'
offered Vaust.

'Daemons,' Reiner spat, under his breath.

'Whatever those things were, we cannot remain here,'
said Heinrich, gesturing to the charred ruin of the door.
'When they return, and return they will, we will be
defenceless.'

'Is there another way out?' Reiner asked, looking out
impassively into the darkness.

'A secret passage leads to the surface from the relic
room,' said Heinrich.

Reiner turned, an inquisitive look flashing briefly over
his face.

'If your priest is successful and banishes the spirits…'
Heinrich let the thought hang in the air for them to finish.

Then we live, Mikael thought.

'The passageway before the relic room is narrow,' Reiner
said. 'It will be easier to defend. We fight in pairs, rotating
as each pair gets tired. We'll make our stand there.'

Without further preamble, Reiner stalked over to the
trapdoor, the others following him.

THEY HAD WAITED for over an hour in the creeping dark of
the catacombs, Sigson's muffled prayers emanating
through the door of the relic room.

Mikael was listening to it when he noticed Veiter looking at him. The Krugedorf knight evoked an uneasy
feeling in the young templar, and he quickly averted his
gaze, shifting it to the other knights.

Vaust was ever watchful over his brother who grimaced in pain next to him. Halbranc and Reiner stood quietly, the former lost in thought, the latter an emotionless statue. Köller sat opposite Mikael and looked sullen, the dark mask upon his face as always.

Of the Krugedorf knights, Goiter and Kurn stood sentinel at the entrance to the passageway. They seemed oddly restless. Even Heinrich, alongside Veiter, appeared on edge.

'What troubles you?' Mikael asked.

Heinrich opened his mouth to answer when the trapdoor caved in and stone fell like rain.

The torches in the passageway guttered and died, engulfing the knights in blackness. Amidst a deluge of broken stone slabs and ruined wood, something large and terrible filled the end of the passageway. The charnel house stink of its breath infected the air.

Goiter turned to shout to Heinrich as something thick and wet lashed out of the dark, and suddenly Goiter was no more, the sickening crunch of bone a macabre echo of his existence.

Overcoming the mind-numbing terror threatening to unman him, Mikael drew his sword.

'We cannot prevail here,' Heinrich breathed, fear in his voice.

Reiner, backing away from the beast, looked over his shoulder at the solid stone door behind him.

'Into the relic room!' he bellowed.

Acting quickly, Halbranc got to the door first. 'Watch my back,' the giant snarled, and heaved on the iron door manacle.

It wouldn't yield.

The massive Krugedorfer, Kurn, appeared alongside him. Together, with the stone grinding in their ears, the knights opened the door.

Inside, Sigson was kneeling on the floor. He'd stepped beyond the cordon of light and was encircled by grave

dust, facing off against the witch. In front of him was a
black candle, its flame casting a bright aura. The warrior
priest was bathed in sweat, his features creased with exer-
tion. Around him, the spirits wailed silently, trying to
tear at him with unearthly claws, only repelled by the
priest's wards.

The knights paused at the portal when they saw the
spirits. The thing in the corridor was a worse terror
though and the knights piled inside. Sigson was
unaware of their presence, entranced as he invoked the
banishment ritual. Kurn heaved the door shut behind
them.

Heart racing, Mikael leant heavily against the wall.
Something fell from his arm greave, dislodged in the
panic. He stooped and picked up a section of cloth. It
was the same piece he'd used to staunch his bleeding
face outside the temple. He hadn't paid much attention
to it. Now that it lay open in his hands, Mikael saw it
bore the crest of the Krugedorf knights: a red shield, two
bearded stags at opposite diagonals. He suddenly
recalled his dream of the stags coming together in a
blaze of flame, and wondered what it meant. He half
heard Sigson chant the banishment rites and felt the
same sadness as he had before. Only it wasn't sadness, it
was something else. It felt like… pleading.

Two stags coming together.

Mikael looked again at the cloth. He held a corner in
each hand and folded them in on each other, then
turned them up, forcing the image of the two stags
together.

His heart quickened as the realisation of what was
before him struck like a hammer blow. In his hand, the
cloth folded over to reveal an entirely different image: a
burning hand.

'Sigson, no!' he cried.

He was too late. Sigson had finished the ritual.

The candle flared impossibly bright, and white light flooded the chamber. The witch screamed, flung back with the force of her broken summoning, the spirits crying out in unison as they were expelled in a blinding coruscation.

The knights were thrown down with the sheer power of the invocation, ears ringing with the screams of the damned.

Blinking back the stark after-image, virtually seared upon his retinas, Mikael saw that Heinrich was on his feet and running towards the arch at the back of the room.

'Slay them!' he cried.

Kurn's zweihander was drawn, and he smashed Vaust aside with the flat of the blade. The knight struck the wall hard and fell into a crumpled heap, next to his semi-conscious brother.

Veiter, eyes aglow with balefire, leapt at Reiner, but the captain of Morr was ready and parried his double-handed assault. The Chaos knight snarled, revealing fangs.

'Knights, to arms, the servants of Chaos are among us!' Reiner bellowed.

Sigson staggered to his feet, drawing his blade with shaking hands.

Kurn's armoured boot put him down as he advanced on Halbranc.

The two giants clashed, zweihander on zweihander, the scrape of churning metal and flashing sparks filling the air around them.

'By the hand of Morr,' Halbranc breathed. Face-to-face with the beast, he saw that Kurn's helmet was fused to his neck, the eyeholes empty voids of hate.

The stone door thundered as whatever was outside tried to get in. Mikael gave it little heed, as he ran past the battling knights. He was intent on Heinrich, who was through the archway at the back of the room and into the antechamber.

'Heinrich!' he cried, flinging his short sword at the traitor captain.

The Krugedorfer turned and parried the blade out of the air with unnatural quickness.

'Unwise to relinquish your only weapon,' he said, licking his lips with a serpentine tongue, and stepping backwards into the centre of the antechamber.

'You want the relics for yourself,' Mikael said accusingly.

'Fool,' Heinrich spat. 'Whatever feeble trinkets reside in this place are of no interest to me. It is the temple that I covet,' he said.

'Ignis!' he then cried and a tongue of flame spread furiously around him, describing a rune-etched symbol on the ground, an unholy icon of Chaos.

Exultant, Heinrich threw his head back and the flames rose to the ceiling.

Mikael backed away from the conflagration. Through the blaze, a hazy silhouette was visible.

'Dormamu, I supplicate myself before you. Make me your host,' Heinrich uttered with a voice like prophecy.

His treachery was clear. He meant to summon a daemon.

The inferno intensified as Heinrich's shadow form was lifted off the ground, the deep and unholy resonance of another voice coming from the fire as Heinrich reasserted his pledge.

'He seeks to re-consecrate the circle,' the witch cried desperately from behind Mikael, vying against the raging din of the fire.

Shading his eyes, heat searing his face, Mikael turned to her.

She staggered to her feet.

'Help me,' she begged.

Suddenly, Kurn loomed behind her, zweihander raised, Halbranc lying prone and defeated, his breastplate smashed.

'No!' Mikael cried as the blade fell. She would be cut in twain.

The blade failed to strike; an aura of blue light surrounding her repulsed it.

Witness to a miracle, Mikael had a sudden epiphany as if the light had opened his eyes for the first time. She was no witch. She was a priestess, the guardian of this place, and he must protect her at all costs.

Mikael took up his thrown short sword and rushed at Kurn, knowing he was no match for the Krugedorfer.

The giant turned his attention to the young knight, exuding menace.

Mikael raised his weapon, awaiting the deathblow that would shatter it and his body. It never came.

Kurn recoiled wordlessly, like an automaton, as Köller's blade smashed down onto his pauldron.

Seeing his opportunity, Mikael came at the Chaos warrior from the front, plunging his sword into Kurn's breastplate. He withdrew it savagely, then watched horrified as black sand spilled from the wound. The knight reached out to crush him with a mailed fist.

Köller cleaved it off with a two-handed blow. Still Kurn lived, and whirling around, smashed Köller into the wall.

Mikael gripped his blade, incredulous that the thing before him still endured.

This was his last chance. 'Morr, guide my hand,' he breathed and thrust his sword deep into the eye slit of Kurn's helmet. The giant staggered, trying to clutch at the weapon embedded in his skull with a hand that no longer existed. At last, he fell, like a hewn oak, thunderously to the ground and was still. But it wasn't over yet. The door to the relic room shuddered, cracks appearing in the stone. Mikael turned to the priestess.

She closed her eyes as she muttered words of power. The knight's defence in her honour had granted her the time she needed to perform some ritual.

The cracks in the stone door widened and finally it split and crumbled. The terrible shadow filling it retreated and a horde of bloodshot, plague-infected eyes regarded them.

Mikael was about to run to intercept the creatures, when he felt the light touch of the priestess on his arm. He looked back.

Her eyes opened, burning with a deep blue lustre. The heat from the conflagration surrounding Heinrich visibly ebbed. Even the mutants paused at the doorway, as if sensing something.

'Stop her!' Heinrich cried from within the inferno, his voice deep and ageless.

Only Veiter remained.

Reiner advanced on the last Krugedorfer, the mutant horde faltering at the doorway.

Flinging his blade at Reiner to distract him, Veiter ran. He fled through the arch at the back of the chamber, lost suddenly behind the inferno.

Reiner was about to give chase. A plague creature grabbed his arm, its rusting cleaver about to strike, when the priestess spoke.

'No.'

The cleaver was blasted aside by some unseen force as her voice echoed through the chamber. It was followed by a terrible wail as the dread spirits returned.

Ghostly faces and ethereal bodies became as one as they coalesced into a swirling, spectral maelstrom.

'Purge this place,' she said.

The spirit host swept through the temple like a cleansing wave, accompanied by a wrathful wind, searing plague-ridden flesh and shredding bone. Holy light blazed furiously as the dust and grime clogging the window was destroyed. A lance of power came through it and engulfed the Chaos circle, extinguishing the flames surrounding Heinrich.

Mikael shielded his eyes against its glory.

Then the light was gone, as quickly as it had manifested, and the vengeful spirits with it.

His vision returning, Mikael saw Sigson crouching down next to the priestess.

Mikael went over to him.

He held her in his arms. She was beautiful, the dirt and grime on her face washed away, her hair golden and pure, her robes no longer torn. A radiant blue aura surrounded her.

'My time here is ended,' she told them. 'The sanctity of this place has been preserved.'

'What do you mean?' Mikael asked, his mind reeling from what he had witnessed.

She pressed something into the young knight's hands.

It looked like a book, old and unadorned, but with a small silver clasp in the centre. Mikael unhooked it and opened it out, revealing that it was no book, but a triptych. Three wooden plates within described a battle. In the middle a temple, two doves flying above in a stormy sky; below them, a force of knights surrounded by holy light, a priestess at their heart; to the left, an army of black-armoured warriors and daemons, led by a mighty dark knight on a fell steed; to the right, a plague ridden horde, their skeletal master holding a scythe aloft...

It was the battle from Mikael's dream.

'This place of power has existed for centuries,' said the priestess. 'The prosperity of the village, the relic in your hands,' she said, looking at Mikael, 'ensures its purity. Every one hundred years it is contested. Every one hundred years a guardian is selected to watch over it, to remain here for another century until it is contested again and the next guardian called.'

'A hundred years,' breathed Sigson, 'but that would mean…'

'Yes, I will die,' she said, smiling faintly. 'When the plague came I was weakened. I could not prevail without help. Now the malady that ravaged this place has been lifted and the new guardian is here to take my place.'

Mikael took a deep breath and exhaled his resignation. The dream had been a sign, he could see that now. It was his calling.

'I am the guardian,' he said solemnly.

The priestess turned, a trace of amusement upon her face, 'No, it is not you of whom I speak,' she said, looking beyond the two knights.

Mikael and Sigson turned as one, following her gaze.

Köller staggered to his feet, the light from the window bathing him was a startling affirmation. He looked shocked at first; then, as if suddenly enlightened, he knelt down, bowing his head and laying his sword before him.

Sigson gasped, as the priestess shimmered and faded, the blue aura surrounding her flaring bright in Köller's eyes as he looked up, bathing the room in azure. Then it was gone, and Köller returned to normal.

The remaining knights of Morr stood around him, their wounds miraculously healed.

'What happened here?' Reiner asked darkly.

Mikael looked back to the corridor. Of the creature and the plague horde, there was no sign; even those mutants who had entered the chamber were gone.

'A miracle,' the young knight breathed.

Reiner walked to the back of the room, apparently unmoved.

He regarded Heinrich's charred remains in a circle of ash. He scattered them into nothing with his boot.

'Our work here is done,' he said, his voice like ice. He turned on his heel, and with a glance at Köller, stalked out of the room.

'What will you do?' Mikael asked Köller.

He looked different, lifted.

'I will remain here,' he said, 'and protect this place in the name of Morr.'

Silence persisted, the gravity of the moment and Köller's undertaking sinking in.

'It is a noble deed, Köller,' said Sigson. 'A great evil has been averted this night.' He bowed solemnly and left the chamber after Reiner.

Valen and Vaust followed, a nod at Köller before they went.

'Fare thee well, lad,' Halbranc said, joining the others.

Mikael handed Köller the triptych. 'This belongs here, I think.'

Köller accepted it gratefully. 'Yours is a great destiny, Mikael. Do not fear it.'

Mikael opened his mouth to speak, but couldn't find any words. Instead, he turned and walked away into the darkness.

OUTSIDE THE TEMPLE, the knights made ready.

'Your orders, Captain Reiner?' Halbranc asked, securing his zweihander.

'We head back to the Road Warden's Rest, get the horses and make for the nearest temple of Morr,' he said. 'There is much to report.'

He stalked off, back the way they had come when first happening upon Hochenheim.

Mikael thought of Köller and found his heart heavy as he walked through the ramshackle village gates and back into the Drakwald. As he did, he looked back at Hochenheim one last time. There, in the village square, he noticed the great tree and upon its branches the smallest of blossoms.

SPOILS OF WAR
by Rick Wolf

'HOW MANY, DO you think?'

'Fifteen? Not more than twenty,' Claus replied in an undertone. They lay on a rocky outcrop. 'We can take them, sir.'

Below, in a hollow that broadened into a small valley of even grassland by a cool brook, Claus could see the creatures below. Some were covered in mangy hair, others wore equally patchy clothes and armour, broken and rusting mail, ripped jerkins and cracked plate. Some loped like beasts, others stood straight like men, but most seemed a curious mixture of the two. They lolled indolently. They had been feasting, the remains of some upland sheep lying bloodied and scattered around them. The wind changed and Claus wrinkled his nose in disgust as their odour reached him.

'I agree,' the captain said. The two men began to work their way backwards, away from the brow of the hill where they might be seen.

The Elector of Nuln's army had spent four frustrating weeks camped close to the market town of Steingart, in the shadow of the Black Mountains, by the upper reaches of the Reik. They were waiting for the force of bandits, mutants, beastmen and gods knew what else that had swept down out of the Great Forest and across the southern Empire. Rumour had it that they had swept aside the forces of Stirland and Averland, burning farmsteads and villages, and putting their inhabitants to the sword. Others claimed that they had been halted in Averland and dealt a decisive blow, others still that the raiders had split into a hundred smaller bands that now wreaked havoc on the soft lands of the south. Meanwhile, the men of Wissenland and Sudenland waited by the Upper Reik for the invaders, anxious, frustrated and angry.

They had looked to the Reiters, mounted pistoliers, to find the enemy. Lieutenant Claus Katzbalger found himself second in command of the scouting party. They were just ten men, including the captain, von Ofterdingen, and Claus sent to search for the raiders. Perhaps they had just found some of them.

THEY REMOUNTED THEIR horses and the men began to work their way carefully round from behind the hill and into the valley. The broad grassland offered perfect conditions for mounted men, but the steep hillside would be hard work for the horses. They might slip and fall or shy, so the riders skirted round the valley, careful not to make a noise.

Now that the sun had risen and burned off the early morning mist, it was hot. Under his armour, Claus felt uncomfortable. The men all wore breast- and back-plates and Claus's armour extended down over his thighs and arms as well. He left his helmet off, but even so the heat of the sun on the blackened half armour seemed to bake him. His mouth was deadly dry and he reached for his water bottle. His stomach squirmed and an urge to be sick swept over him. He gripped his sword pommel closely and whispered a quick prayer to Sigmar that he would use it well.

They paused where the hills flattened out and formed up. Weapons were checked and armour tightened. Claus reached forward to pat his horse as it pawed the ground, reassuring it. Behind him, his men fell into place: Gefreiter Stark, his rank marking him as a veteran of past campaigns, to his left; Trooper von Schwarze to the right; and alongside them, Troopers Tannhauser and Meyer.

'Lieutenant! Your men to the left, I will take the right,' von Ofterdingen said. Four troopers had formed behind him. 'Forward.'

They crested the slight rise and emerged into the valley at a steady trot, the horses gradually building pace. The bestial creatures were still spread out, many sprawled on the ground, utterly unaware of the attack. At the sound of the beating hooves they started, staring round in panic. Claus swung his command along by the brook to cut off any retreat, whilst the others moved to crush them. Claus could see that the captain had drawn his sabre and held it aloft as his men followed him. The ground was speeding past and the horses' hooves flashed and thundered as they hit the earth. Stones were sent skittering into the brook, the horses' footing threatening to slip.

Alert now, the twisted beasts were on their feet. One, a barrel-chested animal, with the body of a man and the antlered head of a stag, was bellowing, throwing its head back and roaring like a rutting deer. Whether in challenge, anger or to rouse others, Claus could not guess.

They swung in from the brook, directly towards the bellowing creature. Claus let the reins slip and pulled two long barrelled pistols from the holsters by his saddle. He knew that behind him each trooper would also be pulling out their pistols.

He heard the cracks of pistol fire as Captain von Ofterdingen's command closed with the beasts. Then he heard the sharper, louder crack of those behind him and squeezed the trigger on the first of his pistols. There was a flash of flame, a burst of smoke, cutting his vision out, and then the horse's charge had carried him past and he could see. He fired again, but this time the wheellock sparked and flashed but the charge failed to catch. Cursing, Claus tried to return the pistol to its holster, but by then he was in amongst the enemy and the battle was on him.

This was the sort of battle that every cavalryman dreamt of: an enemy on foot without ranks or structure. It was barely soldiery. It was butchery. Claus could hear the troopers whooping with the joy of it.

The charge carried him through and Claus, unable to draw his sword, reversed his grip on his long, heavy pistol and brought the club ended grip down on the head of a thin creature with a dog's muzzle. He could feel the crack of bone. He tugged on the reins and wheeled his horse, wrenching his heavy sabre from its scabbard. He saw others do the same – Stark, his sword bloodied to the hilt, Tannhauser, pistol butts smeared with gore – and charged back into the fray. The mutated raiders were breaking, scrambling desperately away from the onslaught, making it easy for the Reiters whose swords fell on the backs of the beastlike heads.

Their screams were a cacophony of animal and human. Claus saw the great stag-like creature speared through the throat as he lifted his head back. He saw the captain firing his pistol into a winged thing, with the face of a young girl; and it was over and the battle was won.

It was then they noticed that Meyer had fallen. His horse must have tumbled; he lay flat on the ground, unconscious. An ugly gash showed in his thigh and marks on his cheeks suggested something had tried to gnaw at it.

'We'd better find somewhere for him to rest,' the captain said, but his eyes scanned the horizon, as if hoping he would see more enemies that he could crush beneath his horse's hooves.

THE SUN WAS beginning to lower in the sky when they arrived at the manor house. It was a stout stone hall, fortified to withstand enemies if need be. Herb gardens and low hedges suggested that defence was not its main purpose, however. A cluster of low stone houses sat below the hall, whilst a few scattered shepherds' huts clung to hills above. It looked beautiful in the sunshine.

They had been forced to a slower pace by the injured Meyer, but there had been no further signs of the enemy, nor had any of the scattered peasants in the area reported any. Claus was grateful of the chance to stop for the night. Now that the nervous excitement of the fight had left him, he was tired. The manor house seemed like a gift from the gods to his weary eyes.

Servants began to appear as the small column of riders filed in. One stepped forward.

'This is the Hall of the von Oppertals. How may we help you?' he asked.

Claus and the captain rode forward. 'I am Captain von Ofterdingen of the Wissenland Reiters. This is Lieutenant Katzbalger. As you can see, one of our men is wounded. You will billet us and provide my man with whatever care you can.'

The man who stood before him was perhaps in his early fifties, grey-haired, with a long, wispy moustache and the beginnings of a paunch. He stood, fists balled on his hips. Claus sensed him bridle at the captain's command. For a moment it looked as if he might refuse, then he tugged at the corner of his moustache.

'Of course, sir. Dieter will help you stable your horses.'

'Is your master here?' the captain demanded.

'No, sir. The new landgrave is at his residence in Nuln. My name is Horst. I am the steward of the lord of Oppertal.'

Von Ofterdingen turned away, unconcerned by the matters of servants.

Claus and Tannhauser carried Meyer into the house while the captain and the others dealt with the horses. They were ushered into an upstairs room where they laid the injured man on a bed. He had regained consciousness a couple of times, and they had forced harsh schnapps down his throat to dull the pain. Now he lay on the bed moaning, scarcely aware of his surroundings.

'Fetch someone who can treat him,' Claus ordered.

The steward said he would send for a healer, the village wise woman, before bustling off.

Claus left Tannhauser with the injured trooper and went back down to the main hall. The others were still seeing to the horses or carrying supplies and saddlebags in.

Claus had time to examine the hall. It was cool and, after the bright sunshine of the day, dark. The manor house must have originally been one single hall, which, at various times, had been added to. The main hall, however, remained. At one end stood an imposing chair. Above that was a wooden gallery for entertainers. The rest of the space was empty but for three great oak tables and cupboards on the wall by the door. Crossed swords completed the decor.

There were small high windows through which shafts of golden sunshine streamed. Claus watched motes of dust dancing in them. He followed the light upwards. A huge, discoloured sheet was draped on the far wall, by the windows. That was odd. He looked around. A servant hurried past, water jugs and bowls in her arms.

'You there. What is beneath that sheet?'

The woman turned to him. She was young, no more than twenty perhaps, and dark curls framed her face.

'The painting, sir.'

Now that he studied it, Claus could see the sheet did not quite cover the entire wall. Around the windows he could see marks, indistinct in the light, but colours and shapes.

'What painting? Why is it covered?'

'I'm sorry, sir. You'll have to ask the steward.'

She tried to curtsey and her face flushed. Claus smiled to himself as he watched her leave, his eyes trailing after her departing body. Then he turned back to the wall. One edge of the cloth hung lower than the rest, the tacks that fixed it in place having worked loose. He strode up to it and gripped the sheet in his hand. He lifted the sheet away as far away from the wall as he could. The angle and the light made it hard to see the pattern behind, a confusion of reds, ochres, greys and a flash of aquamarine. Then, slowly, the shapes formed, and Claus could see armoured knights mounted on barded steeds, pennants fluttering from the ends of lances, he could pick out standards and banners of regiments of pikemen and footmen and horses prancing, and he had to catch his breath. This was magnificent. He tugged at the shroud that covered the wall painting until he felt it give and collapse to the floor in a shower of dust. He stepped back to admire the fresco. It must be the work of a master.

'Sir, what are you doing?'

Claus turned to see the steward, Horst, red-faced, barely trying to conceal his irritation.

'What are you doing?'

'It seemed a shame to cover it,' Claus said simply.

'But that was his lordship's wish,' the steward retorted, 'I mean his *late* lordship.'

'Well,' Claus smiled, equable, 'then he is no longer here to be offended. What does the new lord make of it, anyway?' he continued.

'He has yet to visit us. He has been in the city for three years.'

With this man as his servant Claus felt he could hardly blame the new lord for his lack of interest.

'It is impressive,' Claus said, taking in the dimensions of the painting. 'What is it of?'

'The Battle of Zapochka, in Kislev. Our lord's great-great-great-great-grandfather performed a great service for the sainted Magnus the Pious in his war against the Chaos invaders.'

The Battle of Zapochka, a name that Claus had barely heard of, a footnote in the history of Magnus's war against the Great Incursion. Tribesmen from the far north, beastlike creatures, mutated perversions and daemons summoned from the pits of darkness had swept across Kislev in vast armies, threatening to utterly overwhelm the Empire's northern neighbour. Zapochka had been, like many other engagements in the campaign, a desperate action to preserve the flanks of the Empire's combined forces, to stop attempts to cut it from its supply lines and halt the advance. Few histories would record it, the glory going to the main force that routed the Chaos invasion at the Battle of Kislev Gate. But here, in a small manor, forgotten even by its lord, was a reminder of the heroism of those that had marched north and met the invaders in a battle that had made the final victory possible. It held Claus in wonderment.

'The von Oppertals were ennobled by Magnus himself for their actions that day,' the steward, Horst, said, a note of pride at this reflected glory in his voice. 'Afterwards, the first landgrave returned here, bringing with him money and reminders of the war.'

The artist had included grateful-looking Kislevite shepherds in the foreground of the painting, watching the combat. Magnus the Pious, encased in golden armour, stood on a gilded chariot, his arm raised to point towards the battle. The armoured electors of the Empire stood around him. Of course, neither Magnus nor the electors would have been there, but the von Oppertals had not let that stand in the way of art. Beyond them, in a gentle valley filled with summer flowers, the armies clashed.

'They say that the two-handed sword on the wall came from a barbarian he bested in single combat,' Horst continued. 'It was the second landgrave who had the fresco painted.'

'Magnificent,' Claus said, barely hearing. 'Leave it like that. It'll give us something to look at when we eat.'

IT WAS MUTTON stew that evening. Horst had apologised repeatedly when he saw the look on von Ofterdingen's face at the news, but, he said, the group had been so unexpected that there had been no chance to get anything else. They were lucky that there was enough to go round. It had taken a viewing of the wine cellar to mollify the captain. Then he was delighted.

'Drink deep!' he told his men as they cleared their platters on one of the great tables in the hall. 'Today, we struck a blow for Wissenland against the foul creatures that would destroy our lands!'

The small company of soldiers roared their approval. They were all there, save Meyer, who lay in his room tended by the healer. Claus banged his fist on the table, causing cutlery to clatter.

'This, gentlemen,' von Ofterdingen said, warming to his theme and indicating the glass of good Reikland Hock in his hand, 'is a fitting reward from our generous, if sadly absent, host.'

Again the soldiers joined in.

'These good bottles are, for us, the spoils of war! So let us raise a toast to our good fortune, good swords and good host. Gentlemen, the spoils of war!'

The company rose to its feet. As one they echoed the toast and tossed back the wine.

The servants stood just out of sight, unsure what to make of this band of drunken men.

CLAUS PICKED UP his wine glass. Tannhauser was sprawling across the table and von Schwarze did not seem too far behind. He looked up at the painting he had uncovered earlier. His painting, Claus half felt, since he had found it. It was extraordinary. He let his eyes drift across it. The candles and fire seemed to lend the battle extra life, as the light flickered and shifted, suddenly catching and illuminating portions and figures before casting them back into shadow. There, facing the couched lances of mounted knights, were barbarian northerners in outlandish fur-edged armour. Another flicker, and Claus saw a goat-like monster, surrounded by other mixtures of man and beast. They were vital and raw, sensuous and supple. He shuddered. The depiction of the battle was a little too close to the events of earlier in the day.

Von Schwarze stood, unsteadily. 'I'm off for a piss,' he announced. Claus, looking towards him, only saw the movement in the picture out of the very corner of his eye. He turned back to the painting. It was impossible, of course. The figures could not have moved. He stared at it suspiciously. That giant beast, an amalgamation of man and buffalo, had its head been lowered so, or its arms raised?

It must have been. He must have had more to drink than he had realised.

He knocked the rest of his glass back and got to his feet. Bed, he thought, and moved away from the hall to his room, but, as he did so, he kept half an eye on the strange painting.

CAPTAIN VON OFTERDINGEN gave orders the next day. Questioning the locals had revealed nothing. The captain decided that the group must separate. They would be able to cover more ground that way. He and four troopers would continue further into the hills and leave Lieutenant Katzbalger and his men, including the injured Meyer, behind at the manor house. A dispatch needed to be taken to the army to report their position and findings; von Schwarze would act as courier. That left Katzbalger, Stark and Tannhauser. They were to patrol the valleys immediately surrounding the manor of the Oppertals. They would rendezvous at the manor house again in one week. Having given his orders, von Ofterdingen scribbled his report and handed it to von Schwarze. They rode out that afternoon, von Scharwze back towards Steingart, the captain and the four troopers deeper into the hills.

Claus Katzbalger was in command of those remaining behind. He hoped to the gods that he would not screw it up.

MEYER APPEARED TO have improved slightly. He was conscious and even managed a weak smile when Claus came to see him. He sat slightly propped up in his sick bed, a water jug on a small table nearby, in his whitewashed, cell-like, room. The sun streamed through the window in long golden shafts. Claus left him bathed in its warm glow.

The food was much improved that evening. Perhaps it was because there were fewer of them, but Horst had managed to rustle up roast beef. Claus, Stark and Tannhauser sat and ate in companionable silence. Claus had decided that they would not drink that evening. He was relieved that the painting opposite him did not appear to move now. He found his eyes drawn to it again and again. Eventually, he noticed, in one corner, an artist's joke: a goat-faced beastman, sharply bearded, dressed in an artist's gown and cap, with a paintbrush in its hand.

A SOFT SUN played on the upland valley. Wildflowers grew by the side of the path: a profusion of cornflower blues, startling yellows and deep violets. It was hard to believe that any of the vile monstrosities they had encountered two days before could have been near this place.

'Nothing,' Tannhauser reported as he brought his horse back from the rocky promontory where he had scanned the rest of the valley. It was long, but broadened out into a lush landscape between steeply banked hillsides. It had taken them most of the day to reach this point, no more than three-quarters of the way up the valley, and soon they would have to return to the manor house in the hills below.

Claus nodded. 'We must hope that the captain is having more luck.'

Stark coughed. 'With permission, sir? We're not covering enough ground.'

Claus considered. At this rate they would have hardly scouted half the land he wanted to investigate by the end of the week.

'Yes, gefreiter. Tomorrow we will have to split up. I will take the rest of this valley, and you and Tannhauser the neighbouring ones. We'll have to work outwards from there. I shall stay based at the manor, but you two can press on. We can meet up in three days. If either of you find anything, let me know.'

The others nodded. They turned their horses and began the long trot back to the hall. A part of Claus wished he could stop and simply admire the beauty of the valley in the late summer sunshine.

THE HORSES STABLED, fed and watered, the three men carried their saddlebags into the main hall. Claus set his down by the door gratefully. Hours in the saddle took their toll even on someone used to it. They sat at one of the tables, happy simply to rest. The painting dominated the wall before them.

'You know,' said Stark after some time, 'the oddest thing. You said that painting was of a battle in Kislev?'

'Hmm,' Claus grunted.

'Only, don't those hills there look like the ones in that valley we were in today?'

'How do you mean?'

'Look at that one on the left shaped like an Altdorfer bun, see? And next to it, there's one with a jagged top and pine trees in a row. There were hills just like that at the top end of the valley today.'

'Are you sure?' Claus knew better than to doubt the gefreiter's scouting skills but he could not really see it himself. 'It must be a coincidence. I'll keep an eye out tomorrow,' he said with a smile.

SLEEP DID NOT seem to come easily that evening. In his mind he kept turning over the idea that the valley in the picture was the valley they had been in earlier that day. He knew that sometimes artists chose to change details to bring them closer to the experiences of the viewer: gods or heroes might be painted in the armour of the day, the landscape of legend changed to that of the modern Empire, but why would an artist choose to paint a valley in the hills above them?

He picked up the candle at his bedside and, quietly, sneaked downstairs. In front of the wall painting again, he studied the landscape carefully. Was that hill the same

as one he had seen for real, or that fellside the same as
the steep escarpment he had noted that afternoon? Some
of the details of the landscape were obscured by the boil-
ing mass of Chaos creatures that poured out of the hills.
There, for instance, in amongst a collection of half-beast,
half-man things, was a small black building; had he seen
that? It appeared to be a stone-built shrine, perhaps a
way temple for travellers to shelter in. The beasts were
dancing round it unconnected, it seemed, to the main
battle, covered in sticky dark blood that matted their fur.

He could not be sure, but he felt he had seen that
shrine before.

THE SUN BEAT down on him as he rode up the valley. It
was there. Now that he was looking for it, the low black
stone shrine was obvious against the hillside. He had
hoped all morning that he would not see it, that he
could write it off as imagination, his mind playing tricks
with him, but a part of him had known that he would
find it. Even the way the shrine sat on an outcrop that fell
away more steeply than most of the land around it mir-
rored the shrine he had seen in the painting.

He cursed, looking across at it. He ought to be scouting for signs of the marauding beasts, but he and the
others had searched half this valley the day before and
seen none. Now Stark and Tannhauser should be trailing
through the hills and dales surrounding it. If there was
anything around, they would find it and let him know.
He had time to take a look at the odd little shrine. He
swung his horse towards it and kicked his mount forward.

He had to kick the horse under him several more times
as it climbed the hillside. Claus had had to let it stop and
catch its breath, as it panted in the hot summer sunshine. The shrine had become hidden by the folds of the
land at times and Claus had lost his bearings more than

once, but now it stood before him. This could not be any way temple, he realised. There was no road or path beside it. Indeed, it seemed to be in a spot chosen for its isolation.

He dismounted and walked towards it, glad to be out of the saddle for a while. Ivy and bindweed competed to crawl over and cover the dark stone walls of the shrine, if that was what it was, for, as he approached, he could see no markings of any faith he recognised. A small shrub grew from a crack by the base of the angled roof.

The ground in front of the building was a flattened area of stone and gravel large enough for a small crowd of people or a few carts. There was a large darkened patch at its centre as if something had been spilt there. What it might have been or when it had happened, Claus could not guess. There was a doorway into the black stone. Nothing hung in it, but it was so dark inside that Claus, standing in the sunlight, could not see the interior at all. He walked steadily towards it.

Under the ivy and the bindweed, with its heavy headed white flowers, the building was made from well-dressed stone. Care had been taken in its construction, but there were odd gashes in its stonework, jagged crevasses and brutal chisel marks. On the lintel, above the doorway, someone had clearly attacked the stonework with venom. Where once, Claus supposed, there must have been carvings, these had been shorn away and chipped off. In places, the faint ghostly outline of carvings of people could still be made out, just.

All the marks on the walls, Claus realised, must show where the shrine had once been richly decorated, for the marks convinced him that his guess had been right. Why would someone systematically destroy all of the carvings and markings?

A slight breeze brought a sudden rich scent of jasmine with it. The smell was thick and pungent. It seemed to cloy and stick in Claus's nose and mouth.

He stopped in front of the building. His eyes drank in the chipped dark stone, his nostrils the heavy sweet odour. Some instinct told him that, somehow, something was wrong and that he should turn and run from here, but his senses held him captive where he was.

His horse was stamping and whinnying. He turned back towards it, wondering what had spooked it. He gave it a pat and rubbed its flanks. Puzzled, he looked back at the shrine. Despite the heat of the afternoon, he felt a chill.

The shrine, or whatever it might be, did not hold any clues to his mission, and he told himself that he had wasted enough time. He remounted. The horse did not need to feel his spur or be kicked into life this time; it seemed happy to be on its way.

HORST, THE STEWARD, had denied any knowledge of the building at all when Claus had asked about it on his return. Perhaps the shepherds whose flocks grazed those pastures might be able to help, he suggested. In any case, Horst would have to absent himself from the manor that evening, he said. He would arrange for food to be served to Claus and the injured man. Claus nodded. The steward hardly made for the most congenial company, anyway.

Claus checked on Meyer. He gave no response when Claus greeted him. The room was stuffy. Claus went to Meyer's bedside. Water and some food lay untouched on the table next to him.

'Meyer?'

The trooper moaned, but his eyes remained closed. Claus reached out his hand to touch the other man's

brow. It was burning. Meyer twisted in the bed and let
out a low anguished sound.

Claus left him quickly.

'Horst! Horst! Damn it, where are you, man?'

The servant appeared as Claus rushed down the stairs.

'Meyer has turned feverish. He needs help. Get your
healer.'

'Of course. I will attend to it at once. Food has been
laid out for you. Ilke will tend you.'

ILKE WAS THE dark-haired maid he had seen on his first
afternoon at the manor house. She smiled shyly at him
when she poured wine into his glass. It was a light red,
smelling of elderberries and resin. There were platters of
cold meats, hams and sausage, that Claus helped himself
to, and cheeses and bread spread on the table.

'Come,' Claus said, 'have something to eat with me.'

The maid refused at first and then, at his insistence,
had a slice of salami, but she would not sit with him and
barely spoke. He swallowed his wine and poured himself
some more.

The dancing animals and the shrine pulled his eyes
towards them. He tried to concentrate on something
else, his food, the maid's dark eyes, other figures in the
painting, but he seemed drawn back to the same point in
the picture. He had no desire to remember his visit to the
shrine earlier that day, and no wish to think about Meyer
lying injured upstairs. He knocked back more of the
wine.

He looked at the painting again, and saw that some of
the warped creatures by the black shrine seemed to be
carrying something. He got up and walked to the wall,
his wine glass still in his hand. In amongst the cavorting
shapes was a huge vessel held aloft by leering-faced apes
and ram-headed men. From it spilt a dark red liquid: the
blood that covered many of them?

He sipped from his glass. Some of the creatures were drinking the liquid, in the painting. He could see their tongues stained deep purple by it. Then he realised: perhaps it was not blood in the picture but wine. He turned away suddenly disgusted. He needed something to distract him. He was becoming obsessed.

The maid, Ilke, was clearing the remains of his meal away. He watched the back of her shapely form and a smile formed on his lips.

'The spoils of war,' he murmured softly to himself, as he moved to follow her.

THE SUNLIGHT WAS streaming through the window when he woke. It seemed horribly bright. His head felt thick and his mouth dry. How much had he drunk last night?

He stumbled up and out of bed. There was a pitcher of water in the corner, and he splashed his face with it and then gulped some down. He paused to breathe and then poured the rest down his throat. He felt dreadful.

It was much later than Claus had meant to get up; the sun was already high in the sky. He swore. He needed to be up and out. He had meant to travel beyond the valley he had scouted the last two days, but knew that would prove difficult now. He half tumbled down the staircase and out into the hall grounds.

Horst found him as he saddled his horse.

'There you are,' he said. There was an edge to his voice. 'You enjoyed yourself last night, I take it, whilst I was away.' It was a statement, not a question. Claus did not reply, concentrating on the straps and horse tack.

'You may be interested to know that Ilke has had to return to her family after your treatment of her.'

What the hell was the steward talking about? Then a memory came, of dark eyes and soft skin.

'You may be billeted here, but do not abuse our hospitality again!' Horst spat. He was close enough for Claus to smell his breath.

Claus wished he could explain. He could not. What had he done last night? How much had he drunk? He needed to be on his way.

'I'll speak with you this evening,' he said and swung himself up into the saddle.

THE HEAT OF the day and the motion of the horse made him feel sick. He had to stop twice within an hour. He wished he had found something to eat this morning. At what he guessed was an hour after midday, he found himself on the hill just below the shrine. It seemed as sensible a place to stop as any. He dismounted. The anxiety that the shrine had produced the day before had melted away, and today he was aware only of the view over the valley, the smell of wild flowers, the buzz of bees and the warmth of the stones under him when he sat. He chewed at some dried meat he had in his saddlebag and swigged at his water bottle.

He tried to remember what he had done the night before, but it seemed to be hidden in his mind behind a fog. He could not believe he would have hurt the girl or forced her, but no memories came to him.

He was tired still. His eyes began to slide closed.

Zapochka. He dreamt of the battle. He heard the cries of the armies, the blare of trumpets, the beat of drums, and words spoken in tongues he did not know. Somehow he was in among the horned beasts as they danced at the edge of the battle. One of the ram-headed men who held the great bowl he had seen in the painting came towards him. It rubbed its soft wool against him. A hand stroked his face. It was Ilke the maid's and the beastman was gone. She kissed his cheek tenderly and her hands sank lower down his body. She gripped his torso and stroked his thigh. It was no longer Ilke but the winged thing with the girl's face that the captain had shot days before and that they had left cold and stark for carrion.

He was awake again. For a moment, he was unsure where he was. His dream left him confused. He must have slept most of the afternoon, for the shadows were lengthening. He cursed loud enough to disturb his horse as it cropped the grass nearby. He had lost the whole day to his drunkenness of the night before. There was nothing for it but to head back.

EVENING HAD FULLY set in by the time Claus returned. Horst was not about. In fact, there appeared to be no one at all to serve him. He checked on Meyer, who seemed peacefully asleep. After a while, Claus found the kitchens where a man he had never seen before was able to point him to some food. After a pause, Claus picked himself out some wine too. He had no desire to sit in front of the painting again so he went to his room and ate. Then he lay back, determined to go to sleep. He needed to be up early. But rest would not come; perhaps he had slept too long in the afternoon. He lay wide-awake in bed. He thought he saw shapes and colours in the darkness, shapes that resolved into the charging knights and twisting creatures of the painting.

What was happening to him? He sat up and pressed the balls of his hands against his eyes.

Still the images swam in front of his face: buffalo-headed creatures, goat-faced artists, bowl carriers with ram's heads. Sigmar! Why did it not stop?

The painting was an obsession, dominating his evenings and even now, when not in front of it, he could see it. And during the day there was the shrine from it. He had to escape.

Stark and Tannhauser should be back the next night, the captain and the rest at the end of the week. Could he hold out that long?

SLEEP MUST HAVE come eventually. Claus found himself lying on top of his bedclothes, naked. There was an iron tang in his mouth. He rolled forward and rubbed his eyes. That was when he noticed the blood on them, drying, not yet crusted. He felt his face. Congealing blood covered his chin. Gods, there was blood in his mouth too. He spat, and then reached for the water and began to scrub.

It was early and the sun had only recently broken the skyline, but it seemed as if everyone was up. The courtyard of the Hall was buzzing with life.

'It seems your monsters have arrived, Lieutenant Katzbalger.'

'What?'

It was Horst. 'There was an attack last night. Sheep were gutted, ripped apart and strewn for miles, apparently, and a man.'

Claus stood, numbed. Men and women rushed around him, dizzyingly.

'All of their heads were taken. That poor man was unrecognisable: head ripped away, flesh torn from the bones, heart cut from the chest, a leg crushed. It must have been the foul beasts of Chaos you were searching for.'

'A man?' Horst's words barely seemed to sink in. The heads missing. Why had he felt he had already known that?

Where had the blood come from? Where was Meyer? He dashed back into the hall, leaving Horst behind him, still talking.

He was not surprised when he found Meyer missing, his sick room smelling sweet, like death. Coming down the stairs, he found the painting in front of him. He did not have to study it to notice the groups making their way towards the shrine. In their arms, they were carrying the heads of sheep and men. Claus felt his gorge begin to rise.

He snatched food from the kitchen, ignoring the looks he got, pale-faced and sweating. He needed to leave.

Horst found him as he swung himself up into the saddle. His fingers had fumbled as he had tied the straps around the horse.

'I have to go.'

'Sir,' Horst said, 'we need you to protect us.'

'I can't. Tell the others when they return. Say I've... I've gone to get help.'

He lashed the reins and kicked his spurs into his horse so that it bolted forward and away.

CLAUS RODE BACK towards where he and the others had routed the mutated raiders almost a week before and the road to Steingart, kicking the horse, forcing it forward. Slowly, the horse reduced its pace as Claus's panic began to wane. He let the horse find its own way.

What had happened to him? Tears began to slide down his face. His limbs ached. He needed desperately to get away. He felt as if he had not slept all night.

Had he killed Meyer? It barely seemed possible. Then he remembered the blood in his mouth.

The tears blinded him. He tried to wipe his eyes clear. His horse trotted steadily away from the manor house and the hills. As the fear receded, Claus slumped in his saddle and, eventually, rocked by the horse's motion, sleep claimed him.

HE WAS AWAKE again. The shrine was before him, its black walls scuffed and bruised. He had fallen from the saddle and lay sprawled on the stony ground. He had given the horse its head and somehow it had brought him here. It had been so anxious to get away the first time they had come here. Why had it brought him back?

His face hurt. It felt puffy and he winced when he touched it. He must have hit it when he fell. He pushed himself up. He thought he caught the scent of jasmine in his nostrils.

As he looked up, he saw a sheep's head, bloody, grinning, decapitated, in the shrine's doorway.

He dragged himself towards it.

THE NEXT MORNING dawned with a red smear. Stark rode down from the hills and into the manor house of the von Oppertals. He ached from the ride and nights beneath the cold stars.

'Hello?' he called.

Horst appeared a few minutes later.

'Where is the lieutenant?'

'He said he returned for help, gefreiter.' The steward began to explain something about some dead sheep.

'How is Meyer?'

'It seems he went too.'

Stark was puzzled. He rubbed the stubble that covered his chin, only half listening to the tale Horst told him. What should he do? Wait for the captain or follow the lieutenant? Entering the hall, he stopped before the wall painting.

He did not like it. It disturbed him. Its forms and colours somehow trapped the eye. It seemed to him that he noticed new details each time he looked at it. There, for instance, that figure grinning dementedly or screaming in terror by that old, black, ivy choked building, it was so like the lieutenant. He was certain he had not seen that before.

'Horst,' he said. 'Get that thing covered, would you?'

THE GIFT
by Jesse Cavazos V

THE SUN WAS setting, and it looked like it was going to be a beautiful evening as Johann and Sigismund von Schadt sat on their horses in the middle of the road, craning their necks to peer into the distance. Simultaneously, the two brothers leaned back into their saddles with sighs and looked at each other. To an onlooker, it would have been easy to spot the similarities in their appearance, similarities only enhanced by the clothes they wore: the uniforms of off-duty Reikland soldiers.

Johann, the younger of the two, shrugged. 'I can't see it,' he said at last. 'Are you sure?'

'Of course,' his older brother, Sigismund responded, pointing. 'See? The white spot above the tree there. That's the roof. And if you look to the left and down, you can see a break in the tree line where the yard is.'

'There are trees and breaks everywhere.'

'You're blind, I say. That one, that one. See now?' Sigismund began making jabbing motions with his finger.

Johann looked at his brother. 'Yes, wave your finger some more. You've just pointed to thirty or so trees with all that gesturing.'

'I'm telling you, it's this way. I am absolutely positive,' he said, raising his hands to forestall Johann's inevitable 'Are you sure?' 'Good Sigmar, you should know this by heart by now, after all the times we've gone up and down this road?'

'Some of us don't remember directions well.'

'Some of us can't find our way out of an empty room, you mean, a room with only one door. And the door's open, so you can see it's the exit. And... and there's a sign.'

Johann looked at him.

Sigismund waved his hands as if fanning away his poor oratory. 'Anyway, this is definitely the way, I'm sure.'

Johann shrugged. 'If you say so, then it must be true.'

'So glad you see it my way.'

There was a moment of silence between them as they stared down the road thoughtfully.

'Four years,' Johann said suddenly.

'Aye.'

'Feels like a long time, eh?'

'Aye.'

'Well then,' Johann urged his horse forward, 'let's go home.'

THEY DISMOUNTED IN unison and led their horses into the yard of von Schadt Manor, passing their reins off to a waiting stable boy. With an ease of familiarity honed by a great deal of practice, they strode up to their father and snapped perfect, parade-ground salutes, more for the benefit of the gathered servants than for theirs or their father's.

Otto's face was the image of constructed solemnity. He eyed his sons and growled, 'And where have you been?'

The two brothers exchanged knowing glances and looked him squarely in the eyes. 'The Emperor had need of us,' Sigismund said first.

'The Enemy had returned,' Johann added. He threw a glance at the robed figure standing at his father's side and was startled to see it was a stranger.

'And did you meet the enemy on the field of battle?' Otto asked.

'Yes, father,' Sigismund and Johann chorused.

The robed stranger stepped forward with a noticeable limp. He was exceedingly tall and well-muscled. A hammer pendant, the symbol of the man-god Sigmar, hung around his neck, and in his hand he held a heavy, spiked warhammer, the traditional weapon of a warrior-priest. His eyes, grey like mountain stone, stared at the two young noblemen.

'What did you do when you met him?' he prompted.

The two sons responded instantly. 'We killed him.'

Their words brought a smile to Otto's face. He grabbed both his sons and pulled them closer, gripping them in a tight bear hug. 'As well you should! The war will be won by men like you!'

Around them, the crowd was reacting with delight, surrounding the three men. After a moment Otto let go of his sons in order to shoo away the servants. 'It's good to have you back!' he said, grinning.

But Johann's attention lay on the robed stranger. 'And who might you be, Herr...?' He asked.

The bald priest smiled warmly at Johann. 'Einhardt Koenraad, and you are Johann, correct?'

Johann nodded, unable to keep the disappointment from his face, and began to scan the crowd.

After a moment the priest continued speaking, a note of forced jollity in his words. 'Johann, named for Grand Theogonist Johann Helstrum, I presume? A good name.'

'It was my grandfather's.'

The priest frowned. 'If you are looking for Father Dunn,' he said softly, 'he has passed away. I am his replacement.'

'How did he–' the young noble began, before Otto interjected. 'Sigismund, this is Father Koenraad. He is our new resident priest. He has been very interested in the two of you.'

'Oh?' Sigismund said, smiling. 'And why might that be?'

Father Koenraad laughed. 'I believe young men like you will change the fate of the Empire.'

'I'm sure they will,' Otto said, keeping his attention on his sons. 'Are either of you hungry?'

'No sir,' Johann said quietly. He couldn't believe Father Dunn was dead. His mind reeled. 'I'm going to retire, if you don't mind.'

'I think I will, too,' Sigismund agreed. 'We've been riding all day to get here, and I'm exhausted.'

'All right, but if–' Otto began. Before he could say any more, Johann bowed politely and, without looking at Father Koenraad, hurried into the house.

Otto raised an eyebrow at Sigismund, who was frowning after Johann.

'I hope you'll forgive Johann,' Sigismund said, noticing their father's look. 'The war tried him a great deal. I think hearing about Father Dunn's death must have troubled him.' He looked over at Koenraad. 'I overheard your conversation. Hard for me not to, since you two were standing right next to me.'

'How was it?' Otto asked quietly.

Sigismund shrugged. 'It was war.'

Otto von Schadt was a retired Imperial general. He had led the forces of the Empire against every conceivable enemy and seen more battles than most living men had even heard of. He nodded grimly. 'Fighting against the Enemy,' he muttered. 'I wish you two had fought some other foe at your first battle.'

'Middenheim wasn't that bad,' Sigismund said, the forced levity in his tone telling his father the exact opposite. Middenheim *was* that bad.

Sigismund coughed politely. 'Shall we continue this tomorrow morning?' he asked. 'I'm a bit tired.' With a muted farewell, he turned and entered the manor, leaving his father to stare after him.

SIGISMUND'S THOUGHTS WERE filled with exhaustion as he finished unpacking and collapsed onto his bed. Sighing deeply, he withdrew a pendant that had been hanging around his neck, holding it up to examine it.

The lamp's guttering flame sent flickering yellow light playing over the pendant's surface. Somehow, despite being completely solid, when Sigismund held it up to the light, he could see a dull glow shining through it. A single silver wire wound around the stone, connecting it to a silvery chain from which it hung. At first glance, it appeared to be a simple shade of amber, but when viewed closely he could make out silvery streaks and whirls within it.

Sigismund's heart began to beat faster as he stared at the stone, and his mind began to cloud. The whirls in the stone appeared to wind directly through it, as if he could see right inside it. He looked at it closely and opened his mouth, as if he wanted to say something, but he didn't know what.

There was a knock at the door, startling him. 'It's Johann.'

'Come in.'

The door opened and Johann slipped in, grinning slightly. He noticed the pendant and raised an eyebrow. 'Where did you get that?' he asked.

'I found it in a barrel,' Sigismund said.

Johann looked at him.

'Does it matter?' Sigismund asked, trying to cover up his terrible attempted subterfuge. 'Anyway, what is it you wanted?'

Johann nodded towards the pendant. 'I'm serious. Where did you get that?'

Sigismund held it higher, letting the light from the bedside lamp illuminate the dark yellow stone. 'Isn't it lovely?' he asked.

'Absolutely, but that doesn't answer my question.'

Sigismund sighed. 'Do you remember Middenheim?'

'Could I forget?'

Sigismund gave him an annoyed look and leaned back against the wall next to his bed. 'It was at Sokh, when we ran into those beastmen looting the city.'

In his mind's eye, Sigismund could see his demi-lancer troupe as they wheeled through the city, searching for the enemy. He could starkly remember every moment of that battle, and he suspected Johann could as well.

'Yes,' Johann said blankly. Sigismund could see that Johann remembered the event well.

'The captain believed they'd been sent to try and flank us but had gotten distracted looting. I do remember,' Johann said.

'We had just charged when their leader, the shaman, came out of a building, carrying some loot in its hands.'

Johann bolted to his feet. 'Don't tell me!'

Sigismund winced. 'Yes,' he said. 'I took it from the beastman's body after we killed him. He had it in his hand when he came out.' He grimaced at Johann's expression. 'What? There's nothing wrong with it.'

'How do you know?'

'I just do!' Sigismund shouted, making Johann flinch. 'Just look at it,' he said, more quietly this time. 'It isn't some crude Northern trinket, hammered together by some heathen animal that just recently discovered fire, and decorated by the fingerbones of whatever child he had just finished eating.' Where did this blasphemy come from, he wondered?

Johann's face turned pale. 'How can you say something like that?' he asked, shocked. 'How can you even think about being so dismissive?' He shook his head. 'And so what if it looks fine? That's what concerns me! The Ruinous Powers don't always come in malign guises! Sometimes they appear to be extremely beautiful or magnificent. That's how they seduce us with their lies!'

Sigismund looked at him. 'Can you hear yourself? You sound like a flagellant. Do you want me to start calling you one? Do you want me to get you your scourge, Herr Flagellant? How have you been, Herr Flagellant? Busy day of self-mortification, I trust? Is your–'

'This isn't a joke!'

The smile on Sigismund's face slipped away. For a moment, neither brother spoke. The lamplight flickered wildly, sending their shadows dancing on the wall.

'I understand your worry,' Sigismund said slowly. 'Trust me, I do, but there's nothing wrong with this pendant. How could there be?'

Johann shook his head. 'What happened to the brother I knew?' he said, more to himself than to Sigismund.

Sigismund clenched his teeth. 'What are you implying?' he hissed. 'Are you saying that I've changed somehow?'

Johann gestured at the offending pendant. 'Why else would you do this? May I remind you that not only is looting a crime, but looting from a *beastman*, of all things? You could put your life at risk if a witch hunter were to find out, never mind the risk to your soul!'

'You're so damn self-righteous, Johann!' Sigismund snarled back. 'On the topic of who has changed, what about you? Always preaching to the rest of us, always so solemn. After every battle do you head off to get good and drunk like the rest of us? Hell no! Let's go straight to the chapel instead! You would make a better priest than a soldier!'

'You think I don't know that?' Johann snapped. 'If it wasn't for the fact that it would kill father for me not to follow in his footsteps, I'd already be doing that. But here I am, stuck in this life that I don't want, trying to save the soul of a brother who doesn't even want my help!'

The anger immediately drained out of Sigismund, and his jaw dropped. For a moment, he sat stunned before responding. 'Sigmar, Johann... I had no idea.'

'No one did,' Johann said quietly. 'No one knew except for Father Dunn.'

There was an uncomfortable silence before Johann spoke again.

'He was going to try and talk to father when we got back,' he said. 'I want to fight for the Empire, but I also want to fight for Sigmar. I thought... If I spent *some time* in the military he wouldn't have a problem with me becoming a warrior-priest.'

He gestured at the pendant again, but this time it was muted. 'What makes that so important to you?'

The anger began to rise in Sigismund again, for no reason at all, but he forced it down. What is wrong with me? What am I getting so upset for, he thought, shaking his head? With a sigh, he leaned back against the wall. The bed creaked as he shifted his weight.

'Greta Luitpold,' he said.

'Oh.'

Sigismund managed a weak grin. 'We've known her for... a long time,' he said. 'I've loved her almost since we first met, and I think she feels the same. When I saw this, gripped in that dead shaman's hand, I acted without thinking.' He held the pendant up to the light. 'I spoke to father earlier. He told me that Greta and her father will be here tomorrow to visit us. If memory serves correctly, she'll go to the chapel first to take her blessing from Father Koenraad. I want to, ah, ambush her there and give her this.' He sighed. 'I want to ask her to marry me.'

Johann stared at him. 'I can understand that, but I don't think that pendant's necessary. Like I said, we've known her for years. She wouldn't decline, and neither would her father. What do you need that trinket for?'

Sigismund shrugged. 'You know, father gave mother her necklace when he proposed to her. Do you remember how much she loved it? It meant everything to her. Well... I just want Greta to have something to remember our engagement by.'

'You mean apart from the engagement itself?'

Sigismund frowned. 'Of course. I just want it to be special. How can you argue with that?'

'"All who profit from the spoils of Chaos shall be doomed",' Johann quoted.

'Grand Theogonist Vilgrim III. I am familiar with the teachings of our elders, brother.'

Johann looked him in the eye. 'Are you?' He asked. 'Is merely being "familiar" enough?'

FATHER KOENRAAD LOOKED away from Sigismund's door, thoughtfully digesting everything that he had heard from outside the older brother's room. Without a word, he turned and made his way back to his chapel.

THE CHAPEL APPEARED to be empty as Sigismund pulled the wooden doors shut behind him, wondering where Koenraad was. With a shrug, he sat down and waited for Greta. He hoped that he didn't have to wait long, or else he might chew his arm off with anxiety.

The door opened a short while later and she entered. It may have been his imagination, but she looked even more beautiful than he remembered. Her hair was a shade of amber that perfectly matched that of the stone, and he could see her bright green eyes from where he sat, a short distance away. She bowed her head as she entered the chapel, and then paused, noticing him. The sight of her face after so long made his mouth dry as he stood and walked to her side.

'What are–' she began, before he held up the pendant, smiling as her eyes widened at the sight. 'Sigismund, where did you…?'

'It fell off the back of a cart,' he lied, horribly.

She looked at him.

'It doesn't matter, does it?' He looped the chain over her head and draped it around her neck. 'It's yours. I… I want you to have it,' he said before pausing, and then drew a breath, 'to remember our engagement by.'

She stared at him for a moment, mouth open in surprise. 'I will!' she promised, throwing her arms around him as he kissed her.

Sigismund would remember that moment with perfect clarity for the rest of his life.

'WILL YOU BE here for long?' Sigismund asked Greta as he walked her back to her room. She was still looking at the pendant as she walked.

'Hmm?' She asked. 'Oh, well, we should be here for dinner, and perhaps to stay the night. It all depends.' She smiled at him.

His heart skipped, and he smiled back. He could hardly believe that he had just asked her to marry him, or that she had said yes.

'This is my room,' Greta said, standing on her toes to kiss him on the cheek. His heart skipped a beat. 'I'll change and see you at dinner, then?'

'Yes. You will,' Sigismund said, cursing inwardly at his sudden clumsiness. 'I'll come by to get you then.'

He could tell by the light in her eye that she was aware that he was off-balance, and she determined to make the most of it, teasing him. It had always been her favourite hobby as they had grown up, especially once she had realised his feelings for her.

'I can go inside by myself,' she ribbed, gesturing for him to leave. 'Go away!' She grinned as he held up his hands in surrender. With a final teasing smile, she opened the door and stepped inside, closing the door behind her. When she did, *her* heart skipped a beat, and it wasn't due to joy.

There was writing on the wall over her bed. It had been hidden by the open door as she'd entered, but she could see it clearly now. She couldn't look away from it, even though its very presence filled her with a dull sense of horror. It was a single word that she had never heard before.

'*Nakhan,*' she whispered to herself. What did that mean?

Without warning, the word's meaning became the last thing that she had to worry about as pain lanced through her body. The pendant on her chest was burning with an inner light, and she staggered as the intelligence within responded to the name and tore its way into her mind. As she lay convulsing on the floor, her last thought was of Sigismund.

It WAS LATE evening as Johann spoke to Otto in his study. He had wanted to bring up the topic of becoming a priest, but whenever he was about to mention it, he couldn't bring himself to do so. Instead, he had rambled on about a number of other topics until reaching Sigismund's engagement.

'It's about damn time,' Otto said simply. 'When is he supposed to make the announcement?'

'At dinner,' Johann said. 'I managed to–'

There was a furious banging at the door. 'Otto!' Koenraad's voice came through the door. 'The chapel. It has been desecrated!'

Otto and Johann stared at one another in shock before Koenraad opened the door and barged in. He looked at them as he tightly gripped the handle of his hammer. 'The chapel has been desecrated!' he said again.

Otto and Johann were stunned. It was only when Koenraad gestured for them to follow that they leapt to their feet.

The three of them left the room and hurried towards the stairs leading down to the chapel. It was directly attached to the main house so that any of the pious von Schadt family could go there whenever they felt the need.

The three of them hurried down the hall. 'How?' Otto growled. 'How could this happen?'

'Beastmen?' Johann suggested. 'The woods are thick with them since the end of the war.'

'No,' Father Koenraad said, 'not beastmen. It's too subtle… I fear this is something more insidious. My lord… there may be a heretic amongst your staff.'

'What?' Johann gasped. 'Really, that's a bit unlikely, don't you think? I mean, what led you to that conclusion?'

Father Koenraad turned and looked at Johann menacingly. 'You can be surprised at what can carry taint with it.'

Taint, Johann thought, and then remembered his conversation with Sigismund. *What? How did he… does he know?*

Otto spotted the priest's glance and stopped. He stepped up to the priest, gritting his teeth in rage. 'What are you implying?' he growled.

Johann stepped back. He had never seen his father this angry before and was concerned that he might even attack the priest.

Koenraad raised his hands defensively. 'I meant no insult, my lord.' Even he seemed shocked at the older von Schadt's furious glare.

Otto's head lowered. 'I should be apologising, Einhardt. It's just …' he looked up with tears in his eyes. 'This is our home. The war should not be able to follow us here.'

'The Enemy is never considerate,' Father Koenraad said, resting a hand on Otto's shoulder.

'Hello!' Sigismund's cheerful voice startled them all from down the hallway. He smiled at them, but his expression faded as he noticed their looks. 'What's going on?'

'Sigismund!' Koenraad said, stepping forward. 'What are you doing here?'

'I was just looking for Greta,' he said, wary of Koenraad's forceful question. 'I was going to escort her to dinner, but she didn't answer her door. Have any of you seen her?' He frowned. 'I… what *is* going on?'

Otto and Johann looked at one another, their faces troubled.

Koenraad looked back at them. His face was grim. 'We must find her,' he said.

'What is going on?' Sigismund asked again. 'What aren't you telling me?'

'The chapel has been desecrated,' Johann told him. 'We don't know who did it.'

'What?' Sigismund asked, looking around. 'Are you joking?'

Their expressions answered him. He shook his head, unable to believe them. Finally he looked up. 'I have to try to find her,' he said.

'We will send out search parties,' Otto said. 'If Greta is in danger, we must do whatever we can to try and save her. We should also send for the witch hunters. I don't believe there may be a heretic in our presence, but if there is…'

There was silence as his words sank in.

'I would advise against that, my lord,' Koenraad said, surprising Johann. 'The Templars are notoriously exuberant in the persecution of their duties, and if they come here I fear heretics will burn even if there are no heretics *to* burn.'

Otto shook his head. 'That's a risk I am prepared for.'

'I have to find her before that happens,' Sigismund said. He turned to his father. 'Please.'

'Go,' Otto said.

Sigismund turned and ran down the hallway. Johann started after him, but his father stopped him.

'I need you to help me gather the servants together,' Otto said. 'I can't believe that there are any heretics amongst us, but we must keep them safe.' He turned to look at Koenraad. 'I know your reservations, but you must contact the Templars. I feel that only they can uncover what is happening.'

Koenraad bowed his head. 'Then I will do as you ask,' he said grimly.

HOOVES THUNDERED AS Sigismund drove his horse forward. Having failed to find Greta inside the manor, he had no other option than to search the surrounding area for her. His heart was filled with worry and disbelief. How did this happen? Where could she be?

This is my fault somehow. He cursed himself. *Oh, my love, where are you?*

Where was he, for that matter? He slowed his horse and looked around, trying to re-orient himself. After a moment, he noticed with a start that he was not far from the place where he had met Greta for the first time.

It was a tree at the edge of the river. Sigismund remembered he had been reading when his father had joined him, introducing him to his old friend from the army, General Luitpold, and his daughter. The memory clenched at his heart, and he could feel tears coursing down his cheeks.

I can't bear to lose you, he thought. *Please, please, please be all right.*

He wheeled his horse and rode forward, heading for the tree. His hopes of finding her there were dim, but maybe there Sigmar would give him a sign as to where she might be.

When he rode onto the bank, his hopes died.

He slid from his horse, dropping to his knees as he beheld Greta's body at the edge of the river, blood staining the ground around her arms where she had slit her wrists open with the kitchen knife lying nearby. He crawled to her side and lifted her into his lap, sobbing helplessly as he cradled her head in close to his chest.

'Greta…' he moaned, burying his face in her shoulder. 'Why?'

He stayed there for a while, rocking back and forth with her, before noticing the chain around her neck. The pendant! When he saw it, a wave of sudden nausea made him stagger. Without warning, he suddenly *needed* it. He wanted to look at it, to hold it in his hands again.

This is wrong, he thought, pulling the chain from around her neck. The stone was glowing brightly, and his mind reeled. *This is… it is cursed! Johann was right!*

He fought with all his will to keep the pendant away, knowing inwardly that if it fell around his neck, something bad was going to happen. His hands still looped it over his head, despite his struggle.

'No. Stop it!' he snarled as the chain settled around his shoulders.

His horse's ears twitched as Sigismund's body began to shake, and it dashed from the clearing as his agonised scream tore the night air.

'LOCK THE DOORS and make sure no one leaves,' Father Koenraad said grimly as he mounted his horse. He wheeled it to face the road. 'I will return shortly with the witch hunters and we will see an end to this!'

'Wait!' Johann said, holding up a hand. 'Here.'

He stepped forward, pulling his sword, scabbard and all, from his belt and handing it to Koenraad.

'You are wrong,' he said, meeting the priest's eyes, 'there is no heretic here.' He gestured towards the woods. 'Whatever did this, it did not come from here. That warhammer will be all but useless on horseback, so you should take this in case the real culprit tries to stop you.'

Koenraad nodded. 'I agree with you, Johann,' he said. He raised the sword in salute. 'May Sigmar protect us all!' he shouted. His horse leapt forward, charging down the road to Altdorf.

Johann and Otto stared after him, their faces equally filled with dread.

'I've re-called the search parties,' Otto said. 'All of the servants are inside the main hall, save for a few. I'm going to take some and search the house for whoever's left.'

'I'll come with you.'

'No, I want you to find Sigismund,' Otto said, heading for the door leading back into the house. He stopped with his hand on the handle, turning to look at Johann. 'Sigmar be with you,' he said before going back inside.

Johann stared after his father, his heart filled with sorrow. He knew what was going to happen when the witch hunters arrived. Someone would have to pay the price for letting heresy, real or imagined, foster within the household. It was clear who.

He turned and ran to the stables, praying he would find his brother and Greta before it was too late. Within moments he had mounted his horse and charged into the woods.

It was an hour before he found Greta, and wept at the sight of her body lying in the dirt. He dismounted and chokingly covered her face with his cloak.

As he turned away he noticed tracks other than his in the dirt. *Sigismund's already been here*, he thought, *but where-?*

He mounted up again and rode his horse hard back towards the house. He felt like an idiot for having probably passed Sigismund in the dark without noticing him. Without warning, his horse shrieked and reared. It was all Johann could do to remain in the saddle.

'What is it?' he asked, peering into the woods and cursing himself for handing his weapon away to Koenraad. After a moment a rank stench hit him and he reeled, gagging. 'What-?'

In the dark he could barely make out a large shape lying on the ground a short distance away. He moved closer and stopped when he realised it was a body that had been torn apart as if by an animal.

Sigismund's horse! he realised. *How did... there must have been beastmen after all!*

Beginning to panic, he shouted and kicked his horse forward, not stopping until he reached the edge of the woods and burst from the underbrush. The von Schadt manor loomed in front of him, but any sense of relief he might have had died when he spotted the heavy double doors smashed in.

'No, Sigmar no!' he shouted as he dismounted and ran into the house.

Inside, there was only chaos and the stench of death. The bodies of servants lay all over the main hall, their blood staining the floor. He gaped at the sight, his mind reeling, before the sounds of screaming from deeper within the house stirred him into action, and he charged after them.

He pursued the screaming to the doors of the chapel and kicked them open as the last ones faded. He leapt in, shouting a prayer to Sigmar that died in his throat when he saw what awaited him within.

Whatever it was, it wasn't human, though it had once worn a like shape. As he watched, the gnarled, warped creature standing by the altar dropped Otto von Schadt's mangled body to the ground. As it turned to Johann, he could see a chain around its neck from which a pendant hung.

'Hnnnnggghh… *brotherrr*…' it moaned, raising its heavy head to the ceiling and letting out an anguished howl.

'No,' Johann gasped, unable to believe his eyes. He reached for his sword, remembering that he had given it to Father Koenraad.

The creature staggered forward, falling to the floor as if its legs refused to work, then began crawling slowly towards him.

In his terror, Johann grabbed the closest weapon he could find: a pole-mounted brazier next to the door. The creature's shape blurred forward as it sank serrated teeth into his leg, making him stumble to the ground. The brazier rolled away, hitting the wall and catching some of the hanging tapestries aflame.

The creature pulled itself as upright as it could manage, raising its claws into the air above its head. Its eyes, horribly, were still the same as Sigismund's.

'Nnnngghhh!' it groaned. 'Can't… *stopp*…' The pendant was glowing brighter than a star as it prepared to bring its claws down.

The pendant!

Johann's hand lashed out and he grabbed it. He howled in agony as it burned his hand, searing his flesh as if it were made of fire. He broke the chain with a jerk and the creature collapsed, gasping. The glow and the agony faded into nothing as Johann rolled away. He grabbed the fallen brazier with his good hand as Sigismund, or what was left of him, sprung up on all fours and lunged for him. Flames licked the walls as they surrounded the two brothers. A loud howl filled the chapel, and then there was nothing.

'JOHANN.'

Johann moaned as he stirred himself awake, blinking as he regained consciousness. There was air on his face and he winced as he opened his eyes.

Von Schadt Manor, or what was left of it, stood before him, smoking ruins replacing the place where he had grown up and spent his childhood. He could feel tears welling in his eyes as Father Koenraad crouched next to him, his shadow blocking out the light of the rising sun.

The sun? Is it morning?

'Johann,' Koenraad said again quietly. 'Johann, what happened here?'

The young nobleman groaned as he stirred, registering pain all over his body. Memories returned to him: riding in the darkness, fighting what was once his brother, and pulling himself from the fire. In a cracked, broken voice he told the priest everything, feeling his tears running down his cheeks as he spoke. As he finished, he held up the pendant in his scorched hand.

'This is it,' he gasped. 'This is what did it all. I don't know how or why, but this is it.'

'The Eye of Nakhan,' Koenraad said. 'That explains it. It contains the essence of a powerful Chaos sorcerer named Nakhan. He created the Eye in order to contain his soul in case anyone was ever able to destroy his body. It was a way of keeping himself alive and, essentially, immortal. It must have quietly worked at Sigismund's mind while dormant, slowly changing him. Fortunately for you, you haven't been exposed to it long enough for it to begin influencing your actions. Now that it's awake, you are lucky that you didn't try to put it on.'

'Changed...' Johann said, remembering their argument. Suddenly he thought of something. 'How did you know what it was?'

'You'll be fine,' Koenraad said, ignoring him. 'These burns may be painful, but they won't kill you.' The priest leaned down to stare into his eyes. 'But I will.'

The nobleman lashed out, swinging his hand through the air to knock the priest away, but Koenraad caught his arm and pried the pendant from his fingers.

'Thank you,' Koenraad cooed. 'You have no idea,' he said as Johann tried to crawl to his feet. 'You've no idea how much effort I put into this: the years of manipulating fate until I could bring this into my grasp, the shame of dressing like a complete idiot in order to lie in wait.' He gestured to his priestly vestments, which were darkening from brown to a deep blue in front of Johann's eyes. He kicked Johann in the side and leaned over him again, grinning wildly. 'But it was all worth it,' he said. 'With the Eye of Nakhan, nothing can stop me, least of all you.'

He pulled Johann's sword from its sheath and slowly inserted it into Johann's side, making him cry out. Koenraad laughed.

'I killed that doddering old priest,' he crowed. 'I wrote Nakhan's name on the wall of Greta Luitpold's room to awaken the sorcerer's will in order to overcome her and then Sigismund. I played you all, and you fell for it!'

He laughed as he wrenched the blade from Johann's side. The nobleman's eyes misted as Koenraad tied the broken ends of the chain together in a knot and placed it around his neck, grinning wildly.

Suddenly his smile faded. His body shook and he fell to his knees, staring in awe at the glowing pendant around his neck. Within moments waves of agony had him crying out and convulsing on the ground wildly before he collapsed, limp.

As the life faded from Johann, Koenraad got back to his feet, dusting his robes off. He hardly seemed to notice Johann die as he examined himself, smiling cruelly.

'No, Koenraad,' Nakhan said as he looked at his new hands, 'you played no one.' He smiled. 'It was not your manipulations that brought all this to pass.'

Without a backward glance, the reborn sorcerer turned and strode towards the road leading to Altdorf. The sun was rising, and it looked as if it was going to be a beautiful day.

RIVER OF BLOOD
by Steven Eden

THE INVADERS CHARGED across the churned field, through
sheets of arrows, until the archers scrabbled fretfully at
empty quivers. Orcs, Kurgan marauders from the north,
and goblins tumbled into the long ditch, buckshot and
balls blowing gaps in the heaving mass that closed almost
immediately; they tore at the abatis with axe and fist while
handgunners called frantically for powder. For the most
part, the line held, the ditch carpeted with the slain. But at
one point, a roaring mob of orcs surged over the breastworks, pressing back the bristling hedge of pikes.

Two hundred paces to the rear, Eliak Debretton gauged
the fight with a practiced eye. Rumours had started a
month ago, of a great host gathering in the World's Edge
Mountains, but there were always rumours. A fortnight
later exhausted survivors reported the loss of several
frontier outposts and the massacre of farmers stubborn
or desperate enough to try to scrabble a living from the
borderlands. Those still coherent spoke of an endless
stream of invaders, but refugee tales had to be taken with
a pinch of salt. Nevertheless, the County of Stirland, as it

164

had many times before, gathered its sons, supplemented by mercenary bands, and marched forth under the general, Hulger Trank. A week ago, its advanced guard disappeared into the foothills where the River Stir emerged from the mountains. The next day, its remnants stumbled into camp, the invaders' spearhead hard on their heels. Still confident, Trank entrenched his army between the river and a granite outcrop of the Worlds Edge Mountains, a narrow position held many times before during the endless wars to maintain the border, and for three days the invaders had raged uselessly against it. But each day more defenders had died, the stocks of powder had dwindled, the margin of victory had grown thinner, and still there seemed no end to the masses descending upon them.

Debretton loosened his sword in its scabbard, and turned to the Norscan mounted next to him. 'See, Vanir, how the rear rankers begin to drift back, to glance behind them. Here and there a man falls and no one takes his place. A nervous line is like a failing dam. Cracks appear and spread before there is a hint of water, but when it gives way it goes all at once.' Vanir merely grunted in reply, busy as he was tucking his long, yellow braids beneath his tunic. Debretton looked over his shoulder to his troop of cavalry, thirty dogs of war from every corner of the Old World. Some, such as Vanir, had been with him for years, ever since… well, ever since circumstances had led him to take up the life of the freebooter. Others, he had recruited over a dozen campaigns, men he had picked out as superb fighters with little to lose. They wore an eclectic range of armour and carried a variety of weapons: lance, bows, hammers, swords, as befitted their personal style of combat. All they had in common was a yen for war and gold.

General Hulger Trank rode up roaring, trailing a stream of attendants, flunkies and standard-bearers, his voice only slightly muffled by the visored helm he wore. 'Damn you, Debretton, I told you to drive that scum back.'

'Aye, so you did, my lord, and I intend to do just that when the time is right.'

Trank tore off his helm, revealing a shock of white hair, and a hook-nosed visage purple with fury. 'They are across the works already. What are you waiting for?'

Debretton leaned over his pommel and adjusted a strap. 'For the moment I judge most propitious. You will have to trust in me. And may I suggest you draw aside to avoid a trampling.'

Trank's mouth worked. He emitted a series of strangled croaks. Finally, with visible effort, he gained control and through gritted teeth swore an oath. 'Debretton, no man speaks to me so. I'll have your head—'

Debretton, one eye on the enemy, interrupted, 'Later on, it will be at your disposal. For now, though, I have need of it, so let me do what you have paid me for.' The two men locked gazes for a long moment, until Trank hurled his helmet to the ground, yanking his horse brutally about to return to his retinue.

'You soiled your name years ago, Debretton, a traitor to your homeland and your family,' he snarled over one shoulder, 'and were you not my last reserve? By Sigmar I hope you are half the warrior you think you are.'

Debretton and Vanir watched impassively as Trank galloped off. Vanir made one last adjustment to his braids. 'He talks too much.'

Debretton motioned his trumpeter forward, a slight lad of fifteen struggling to look unconcerned. 'You've picked a fine fight for your first,' he told the boy with a grim smile, 'just be sure you stay close and blow with all your heart, and watch me for the recall after we drive them past the ditch.'

The mercenary glanced back at the buckling line. 'Trank is a fool,' he said to Vanir. 'He has no idea how to use cavalry.'

The pikemen dug in desperately, scrabbling to hold back a wedge of howling orcs. A huge beast muscled its way forward at the apex, laying men low with a hammer the size of a small anvil. 'Three hundred horsemen would make no impression on that mob, but the orcs have even less discipline in victory than in defeat. Their bloodlust blinds them. If we wait until they are dispersed, out of control, our thirty should be more than enough.' Debretton drew his sword, the trumpeter lifted his horn to his lips, and the troopers steadied their suddenly excited mounts.

The captain watched as orcs overwhelmed the line of pike with a roar and streamed through the gap. Only half consciously, he measured the distance, judged the ground, and predicted the moment when the onrushing line would scatter beyond hope of redemption. 'Twenty more paces... What do you think, Vanir? Is now the time?'

Vanir hefted his double-bladed axe experimentally. 'I think you talk too much.'

Debretton barked laughter, brought his sword flashing down, and the company sprang forward.

'I DIDN'T THINK less than three dozen could do what I saw done today. Your men cut through the orcs as if they were children. You saved the army.' Hulger Trank shifted moodily in the entrance to Debretton's tent, clearly a man unused to issuing compliments or making amends. Outside the small tent the army, or what was left of it, was working desperately through the night to clear the dead away and repair the breastworks where the enemy had broken through. Among the bodies was half of Debretton's troop. The other half snored away drunkenly, bedded down beside their horses, manual labour being beneath their dignity and outside the terms of their employment. Debretton, sprawled before Trank on a pallet heaped with furs, tipped back a flagon of beer. A sleeping woman nestled against his naked chest. He probed gingerly at a shallow cut along the side of his jaw, where a spear thrust had come within an inch or two of tearing out his throat. It would add a prominent scar to his collection, he reflected, should he live long enough for it to heal.

'No, my lord, this army is doomed. You've left it here too long. Tomorrow the line will break not in one place, but in many, and there will be no reserve.' Debretton pushed the woman away. She burrowed beneath the furs as he stood and pulled a tunic over his head. 'While you've wrestled with the enemy here, his outriders have long since passed us by on both flanks.'

'Aye, so you pointed out in council two nights past. But how could I know that this invasion was only a small part of a larger war? Why, the whole border is aflame from the sea all the way round to the Grey Mountains.' Trank clenched his fists so that the knuckles stood out whitely. 'Besides, in forty years of war I have never con-ceded a field.'

The mercenary snorted. 'A fine epithet that will make for your gravestone.'

'Don't mock me, Debretton. I have spent my life hold-ing these marches. Now they burn.' The count's chin fell to his chest. 'My son-in-law fell today, and I will join him tomorrow. I have failed my duty and brought ruin on myself, my line, and my lands.' Trank raised his head. 'But I did not come here to confess my sins. I came to demand one last service of you.' A trace of bitterness crept into Trank's tone. 'With the Empire beset on all sides, His Lordship the Count of Stirland is left to his own devices. He has decided to cut his losses, meaning us, and concentrate the rest of his host at Reiksgrad. It is the strongest fortress within many leagues. It has high walls and broad towers and is practically unassailable, surrounded as it is by the Stir and marshlands, with only a single causeway giving access to the gates. He sent instructions for us to make our way there if possible, but I have informed his lordship that we haven't the strength to make a fighting retreat. We can be of more use standing here.'

The count lifted the flap to the tent and beckoned into the darkness beyond. A young woman came forward hesitantly. She wore an ermine cloak, trimmed in white, her features hidden beneath wimple and veil. Trank put an arm around her and ushered her in. 'This is my daughter. She is with child, my heir. I need to save something from this disaster, so I want you to escort her to Reiksgrad. It may be besieged, but the enemy will not take it by storm. From there she can make her way to safety.'

Debretton shook his head. 'Our contract is broken, my lord. My men and I leave you to your fate tonight. With luck and hard riding we may be able to make it through the mountains, but our chances are slim enough without dragging along milady.'

'I can ride,' the woman said, and Debretton caught a flash of azure eyes above the veil.

'As well as any man and better than most can,' Trank declared proudly. 'We breed strong women on the frontier. She won't slow you down.'

Debretton's features hardened into a scowl. 'There's a difference between riding to the hounds and having to ride down an enemy. I won't put my men at risk in the faint hope of preserving your seed.'

'You vile, lowborn scum,' the woman hissed. She trembled, though Debretton could not tell whether it was from fear or anger. Her father restrained her, making shushing noises.

Debretton stepped close. He was faintly stirred that she did not flinch. 'Yes, scum we are, but angels compared to the beasts, human and otherwise, that range the marches.' His glance shifted to Trank. 'Think, man, the fate you could condemn her to. It would be a mercy to slit her throat now, before milady ends up tortured to death in some enemy camp, or worse.' Debretton lounged back on the pallet. 'I won't have that on my conscience. Now leave me to my beer and my whore.'

It was the woman's turn to step forward. 'How dare you–' she began, but her father laid a hand on her shoulder. Trank pulled the woman back and reached into a pouch on his belt. 'I was warned that an appeal to your honour would fail,' he said, 'and that I would have to give you this.'

Debretton looked up. Trank held a single silver *thaler*. The Empire sigil glinted in the firelight. On the obverse, Debretton knew, would be a crude likeness of Karl Franz; he had seen coins like this before. A small hole had been bored through the coin near one edge. 'Do not ask this of me,' he said, his eyes never leaving the coin.

'I do. His lordship explained to me that you are bound to accept this token and perform any service asked of you. A penance of sorts…'

'His lordship reveals too much,' Debretton snarled. Resentfully he reached forward, taking the silver piece. He regarded it thoughtfully for a long moment, turning it this way and that, and then closed his fist around it. 'My lord, there are fates worse than death.'

For a moment, Trank's face crumpled. He drew in a long, shuddering breath. 'I know. My own is one. But this…' The old warrior straightened. 'Taking this chance is what duty demands.'

'And it is my choice as well,' the woman said, chin held high, her gaze a damning mixture of hope and contempt. 'I will risk anything to save my child. I will ride alone if needs be.'

'I believe you would,' Debretton said quietly. Then, in a more decisive tone, he went on. 'What is your name, child?'

'Ilse, and I am no child.'

'Let me see you properly.'

Ilse pulled back her wimple, allowing long golden hair to cascade down below her shoulders. Her veil fell away, revealing flushed cheeks, full lips, and a firm chin. Debretton rose, eyes fixed on her face, ran fingers through her hair and gently spread her cloak. Her figure was slim, almost boyish, with no swell yet of bosom or abdomen to show her pregnancy. She endured his inspection until at last his hands fell to his side. Ilse hurriedly tugged the cloak back into place.

'How long can you hold on the morrow? No prideful boasting, this is too important.'

Trank bit back a retort, pursing his lips. 'A thousand pike and swordsmen, half that many archers and hand gunners, though the powder is almost gone. I can hold well past noon, with luck perhaps until dusk.'

Debretton grunted. 'This army has had little enough luck. If you can keep the enemy busy through midday, we may have a chance.' His lips twitched upwards. 'Such a fine lady must travel in style. She has a coach, I imagine?' When Trank nodded, Debretton went on. 'We leave as soon as the moon is down. Milady will travel in the coach, with a mounted guard and spare horses, and what of your war chest?'

The count was slightly taken aback. 'I had thought to bury it, or perhaps throw it in the river, rather than let it fall into the hands…'

'I'll want that in the coach, my lord. Full payment for services rendered, in advance. It may be difficult to collect later on.'

As DEBRETTON PULLED his hose up, the whore stirred sleepily. She emerged from the bed coverings, bleary

eyed. When she saw him dressing, she snatched a shift to
her breast. 'Where are you off to, this time of night?' Her
words were slurred by drink, with a plaintive tone that
set his teeth on edge. Nevertheless, he smiled down at
her.

'We're leaving, princess. No fortune to be made here,
too many orcs and bad men to kill.'

'You're not leaving me, are you, Eliak?' The whore
looked beseechingly at him, fear sobering her quickly.
The mercenary knelt down beside her, and took her face
tenderly in both hands, managing not to wince at her
wine soaked breath.

'Never, my lovely,' he purred. 'I have such plans for
you.' He sat beside her, feeling around for his boots. 'Get
dressed,' he ordered, 'and not in those rags, either,' he
said, as she began to scramble around for her things. He
grinned as she stared uncomprehendingly. 'Tonight, you
wear silk.'

THIRTY RIDERS MOVED two-by-two through the dark, as
silently as a column of cavalry and a four-in-hand coach
could manage. Tack, weapons, and baggage were tied
down or swaddled, conversations held in whispers. No
stars showed in an overcast sky, and the gibbous moon
had set hours before. The road they travelled could just
be made out as a faint stripe against the meadow grass,
and then only if you kept the verge in the corner of your
eye. Off to the west, a hundred paces or so, the Stir
rushed northward.

Debretton rode just in front of the coach. He could
barely make out his horse's ears, and could only sense
the riders in front of him through muffled hoof beats
and dust in his face. Brandyn van Herz, captain of
Trank's personal guard, sidled up next to him. Like the
rest of his troopers, van Herz had abandoned his
armour, wearing only a leather jerkin and a steel cap.

'So, Debretton, tell me,' he said softly, 'why in Sigmar's name are we dragging this great wagon behind us, as if we were delivering her ladyship to the huntsman's ball? She can ride, you know.'

Debretton smiled briefly. 'So I've been informed. The coach is not for milady, but for the gold.'

He could feel van Herz bristle beside him. 'Damn the gold! Ten times as much would not be a fair trade for that girl.' The captain's tone was fierce, though he was far too experienced to raise his voice. 'She's the only treasure my lads care for, and she carries the last hope for our lands in her belly.'

'That's as may be, but the only thing that keeps *my* lads here is the hope of laying their hands on that treasure. Otherwise, they'd have flown hours ago to take their chances in the hills, and we'll need every sword we can muster to make it through to Reiksgrad.'

Van Herz was quiet for a long moment. Then he chuckled. 'That's why you wanted us along. We're guarding the gold from your dogs, keeping them from simply taking it and leaving our lady behind. This way they are bound to us by their own greed.'

'For now, but believe me; every damned one of them is calculating the odds. Thirteen of them against sixteen of you: when the balance swings in their favour sufficiently, they'll make a play.'

'You haven't included yourself in that count.'

Debretton leaned towards van Herz. 'Would you take me at my word if I swore that delivering milady was my only concern?'

They rode on a ways before the captain answered with a simple, 'Not yet.' Van Herz lifted his cap to scratch at his scalp. 'But this coach anchors us to the highway. It's far too heavy to go cross-country, and I fear the road ahead will be thick with unfriendly travellers.'

The mercenary nodded. 'True.' He was about to go on when something in the dark caught his attention. Instead, he asked, 'This road crosses over a bridge to the west bank, does it not?'

'Aye, there is a small village and toll bridge. The road branches, one fork to the north-east and the other west across the river and then north to Reiksgrad.'

'The bridge is, say, two to three leagues from here?'

Van Herz considered. 'Difficult to say in the dark how far we've travelled, but, yes, that should be about right. Are you familiar with this territory?'

'No. Look up.' The captain peered into the night, and realised that he could just make out the silhouette of trees that lined the river. They stood faintly against the backdrop of a pale, roseate glow reflected from low clouds.

DEBRETTON AND VANIR crawled forward along the river-bank behind a wiry scout swathed in black cloak and leggings. The scout held up a fist, then pointed word-lessly in the direction of the crackling flames. Motioning the others to stand fast, Debretton wormed his way into a heavy clump of bulrushes until he could see the village, or what was left of it. Miserable huts smouldered in ruins, while a larger building, perhaps a warehouse or barn, still burned fiercely. Bodies lay here and there. Invaders, great, shaggy men in horned helmets, wan-dered back and forth, some with bottles clutched in their fists. A few kicked disconsolately through the ashes, clearly disappointed at the lack of loot. On the stone bridge, just visible from where he lay, Debretton spotted five more. Two stood at either end of the bridge, more or less on guard, while the fifth sat atop a wagon parked midway across the span. Horses appeared to be idly graz-ing on the far bank, though it was impossible to judge how many in the dark.

Debretton backed down to his companions. 'Shlem,' he gestured for the goateed scout, leaning over to whisper in one bejewelled ear. 'How many bows do we have?'

The scout tugged on the tip of his beard, heavy brows knitted in concentration. 'Six bows, all crossbows, but only four bowmen; neither Yvar nor Thaddeus could hit the horse they were riding on.'

A grin flashed across Debretton's face. 'Too true, my friend. Vanir, make your way back to the column and bring forward the crossbows and our best marksmen. From here we will eliminate those upon the bridge. Tell van Herz to stay concealed until he sees them fall. That will be his signal to charge home. Tell him he must kill those on the near bank, cross the bridge, and scatter the men and horses he finds there.' Debretton grasped Vanir's thick shoulder as he turned to leave, and passed on a few more hurried directions. Vanir nodded and melted into the dark.

FIFTEEN MINUTES LATER all was ready. Debretton, Shlem, Vanir and two other mercenaries lay in the stinking, green mud of the riverbank, each man sighting on a target. Without lifting his cheek from the crossbow's stock, Debretton spoke softly. 'Let fly.' As one, five bolts sped away. Debretton saw his man throw his arms skyward as if in prayer, but the mercenary was up and running before the body slid to the ground. Simultaneously, a horn bleated weirdly, followed by shouts and the thunder of hoof beats.

Debretton vaulted onto the bridge. To his right a pair of corpses sprawled, and two more were heaped at the far end. One guard was still up, though, staggering towards the unlimbered wagon with a torch, one arm pinned to his body by a bolt. Debretton slipped a dagger from the top of his boot and cocked it just behind his ear, pausing for a moment to feel its balance and

measure the distance. He threw, and the blade buried
itself in the back of the man's neck, just below the skull.
The man dropped like a puppet whose strings had been
cut, the torch rolling away and coming to rest next to the
wagon's tongue.

The other mercenaries were on the bridge, Vanir's
group re-loading their crossbows as they secured the far
end. Shlem and Debretton checked the bodies, slitting
the throat of one found still breathing. Shlem pulled
back the tarpaulin covering the wagon-bed. Both men
had to stand aside as whooping riders, van Herz at their
head, charged by. In the village itself, Debretton saw his
own men cantering around, chasing down the last few
enemies still standing. A low whistle brought his attention back to the wagon. Shlem had a corner of the
tarpaulin raised, revealing six squat, black barrels of
powder.

Debretton hastily kicked the guttering torch away.
'Looks like we arrived just in time. By the Emperor, there
is enough here to drop a dozen bridges.' Shlem nodded
absently, and out of the corner of one eye Debretton
noted an evil grin slowly spreading across his features.
'What, you old dog?'

Shlem, still grinning, laid one finger against his long
nose. 'I am thinking that the gods have placed this powder here for a reason.' He pointed with his chin in the
direction van Herz had gone. 'What better time to depart
from our travelling companions, with more treasure in
our pockets than we could make in twenty campaigns
and a fine lady to hold for ransom.'

Shaking his head, Debretton scowled. 'No. We stick by
our contract.' Shlem's face fell, and Debretton clapped
him on the back. 'Don't fret. The gold will still be in our
hands when we reach Reiksgrad, and doubtless there will
be few enough of us left to split it amongst.' He
motioned towards the village. 'Now gather the men and

bring forward the coach. Join us as quickly as you can; it is almost dawn.'

Debretton strode away. Behind him a sullen Shlem called, 'Your scruples will cost you much, someday.'

'They already have,' muttered the mercenary under his breath. At the far end of the bridge he waved over Vanir. The northerner approached, nodding imperceptibly. 'Let's go find van Herz,' sighed Debretton. 'One way or another, we'll be moving again shortly.'

THEY FOUND AN irritated van Herz some distance from the bridge, along with his guardsmen. 'You can have your trumpeter back,' he shouted by way of greeting. 'Damn fool boy can't blow a note.'

'Anyone escape?'

Van Herz shrugged. 'Not that I saw. There were a few tending the herd; we killed them and drove off the horses.' He glared at the trumpeter. 'Spent the next ten minutes rounding up my own men in the dark, with no one to blow recall, or I'd have returned sooner.'

Before Debretton could reply, an explosion rent the night.

VAN HERZ DISMOUNTED, and went down on hands and knees to examine the gap. Twenty feet below him the river stormed past the bridge's broken footings. He stood, dusting his hands together, and peered into the gloom. The sun, not yet visible, was colouring the eastern sky blood-red, and he could just make out riders and a coach belting north-east in the far distance. The old soldier trembled with rage. 'Betrayed,' he said. 'Foully betrayed, and the girl I swore to protect in the hands of those… those…' He fell silent, unable to find a strong enough oath. Then, sliding his sword from its scabbard, he turned and advanced on Debretton and Vanir, both men pinioned by a grim soldier on each arm. 'I'll kill

them all, I swear, and I'll start with you two.' He gripped
the pommel with both hands and pivoted to deliver a
killing blow as his soldiers shouted encouragement.

'Stay your hand, uncle.' The trumpeter spoke imperi-
ously. 'And you men, stop gabbling like fishwives on
market day. Remember who you are: warriors for the
house of Trank.'

Van Herz stood frozen for a moment, blade poised,
mouth open. The trumpeter pulled off her leather helmet, the type with broad cheek guards and a strip of
hardened metal to protect the nose. The hair was roughly
shorn and the skin stained the shade of young oak, but
the rising sun picked out a pair of azure eyes.

'Waited long enough,' commented Vanir.

'You MIGHT HAVE trusted me, you know.' Van Herz and
Debretton rode at the head of the column as the party
moved north at a brisk trot. On their right, the river
churned ceaselessly, outpacing the riders. Bodies had
begun to appear, bobbing in the white water, heralds
from the slaughter that was undoubtedly still going on
upstream.

'I might have,' Debretton allowed, 'but I prefer not to
when circumstances allow.'

Van Herz grunted sourly. 'Still it galls me to think of
that swine making off with the count's war chest.'

'He won't get far.'

'How do you know?'

Debretton never ceased scanning the countryside. So
far their luck had held. They had come across a few
ruined farmsteads and seen the tracks of raiding parties,
but by keeping just off the highway they had so far
avoided the enemy. Once the rear guard spotted a company of orcs and goblins, mounted on wolves, but they
had sufficient warning to hide in a copse of trees.
Though the wolves had certainly smelled something,

their riders were too intent on the prospect of plunder to investigate, and they had urged the snarling, snapping beasts northward. 'I thought Shlem or one of the others might try to take advantage of the situation, though I did not anticipate the wagon full of powder. So I had Vanir loosen the hubs on the coach's rear axle when he came back from our forward scout, just enough so that an hour or so of travel would cause them to fail. By now Shlem is cursing over that strong box next to a disabled coach, trying to hack or pry it open before the enemy arrives. Even if he succeeds he can't carry it all away, though I imagine he will try. In any case, he'll lead our pursuers a merry chase and buy us some time.'

Van Herz considered for a moment. 'And if he had not deserted us, you'd have retightened the hubs before they gave way?' Debretton nodded and van Herz laughed heartily. 'By Sigmar, you are a devious one. You can't have planned this out completely from the start.'

'No, I'm no seer, but I've learned over the years how to improvise.'

LATER THAT DAY, and just short of Reiksgrad, their luck came to an end. The river and road ran through a narrow gorge where more corpses bumped their way along, headed for the fortress. Rather than chance sneaking through the bottleneck, they climbed the shoulder of the gorge and paused along the ridge. Below them the ground fell away to the north, and Reiksgrad was plainly visible nestled against a loop in the river, only a few leagues distant. The granite walls of the fortress were untouched, and Debretton could just make out the pennons of Stirland fluttering from the numerous watchtowers. Men and orcs moved restlessly along the river, while thick columns of smoke towered over fields, humble farms and walled estates.

'Damn.' Debretton stood, hands on hips, surveying the terrain. It was open country with no way to sneak through. Already he could see palisades going up to block the causeway into Reiksgrad, though most of the enemy seemed content to loot and burn the surrounding countryside. 'There are more of them here than I had hoped; too many to fight through.'

Beside him, van Herz looked southward through a spyglass. 'More bad news in this direction, I'm afraid. I do not think the old warrior delayed them for long this morning.' He handed Debretton the instrument.

The mercenary cursed again. To the south a black carpet undulated on both sides of the river. Closer, mounted units could be seen scouting ahead of the main body. 'Shlem may have bought us some time drawing off his outriders,' van Herz commented, 'but not enough, it seems.' The old soldier looked westward to the mountains. 'Perhaps we should take our chances in the high country.'

Debretton did not respond immediately. He scanned the river valley once more, and then closed the spyglass with a snap. 'How long before the main body reaches us? Before dark, do you think?'

Van Herz looked at the sun, already well below its zenith. 'No. Some will, but the mass not before sundown.'

'And would you care to move an army through that defile at night?'

'Never. They will certainly make camp on the southern side. Why, do you think we will be safe here?'

Debretton shook his head. 'Not entirely. Assuming the commander is no fool, he will picket the high ground. But we can move down the reverse slope. It's unlikely anyone will want to pick their way down those gullies in the dark.'

'And then what? Even if we remain undetected through the night, we'll still be trapped here in the morning, between hell and high water.' When Debretton remained silent, van Herz grew irritated. 'Speak, man. Do you have a plan or not?'

Debretton watched a corpse drifting by. 'Not yet.' His eyes narrowed. 'But I think we have a few hours to come up with one.'

THE GROUP MOVED carefully down the northern slope, ensconcing themselves in a ravine choked with gorse. For the rest of the day they remained undetected as small parties of invaders made their way along the road towards Reiksgrad. Enemy scouts could be heard as they sniffed around the top of the ridge towards sundown, but failed to see them in their hide. As the sun disappeared, the scouts thrashed away through the underbrush to light a watch fire on the crest just above the fugitives. Debretton sat silently until full dark, idly plucking at gorse-berries that grew in profusion all around them. An hour later, Vanir slid next to him, wiping blood from a short blade.

'No more scouts,' he announced.

'How many were there?'

'Only four.'

'Sure you got them all?' When Vanir did not dignify this with an answer, Debretton went on. 'And the rest?'

'Many camp fires, but all on the other side.' Debretton nodded and picked his way through the brush to van Herz, with Vanir following silently. Ilse, the captain, and his soldiers looked at him expectantly.

'The enemy main body has camped on the other side of the defile,' he began, quietly. 'We will lead the horses down to the bottom of the ridge, and then ride for the fortress. There are quite a few of them between us and the walls of Reiksgrad, but they are scattered and disorganised. In the dark we may pass as just another group of prowling bandits. With the blessing, we might reach the end of the causeway without incident. Doubtless we'll have to fight through there, but if we can catch them unawares all should go well.'

'There are many a "might" and "may" in that plan,' van Herz pointed out.

'Aye,' conceded Debretton, 'but that is all we have left.' He grasped the reins of his horse, and patted its neck. 'Let's be on our way.'

Vanir led them as they picked their way cautiously down the hillside. To Debretton their progress was only slightly quieter than a procession of circus pachyderms, but nothing stirred in the low ground. Finally on the level plain, they mounted and made their way carefully towards refuge.

At first they had little difficulty in threading their way between the silent enemy camps. From time to time they paused as Vanir scouted ahead, and once they surprised and quickly silenced a patrol on some night time errand. As they neared Reiksgrad, however, the enemy posts grew thicker and more alert. Hammering and guttural commands sounded through the still air as they approached the siege works being thrown up to surround the place. The halts grew longer and the escapes narrower, until at last Vanir emerged from the dark to report that there was no way through the lines.

'None?'

'Not without fighting,' the northerner reported laconically.

Debretton stood in thought for a moment, and then spoke to van Herz. 'Here is where milady and I must part company with you. We will make our way down to the river and into the city from there. You can either cut your way through or withdraw back into the hills. There is still enough time before dawn for that.'

Before van Herz could reply, Ilse stepped forward. 'I've proved I can ride with you in a charge, uncle.'

'Aye, that you have, girl,' the old soldier smiled. He glanced at Vanir. 'What do you think our chances might be?' The northerner simply grimaced and shook his head. 'I think you should go with Debretton.'

Ilse bit her lip. 'Only if you promise to head for the mountains, uncle.'

Van Herz looked to Debretton. 'What do you say? Would a distraction help?'

Debretton hesitated, but finally nodded. 'For what I have in mind, yes,' he said.

'That's settled then.' Van Herz placed a finger on Ilse's lips before she could protest. 'Listen, girl, I've spent too long fighting for your family to quit now. If this is the last service I can perform to see you to safety, you wouldn't deny me the chance, would you? And you have the child to think of.' Ilse's eyes watered and she shook her head, clasping van Herz's hand with both of hers. 'Besides, I imagine the finest warriors east of the River Reik can cut through a few slack-jawed orcs, right boys?' The men growled their assent.

'Sigmar be with you, then, uncle, and your men, too. I will see you all in Reiksgrad,' Ilse said to the guardsmen with a tearful smile. They nodded and murmured good wishes in return. Ilse wiped her eyes and turned to Debretton. 'I'm ready.'

'Good. Give us five minutes, captain, and then ride hard for the gates.' Debretton and van Herz clasped hands. 'And what of you, Vanir?'

In answer, Vanir mounted his horse and unslung his axe. 'You sneak, I fight.'

'Fair enough,' Debretton said. As he turned to go, van Herz held him back.

'How do you intend to make it through the lines, Debretton?'

The mercenary held up a pair of empty wineskins and a satchel of gorse-berries. 'Improvisation.'

* * *

STANDING ATOP A bridge barely a bowshot from the outer
works of Reiksgrad, a disgruntled orc leaned on its spear
while its companions roistered among ruined wine cel-
lars and feasted on hot, smoking flesh. It brightened
slightly when a clamour arose to the west, the clash of
arms and shouts that indicated a fight. Hundreds of its
fellows roused themselves and rushed away into the
night, and for a short time it could follow the progress of
the battle by the noise and the clustering of torches. It
was on the verge of abandoning his post when the clan-
gour died away, and it morosely turned back to studying
the dead floating by.

The greenskin amused itself by spitting at the corpses
as they flowed under the low bridge. After a while it had
his timing down quite nicely. It fixed on one swollen figure, its hand stiffly raised out of the water, blood from a
gash on the neck black in the moonlight, eyes staring
blankly upwards. The orc hocked thickly, paused, and
spat past yellowed tusks. The wad of phlegm struck
squarely between the eyes, but the orc's hoot of triumph
was cut short when it saw the corpse blink and screw up
its face in disgust.

The orc gaped blankly, its sluggish brain turning over
with some difficulty as the body passed beneath the
bridge. Then it whirled and scampered to the other side,
spear raised as it bent over the water. A flash of silver shot
up from below, a dagger passing through its throat and
thunking into the underside of its skull. The orc straightened slowly, its spear dangling from nerveless fingers,
and then fell back in a clatter.

A few moments later, Debretton clambered up on the
riverbank, hard against the curtain wall of Reiksgrad. He
was still splashing his face with handfuls of water, trying
to scrub away the vile stink of orc sputum when Ilse
emerged. She stripped the inflated wineskin from
beneath her tunic, and attempted to wash off the mud

and berry juice that marred her features. Finally, she gave up and collapsed, exhausted, into the reeds. 'What now?'

Debretton pulled off his own wineskin. He unwound the cord that bound its neck, pulled out the stopper and deflated it, then tossed it in the river. He looked up at the wall. 'We wait here for dawn,' he said, 'and try not to get killed by our own people.' He pressed a ragged cloth against the spear gash he had reopened just before they had slipped into the river upstream.

The woman raised herself wearily on one elbow. 'Thank you.' Debretton smiled to himself. Ilse was as graceless in apologising as her father had been. 'I know you sacrificed much.'

'No need to thank me, milady, I serve for pay, not for you.'

'What pay? That *thaler* my father gave you? My hand-maiden makes as much emptying chamber pots.'

Debretton fished the silver piece from a pouch at his belt. He untied a cord from around his neck, threaded it through the hole in the coin, and retied the cord. He held it up for a moment, a dozen or so identical *thalers* jingling softly together. 'It is enough for me.'

LIES OF THE FLESH
by Steven Savile

THE WIND-BLASTED moor rolled out before them, rich with the muted shades of heather and gorse, and speckled with white blossoms. A low, scuttling wind whipped across the tips of the vegetation, bullying the dwarfs as they trudged through the boggy peat. The earth had a peculiar acidic smell that stung Skargrim's nostrils and burned the back of his throat as he inhaled. The sun smouldered low in the sky, setting on the Ostermark.

Skargrim ducked his head down until his chin pressed against the chainmail on his chest and struggled on, his boots sinking up to the ankles in the black peat. Few crops could flourish in such a rich bed. It needed to be cut into stonier land, to nourish it. The world was funny like that: too much of a good thing was as poisonous as too little, and just as capable of killing the things it cared for.

The wind picked up, swirling around the dwarfs, forcing them to draw their cloaks tighter around their shoulders. It goaded them on deeper and deeper into the moor. Twice Kragar stumbled, his foot sinking into a hidden pothole. Both times he needed the butt of his hammer to heave himself out of the mire. The rune-priest, Thorbad, was no more certain on his feet.

The wind carried strange sounds with it. It folded them in on themselves, joining them together, like voices of the dead buried deep beneath the peat. The ghostly keening rose into an elegiac lament.

Skargrim shuddered and pulled his cloak closer around his shoulders. Once dusk reclaimed the sky, navigating the moor would go from difficult to dangerous.

As they crested the next low rise, Skargrim saw rooftops: a human settlement. A trick of perspective and failing light made it look as though the smoke emanated from the canted roofs. It didn't. Strips of peat had been cut and dried, laid out at the mouth of the small hamlet and set alight. He counted four pyres.

'Why the fires?' Thorbad wondered, coming up to stand beside him.

A CROOK-BACKED farmer stabbed a pitchfork into the rectangular sods of peat, throwing three more onto the fire. He leaned back, foot resting above the iron tines, and wiped the sweat from his brow. He had an open face, cragged with the wrinkles of time and hard work. His eyes were dark, ringed with fatigue. He saw the three dwarfs and stopped what he was doing to study them suspiciously. His frank appraisal verged on rudeness.

'Evening,' Kragar said.

'Aye,' the farmer agreed, 'that's what they call it when the sun goes down. Not often we see your kind round these parts.'

'Our kind?'

'Aye, your kind, dwarfs.'

'We are on our way back home, to the mountains,' Thorbad told him. 'Is there an inn here, where we can stay the night?'

The farmer grunted and gestured towards a building at the far side of what Skargrim presumed was the village green. There was a well in the centre, the grass around it worn down in tracks leading off to each of the cardinals. A thin-faced woman sat on a bench beneath the only tree, darning a patch onto a threadbare quilt. The branches hung low, as though weeping. She was lost in what she was doing. On the far side of the green two men struggled with a heavy wooden shutter, driving black iron nails into the timber frame of the window to hold it in place.

They left the farmer stoking the peat fire and headed towards the inn.

The battered wooden inn sign creaked and sighed as it rocked softly in the breeze. The steady chime of the hammer rang out in counterpoint to the noise. Eight of the ten houses facing onto the green had new shutters nailed across their windows. The last house on the left had older shutters that bore deep score marks and looked close to splitting along the grain where the wood hadn't been seasoned properly. Typical, Skargrim thought. Humans were always in a hurry to get things done and never took the time needed to do them right.

All eyes turned on the dwarfs as they crossed the green.

'Friendly place,' Thorbad muttered.

Skargrim nodded. It was not the most welcome homestead he had been in, not that he had spent a lot of time in the company of the short-lived ones.

'Notice anything peculiar?'

The four peat fires burned to the north, south, east and west, each tended by an equally dour-faced farmer.

It took him a moment to see what had caught Thorbad's eye. The heads of the nails resembled the sign of the Man-God, and the black iron handle of the well had been fashioned in the image of his hammer. There were more instances of religious fervor on display, including a small shrine to Shallya with a single burning candle set into the well wall. Copper and tin coins had been left as offerings. Not all of the observances were to the Man-God, or the more enlightened pantheon of deities, either. It always amused the dwarf how readily the manlings shifted their allegiance to whatever crude beliefs they thought would help them, especially in backwaters like this place, where the old ways still bubbled just beneath the surface of the collective conscience. Skargrim saw strange fetishes hanging above the doorway of one of the homes. He had mistaken the cluster of feathers for a dead bird, but on closer inspection he saw that it was more than just the evening's meal being bled. It was an elaborate construction of feather and bone, but of no creature that had ever lived. The bones of chicken, dog and sparrow had been stuffed up with feathers from at least a dozen different birds to fashion the fetish. The feet had been removed and stuffed with a pungent salve no doubt meant to ward off some unseen evil.

'Superstitious lot,' he said.

Thorbad nodded.

The hamlet was larger than it had at first appeared. The ground sloped away, and the more distant rooftops had originally been hidden from view. Skargrim could just make out the weathervane above the canted rooftop of the blacksmith's. The doors of the smithy were open, an inviting, lambent red glowing within. No doubt the smith was fashioning more sacred nails.

To the dwarfs, the village felt odd, even for a human settlement.

TWO OLD MEN sat on stools in the corner of the inn, hunched over a game of chance. Another sat at the bar nursing an empty tankard in his thick, grime-stained fingers. A serving girl bustled through the room, four tankards balanced in her hands for the long table at the other side of the room.

There was none of the banter the dwarf associated with tap rooms, serving wenches and drunken young men. The girl placed a foamy tankard before each of the drinkers and disappeared back into the kitchen without so much as a word.

The last man sat alone beside the fire, smoking a briar-wood pipe. He was a gaunt soul with the waxy complexion of the terminally ill. His head was shaved, a blue-grey tattoo that looked almost like an hourglass inked across his brow and the ridge of his nose. He watched the dwarfs intently without seeming to watch them at all.

The barkeep looked up from wiping out a pewter pitcher with a rag. He hawked a wad of weed into the spittoon beneath the bar and placed the tankard down on the pitted wooden surface. He glared at the dwarfs for a while, then finally said, 'You want something?'

'Ale, manling, three mugs,' Kragar said, stamping the stiffness out of his feet. Skargrim looked around the tap room, found a table that suited, and sat. The place reeked of unwashed bodies, peat, piss, and poor ale... very poor ale.

Kragar took half a mouthful and spat it out in a spume, cursing. He slammed the tankard down on the table and shook his head, wondering how to cleanse his tongue of the insipid brew. 'What in Bugman's name is this swill?' he muttered. 'Do humans have no idea what a decent pint's supposed to taste like?'

Before the hapless Kragar could vent his distaste openly, a young girl, no more than eight or nine years old, came charging down the narrow flight of wooden stairs. She threw herself into the barkeep's arms, smothering him with kisses.

'Night, night, princess,' the barkeep said, setting her down on the ground with an indulgent smile.

She blew him another kiss from the bottom step before disappearing back upstairs again.

'She's a whirlwind, that one. Never stops for a minute. Takes after her mother,' the man said, indulgently.

Kragar grunted.

One by one and two by two the other drinkers slowly departed, but the night was still young. In fact, it was barely night at all. Soon the dwarfs were alone in the tap room, save for the pipe smoker still warming himself by the fire.

Thorbad looked up from his brew, his face troubled.

'What is it?'

'Nothing,' the runepriest said, scowling.

'What do you mean nothing?'

'Nothing, that's it.'

Skargrim chuckled mirthlessly. 'Which in itself suggests something is amiss in that warped thing that passes for your brain?'

'Precisely,' the runepriest grunted. 'Something's not right here but I'm damned if I can put my finger on it.'

'This is a human village. It's not our problem.'

The sound of bolts slamming home and the timber brace dropping into place on the main door punctuated Kragar's words. The dwarf turned to see the barkeep brushing off his hands.

'Early to be closing isn't it?' asked Skargrim, surprised. *No love of the finer things.* The brew was rancid and folk hardly gregarious. With the exception of the barkeep and his daughter, no one had said a word to them since they had trudged into town.

'We're done for the night. Folks tend to keep to themselves after dark,' the barkeep said, heading back to the bar. 'Your room is at the top of the stairs. And no stealing any ale while I'm gone.' He balled up his rag and dropped it on the bar.

'As if we'd want any more of that piss water,' Kragar muttered.

The barkeep turned to the old man dozing by the fire. 'We're closing, Iago.'

The man looked up, deep blue eyes piercing the atmosphere, and shook his head slowly. He tapped out the contents of his pipe and refilled it with fresh smoke, drawing slowly on the briarwood. He closed his eyes, seeming to go back to sleep, cradling the pipe in his lap as though he cherished its small heat. He didn't draw on it again, just held it, content to breathe in the subtle aroma of leaf and wood through his nose.

Halfway up the stairs the barkeep turned, almost as an afterthought, and called back down to them, 'Best not to venture out now. The moors can be dangerous after dark.' With that, he disappeared upstairs, his heavy foot-steps creaking along the landing. A moment later a door groaned slowly open, and then closed, settling heavily into its frame.

The dwarfs looked at each other, then at the mugs on the table between them.

'Much as it kills me to say it, I can't drink another drop.'

'I never thought I'd hear such words pass your lips, Kragar.'

THEIR ROOM WAS full of the creaks and groans of the building settling around them.

Skargrim tossed and turned restlessly. Beside him Kragar snored. His tongue rattled against his palate, causing his breath to whistle between the gap in his front teeth.

The moon was a bright silver sickle in the sky, hanging over the dark moors like a scythe.

Thorbad jabbed Kragar in the ribs. He opened his eyes, grunted, and rolled over dismissively, pulling the moth-eaten blanket with him. Within a few minutes he was snoring again, louder than before.

Skargrim gave up trying to sleep. He watched the shadow shapes on the wall as they ghosted over the seasoned timbers and whitewashed plaster. Three narrow cots had been crammed into the gabled room, the heads pressed up underneath the low sloping ceiling, the pillow feathers crushed flat and limp. Mould stained the ceiling blue in cracked patches. It smelled rank, like cheese turned sour.

A scattering of gravel hit the high window.

It took Skargrim a moment to realise what the noise was. He sat up in his cot, almost banging his head on the low ceiling. It came again, like hard rain. He clambered out of bed, went over to the window, and slowly lifted the latch. He strained to see out through the glass but couldn't, so he pushed the window open.

The first thing that hit him was the stench. He hadn't noticed it before with the peat burning. The village reeked of decay, the smell clinging to the wind like a death shroud: putrescence.

He scanned the shadows, looking for something: a movement, a flutter, a shuffle where there should have been stillness. The shadows were unforgiving, the sickle moon threw them into dim relief. Skargrim stared across them. Then, the man moved: a cadaverous figure wrapped in a cloak, utterly at home in the darkest places of the night. He lifted a white hand and beckoned the dwarf down to join him before melding back into the anonymity of the dark.

'This place reeks,' Skargrim muttered, closing the window.

Thorbad cracked his neck bones and rolled out of his narrow cot, his face grim. 'Nothing good ever comes of sneaking about in the shadows.'

Kragar grunted and knuckled his eyes, his face screwed up as though it had been hammered by a steel gauntlet. 'Can't you pair see I'm asleep?'

WHEN THEY CAME back downstairs, the bar was empty. Iago had gone.

The stairs creaked and groaned loudly in the silence. Skargrim crossed the taproom and shot back the black iron bolts, one after the other. The reports echoed through the inn.

'Quietly, fool,' Thorbad rasped. 'We don't want to wake the entire village.'

Skargrim dragged the heavy timbered door open, forcing it back on its huge hinges to let in the night. The smell was worse down here. With the four fires burnt out for the night, whatever filth was behind the smell festered.

The low keening of the moor wind masked the most obvious sounds.

It took him a moment to see the cloaked figure, and then he only saw it because the stranger detached himself from the shadows and stepped out into the village green. The moonlight caught his features, casting a silver death-mask where there should have been a face. The man turned and walked away. He moved with deceptive grace, the folds of his cloak swirling around his legs like eager lapdogs.

The figure disappeared in the direction of the temple.

The weathervane twisted in the wind, the cockerel's head spinning erratically until it came to rest, pointing east. In the distance, a lupine lament tore the night. It was a melancholy sound, filled with sadness.

'Come on, then,' Skargrim said, setting off to follow the shadowy figure through the midnight streets.

THE STRANGER PRESSED a crooked finger to his thin lips, urging silence as he led them down a narrow stone stairway.

The dwarfs followed him into a cramped chamber where a single candle burned, its low light guttering in the sudden breeze. Fitful shadows danced beneath its sway.

The cool air had a familiar, subterranean feel.

It took Skargrim a moment to realise the chamber's purpose: it was a preparation room for the dead before burial. A low wooden table, with deep scores on either side to drain blood and other bodily fluids, dominated the room. Demijohns of preservatives and pickling fluids were shelved on the far wall alongside surgical instruments and cloth bandages.

There was an inscription on the wall as well, which Kragar, who was more familiar with humans, attempted to translate. *This is the place where death lives.* No, that wasn't quite right. *This is the house where death rejoices.*

'What is this place?' Kragar whispered, staring at rows of organs floating inside glass containers. 'And who in Grungni's name are you?'

Behind the door, three small coffins were stacked one atop another.

The stranger pulled back his hood and turned to face them. 'We are beneath the Temple of Morr,' the man said. His voice was almost brittle, as though seldom used, but there was an underlying iron to it. 'I am Eustasius Meusmann, priest of the temple. This is where we prepare the dead.'

The man unclasped his cloak and laid it on top of the small coffins. He wore the austere robes of a priest beneath, but they were rumpled and stained.

'You are strangers. People are always curious about strangers, especially those as uncommon as you. I would not have our business being the gossip of the town,' the priest of Morr explained. 'This place is safe.'

'So talk,' Skargrim said, bluntly.

'Tell me, have you noticed anything strange during your short stay in Mielau?' The priest talked slowly and enunciated every word deliberately.

'Bonfires, fetishes, new shutters hammered down with holy nails?' Thorbad offered.

'Yes, yes, yes,' the man said, 'exactly. Things are there that shouldn't be. But what is *not* there that ought to be?'

'We saw few children,' Thorbad commented.

The priest nodded. 'There is a malady. Someone of a more superstitious bent might call it a curse, but I believe it is more plague than pariah. Milo, the headman, buries his head in the peat and refuses to do anything. It is the same every year. Same time, every year: Pflugzeit. Sickness from the marshes.'

'So?'

'Children are wasting away from a blood sickness.'

'Spit it out, priest,' Skargrim pressed.

The priest met his gaze with deathly sincerity. 'I believe there is a revenant, out there in the marshes. It comes into the village when it wakes from hibernation, needing to feed. It steals the life out of the young ones, bleeding them dry.'

'A revenant?' Kragar asked, incredulous. He looked from Skargrim to Thorbad and then back at the man. He shook his head. 'Here?'

'It sounds preposterous, believe me I know. I am an old man, and a priest at that. The children are all we have. I don't want to be putting them in the ground, wondering if there was something I could have done. Whatever it is, this sickness is striking down our children. Please, stay. Find the cause, be it mundane or supernatural. I beg you. You are our only hope.'

'WE'LL GIVE IT a day, and see what we can find,' Skargrim said when they returned to the inn. The door was open a crack, the taproom empty.

'This place is terrible, and the beer is undrinkable.'

'You don't seriously think there is a revenant hiding out in the marshes do you?'

'Not for a moment,' Skargrim said. 'But something is wrong, and I've half a mind to stick around and fix it. Like the priest said, we're their only hope.'

'You always were a vain bugger, thinking you could fix the world's woes. I say we move on.'

'This sickness, the more I think about it, the more I dislike it,' Skargrim said.

'What do you have in mind?' Thorbad asked, scratching at his scraggy beard.

'Someone was the first to fall sick, someone links all the others together. Disease spreads, it doesn't just appear from nowhere. We've got a list of names. We could visit a few of the families, see what's going on.'

'How on earth are we supposed to work out who loosed a plague?' asked Kragar. 'More to the point, why should we care?'

Thorbad looked at Skargrim and saw through his friend's vanity. 'There is evil at work here. We hunt it down and we destroy it. That is why we care.'

'But we aren't talking about some great hairy beast,' said Kragar. 'We're talking about a disease. It doesn't leave footprints in the peat for a tracker to follow.'

ELIKA FREUND WAS the first name on their list.

She was six and a half years old, and the sickness had taken its toll. Her face was hollowed out, with too little flesh draped over the bones of her head. Her eyes were warm, wet circles of pain amidst the wounded innocence of her face.

Her father, Stefan, lived alone in the shadow of the temple. His wife had died two summers earlier. He was a pig farmer, though he had given up on the animals since his daughter had fallen ill.

He led Thorbad through to the back room where Elika lay among sweat tangled bedding on her small cot.

'She has been like that for two weeks now, getting gradually worse. She used to be so vibrant, so beautiful, so full of life. Now she just lies there. She is dying, and there is nothing I can do.'

Thorbad touched the girl's brow. She was cold, too cold to be healthy. He tilted her head slightly, exposing her neck. There were no wounds around the thick vein, no bruising and no puncture marks.

'IT'S NO VAMPIRE I've ever seen.' Thorbad folded his thick arms and leaned across the stained table. 'I'll say that much.'

The taproom of the White Hart was empty save for the company of dwarfs. The barkeep, Naubhof, busied himself wiping the tankards. He stoked the fire occasionally and moved the chairs, straightening them just for the sake of straightening them. He changed the oil in the burners, and then went back to towelling out the same pitcher.

'It's nothing more than a disease. There isn't a damned thing we can do with an axe or a hammer. I say we're done here. Sooner we are gone the better.'

'WHAT DID THEY say? Anything out of the ordinary?'

Kragar shook his head. 'Nothing. Mind, they weren't exactly eager to speak about a beautiful child wasting away and the unfairness of life.'

'Same here,' Thorbad said. 'Once full of life, now she lies silently waiting to die.'

There was no link there. Happy, beautiful, full of life; those words could have described any child.

Something niggled at the back of his mind. His subconscious refused to accept that the three weren't linked. They must have overlooked something.

'You're clutching at straws,' Skargrim said to himself. Behind him, Naubhof dropped a flagon and cursed as its contents spilled across the sawdusted floorboards. The barkeep kicked it across the floor in frustration and then sank behind the bar, head in hands, and wept.

Skargrim stood, dragging back his chair, and went behind the bar.

The barkeep looked up at him through thick fingers and bloodshot eyes.

Skargrim didn't have to ask what was wrong, he knew: the little girl he had seen running through the taproom last night, Naubhof's daughter. She hadn't been down all night. He knelt beside the weeping man. He tried to talk but couldn't get a word out between the great gulping sobs. His chest heaved, his breath sucking in and out through his nose and mouth simultaneously. Skargrim didn't have to ask, but he did anyway.

Naubhof nodded, tears running down his cheeks.

NAUBHOF'S DAUGHTER LAY unmoving on her small cot. She stared, eyes wide, at some invisible spot in the distance. Skargrim touched her cheek. It was cold. There wasn't a mark on her skin. He clicked his fingers, and her head twisted round sharply at the sound. The sudden movement surprised him, but there was nothing in her eyes to suggest she had actually heard the sound, or was aware of what it was. He moved his hand to the right, towards the window, and clicked his fingers again. Again, the girl's head unconsciously jerked around in the direction of the sound. She responded similarly to any loud stimuli: coughs, claps, even a shout from Thorbad. Other than that there was nothing. It was as though someone had reached in and snuffed her light out, extracting her essence from the shell of her body.

Skargrim looked at the little girl lying helpless, fragile. There was something there, a connection in that thought, but answers continued to elude him.

'WHAT HAPPENED?' SKARGRIM asked Naubhof. The man was disconsolate. He left the tears on his cheeks, letting them run. He sat against the wall beside the dwindling fire. He seemed smaller, shrunken in his grief.

'I... she... I don't know. She just didn't wake up.'

'What did she do yesterday? Who did she see? Did she play with her friends? Visit the marshes?' Thorbad didn't give the man a chance to answer the first question before asking the fourth. 'Anything?'

The barkeep shook his head. 'Nothing. She was fine when she went to bed.'

'Could anyone, or anything, have gotten into her room when she was sleeping?'

'No,' Naubhof said, certain. 'The windows are shuttered tight. The door was barred. Nothing could get in without being let in, and Karla knows better than that. You were here all night, surely you would have heard someone breaking in. They would need an axe to get through that door.' He looked over his shoulder at the huge, thick timbered door, the door that had been ajar when they returned from their nocturnal visit with the priest of Morr.

Skargrim realised then that it was their fault. Their carelessness had let whatever it was into the inn, into that little girl's room. Now she lay there, an empty vessel, and it was because of them.

'This room is the heart of Mielau,' said Skargrim. 'At one time or another everyone comes through here. They drink, they talk, and you listen. Someone told you about the first sickness. Someone cried into their beer. You know who that was.'

'Allan Delain.' The innkeep said the name as though it physically hurt him to do so. 'It was hard for him; he lost everything in just a few months. His little girl, Saskia, died of the sickness. She was the first.' Naubhof sank back as though trying to meld with the stones of the wall. 'Thought it was consumption, myself. She was a pretty little thing, I remember, the mirror of her mother. But she never was the most robust of children, you know? Always coming down with this or that.'

'He lost everything?' Thorbad asked, lifting the black iron poker and stoking the fire, in a vain attempt to warm up the chilly room.

'His wife, Carol, died the summer before, just before the festival. A stupid accident. Then his eldest, Kristyn, hanged herself from the rafters on the eve of her wedding. Allan came home from the field and found her there. Saskia was all he had left. He worshipped that little girl. In the space of a few months his entire world ended. He used to come into the bar, night after night, not drinking, not talking, just quietly weeping. No one ever knew what to say to him.' Naubhof lapsed into silence. For a while no one spoke.

'Tell me,' Kragar asked, breaking the introspective silence, 'why do you keep your doors barred and windows shuttered at night? You don't believe it is sickness, do you? What are you afraid of?'

Naubhof looked at him through tear streaked eyes. 'Come nightfall, evil lurks on these diseased streets,' he said, with such intensity it shook them. 'Can't you feel it?'

ALLAN DELAIN LOOKED at the dwarfs, not bothering to hide his suspicion. 'What is it to you? Why do you want to know about my girls?'

'The barkeep told us about your loss. He believes Saskia was the first of the village children to die from the wasting sickness.'

'Well Naubhof should keep his fat nose out of other people's business.'

'His daughter is ill,' Skargrim said flatly.

'Oh.' Delain's foul humour dissolved in a single sound. 'I didn't know. I... how long?'

'Last night.'

'Will it never end?'

'Tell us what happened. What do you remember of Saskia's illness?'

'There is nothing to tell.' Delain sniffed, stifling bitter memories as they threatened to overwhelm him. 'She took her sister's death hard. She idolised Kristyn, but what eleven-year-old doesn't worship her big sister? She stopped going out with her friends. It was as if she had forgotten how to play. She only sat up in her room, clutching a wretched rag doll that used to be Kristyn's. She wouldn't eat properly. She wasted away before my eyes and there was nothing I could do. I wasn't enough to fill the space for her.'

Skargrim ignored the man's pain. 'Was she a beautiful child?'

Allan Delain laughed bitterly. 'Doesn't every father think his daughter is the most beautiful child in the world? Yes she was beautiful. She was the jewel of the village.'

Skargrim nodded. Apparently as an afterthought, he asked, 'One last thing, if you would, Naubhof said your eldest daughter was to be married. Who to?'

'Iago Kaufmann.'

'Ah. And where would we find this Kaufmann?'

'He lives outside the village now, in a tower within the marshes. He's a peculiar sort, but then, show me a mage that isn't a little odd. He keeps himself very much to himself, has done since, well, you know...'

'WHAT ARE YOU thinking?' Thorbad asked.

Skargrim teased at his beard, tugging one of the steel-grey strands from his chin. He scowled down at it. 'We need to talk to Kaufmann. There might be measures he can take to contain the illness while we root out the cause.'

'A restless spirit of some kind?' Kragar asked.

Skargrim nodded. 'We left the door open last night and something got in and drained the life out of the barkeep's daughter. It's our fault, so we must make it right. There is something evil out there in the night, and we're going to kill it.'

'Well, there's one way to know for sure,' Thorbad said.
'Dig her up,' Kragar agreed.

'THE MAGE DOESN'T exactly encourage visitors,' Kragar
said, his leg sinking knee-deep into the sodden ground.
He shuddered, his face twisting with revulsion, and
jerked back instinctively. Skargrim had to catch him by
the shoulder to stop him from pitching into the bog.

The wind was rising. Mielau was a curious construction; the village straddled the border between the solid
ground of the moors and the bog of the marsh. A mile to
the east the ground turned treacherous, every successive
step more unsure than the last. The grasses grew taller,
reaching up to Skargrim and Kragar's waists, lush green.
Bulrushes popped up in patches where the ground was
saturated, but the path to Kaufmann's tower was by no
means that obvious, even to the ranger. As the grasses
grew taller the waters deepened, and the dwarfs' dislike
for their journey grew.

It was a bleak, hostile environment. A poisonous sun
set redly on the horizon. Curls of mist rose up from the
marsh, conjuring wraiths to patrol the long grasses.
Despite the isolation there was no quiet; insects chirped
and buzzed incessantly.

Skargrim, being a ranger, was more sure-footed than
the others. Kragar was reduced to using a crooked branch
as a staff to feel out firm ground. Masked beneath the
rushes and the tall grass was a makeshift causeway of
banked up earth. It was tortuously slow going, feeling
out each step with the foot of the branch, the branch
sinking into marsh water more often than not. Tangles of
thorny brambles meshed with the gorse and reed, giving
the marshes bite.

Skargrim pushed them aside, opening the way.

'This is an accursed place,' Kragar muttered, stumbling
again. Skargrim made a grab for his collar. It became

more and more difficult to follow the twists of the hidden path the lower the sun sank.

Skargrim scanned the horizon for signs of the wizard's tower. 'Who in their right mind would choose to live out here?'

Beside him Kragar cried out and pointed down the bank. Tied among the rushes was a crude raft of logs lashed together with leather ties, and a long punting pole. He clambered up onto the raft and sank the pole into the mud, using his weight to ease it forward.

Skargrim splashed through the shallow marsh waters behind him, cursing with every step. Kragar helped him struggle onto the raft. He was muttering dark curses under his breath.

Twenty feet on the marsh was almost as deep as they were tall. Noxious aromas wafted up from beneath the waterline every time the pole sank in.

Mielau disappeared behind them. With the sun all but spent, they saw the skeletal finger of the wizard's tower rising out of the tall grasses, accusing the sky.

The dwarfs brought the raft as near the tower as they could. Creepers and climbing plants rose out of the marsh to reclaim the decrepit structure, their tendrils opening cracks in the stones. Part of the conical roof had collapsed, exposing rotten beams and broken slate.

'Even harder to believe anyone lives here,' Kragar said.

Skargrim imagined the wind carrying with it the lamenting voices of all the children who had ever succumbed to the sickness, laying their pain at the wizard's door. The thought wormed its way deep inside the dwarf's skin and wrapped itself around his heart. He felt eyes watching them as they walked up to the iron banded door. A single amethyst was set in the keystone of the arch. Rose thorns twined around each other on either side of the door, the flowers long since wilted.

There were footprints in the wet grass, heel and toe showing clearly. Skargrim knelt, studying the indentations. They were too small to be the prints of a fully grown man, too delicate, the impression too subtle. A woman, maybe, or a girl child. He dusted the residue of marsh soil from his fingers and banged on the door with a clenched fist.

IAGO KAUFMANN OPENED the door, his brow creased in an unwelcoming scowl at the intrusion on his solitude.

'What?'

Skargrim knew the man, even without his briarwood pipe. The shaved head and hourglass tattoo were not features likely to be forgotten. The mage had been dozing the last time they had seen him, hunched against the fireplace in the White Hart.

'We want to talk to you, wizard.'

'I have nothing to say.'

Skargrim put his foot in the way of the closing door. 'There are children sick and dying, wizard. Are a few moments of your isolation that precious?'

Kaufmann sighed, 'Yes, yes, yes, it is a great tragedy, but I don't see what it has to do with me. They don't meddle in my life, and in turn I don't meddle in theirs.'

'Perhaps you should, wizard,' Kragar said. 'Just a few questions, and then we'll gladly leave you to your miserable existence.'

'Oh, for pity's sake, come in then and ask your damned questions.'

Kaufmann ushered them into the chaos that was his home. The first thing Skargrim noticed was the smell: the dank, fungal smell of something rotten, an astringent reek not dissimilar to the stench on the night wind. The second thing he noticed was the mess. Kaufmann's home was more akin to a jackdaw's nest than a grown man's home. Amid the clutter he saw the makings of several gewgaws, much like the ones hanging from the homes of Mielau. Skargrim could imagine the mage walking the diseased streets after nightfall, stringing up fetishes and charms to ward off the sickness.

For all his protestations, it seemed Kaufmann did care.

There was a rumpled cot in the corner, surrounded by shelves of books, sheaves of vellum, and pots of ink, ink that stained the pitted work surface of the room's only table. Beakers and phials filled with curiously coloured liquids steamed, bubbled and fizzed beside embalming fluid, coffin nails and vials of viscous red liquid. And, curiously, there were mirrors: hand mirrors, gilded full-bodied mirrors and silvered mirrors. A pile of white bones in the corner caught his eye: a human ribcage laid bare.

'So, dwarfs, ask.'

'We believe that the sickness afflicting the village originated from the house of Herr Delain.'

'That is not a question, dwarf. That is a statement.' Kaufmann reached for his briarwood pipe.

There was an old panelled door between the two largest mirrors, held shut by a thick rusty chain. Skargrim reasoned that it led to the collapsed second storey of the crumbling tower. There was a second door, a trap set into the floor, built into the ancient stonework but burnished and apparently new. It was secured with a wooden brace.

'Did you know Saskia Delain?'

'Of course I knew her, I was betrothed to her sister,' Kaufmann said. 'She was a beautiful child. Such a waste.'

'That word again,' Kragar said to Skargrim.

'Was her sister beautiful?'

'What are you prattling on about, dwarf? What can it possibly matter if Kristyn was a troll or a swan?'

'Was Kristyn beautiful?'

'Not in the classical sense,' Kaufmann replied, 'but she was beautiful to me.'

Skargrim looked over the mage's shoulder at the huge silvered mirror on the far wall and at their reflected selves captured within it.

Kaufmann looked down at his hands. 'Kristyn came to me, a week before we were to be married and asked for my help, for a séance. She wanted me to use my skills to reach her mother. She was insistent, and I was a fool in love.'

'Why was she so desperate to contact her mother?'

'She was having nightmares. She wouldn't tell me what they were about, not at first, but then she shared. I wished she hadn't.' The wizard fidgeted with the stem of his unlit pipe. 'They were dreams of when she was young. She needed to know if they were true or not. Her father refused to tell her.'

'So you helped her?'

'I wish to all the gods I hadn't, believe me. No one could have lived with what she learned. Whichever way you choose to look at it, I killed her. I was responsible.' Kaufmann sank down onto a tatty chair, the upholstery split and spilling stuffing. He fumbled the pipe, dropping it on the floor at his feet. Salt tears stained his wan cheeks. 'She was a twin. Her sister was smothered on their third birthday. Kristyn killed her own sister, dwarf. That was her dream. Over and over, every night, she dreamed of suffocating the life out of a child she thought was herself. It has nothing to do with the sickness taking these poor children; it was Kristyn's personal shame. Now, please, I beg you, let her shame stay dead with her. She deserves that little dignity, surely?'

'She isn't at rest, mage, and you know it. I can tell by looking around your chamber, at your face. She has become a restless spirit, a revenant shade. Forget what she was, she is now a thing of evil and must be sent screaming back to the underworld. Redeem yourself, wizard. This has to end, for the sake of all the children curled up in their beds tonight.'

THORBAD STOOD KNEE deep in Kristyn Delain's grave.

He had come prepared to burn her bones and release her vengeful spirit, once and for all laying to rest the evil that had invaded the quiet hamlet of Mielau.

'I remember the funeral rites. It's as if it happened yesterday,' Meusmann, the priest of Morr, said. 'Such a tragedy, a young girl taking her own life. Her father was beside himself, so soon after losing his wife.'

Wiping the sweat from his brow, the runepriest asked, 'What about Kaufmann?'

'Grief comes to some later than others. He was silent. Refused the comfort of others. He paid his last respects and went home to his solitude. I doubt he even believed it had happened.'

A small stone, beneath a weeping willow tree, bore her name. The grass around the grave had yellowed and died.

Thorbad drove the shovel into the hard earth, forcing it deep with all of his weight. The pile of black earth rose beside him. Again and again the shovel bit into the soil, until it finally hit something harder. He dropped down onto his hands and knees and began clearing the dirt away from the coffin lid.

The twin moons of Morrslieb and Mannsleib were in ascendancy long before they cracked open the lid on Kristyn Delain's empty coffin.

There was nothing to burn. There would be no easy release from the scourge they faced.

'YOU BURY THE boy tomorrow?'

'At first light,' the priest said, frightened by the look of grim determination on Thorbad's face.

'Last light would be better. We could use the corpse to lure out the dead. The creature obviously needs to feed, so we put temptation in its way.'

'That is wrong, dwarf. The boy deserves peace. I will not sanction the violation of the ceremony.'

'You asked for our help, priest. We bury the boy at dusk.'

'WE HAVE AN empty grave, a great love lost to suicide, and a mad wizard: all the makings of a classic Tilean tragedy,' Kragar said. 'We also have our cause, but we don't have the slightest clue exactly what that cause is. An empty grave smacks of a bloodsucker, but there were no bite marks on any of the young ones. And what's with all of those damned mirrors?'

'Beauty,' said Skargrim. 'Vanity. What else is a mirror for? She lived in his tower, preening and posing before those huge mirrors. The only reason they haven't been destroyed is because they remind the idiot mage of his lost love. His bed was turned towards the largest. Maybe he dreams he can see her reflected in their silver.'

'So what are we going to do?'

'The priest was right, at least in part,' Thorbad said. 'This is no natural sickness. Find the Delain woman and we find the cause. Rid the world of her accursed presence, and we wipe out the disease.'

'Tonight,' Skargrim nodded, 'we'll find the girl and put her out of our misery.'

SHE WAS NO longer a thing of beauty.

She was no longer anything. But she remembered. She remembered her love for him. She remembered her mother's hand, her sister's face. She hungered.

She had promised to stay in the marshes.

She remembered their screams, new and old. She remembered the sudden blossoming of vitality inside her body, the blush of youth, the strength, the living. She remembered death, and she craved it.

The more she fed, the more her failing flesh needed it.

She remembered her reflection in the glass, the anger at seeing her flesh decaying, her beauty eroding. And she surrendered to the hunger inside, the need to consume the very essence of all things beautiful: children captivated by all that the world had to offer.

She did not remember how she came to be damned to this unlife. She did not remember the hand that fashioned her doom.

But she remembered why. 'He loved me,' she told the abomination in the glass.

She opened her mouth, sharing the screams of the souls she had consumed with the night, savouring their innocence even as it surrendered to the maelstrom of her corrupt flesh.

She called the dead children to her, and they answered her call.

THEY HEARD THE cry as they stepped out into the darkness. It was both more and less than human.

'I've got no liking for this,' Kragar muttered. 'Even the air tastes wrong.'

Thunder echoed across the sky, a single rumbling call before the first fat drops of rain hit their faces. Within a minute it was torrential, the driving rain transforming the hard-packed earth to mud.

'Do you think the wizard will keep his end of the bargain? We are about to slay his true love.'

'Kaufmann is of the Amethyst Order, dwarf.' Eustasius Meusmann explained. 'None understand the transience of life better than the magisters of the purple wind. They touch the essence of death with their work but do not follow the path of shadows. It is their sacred duty to undo all the works of necromancy. He will come when he is called, have faith.'

Karla, the barkeep's daughter appeared around the street corner, directly across from their hiding place. Her face was empty, her eyes hungry. She moved with a curious shuffling gait, struggling to put one foot in front of the other.

A low moan escaped her lips, answering the cry of a moment before. The same call echoed like thunder across the small hamlet, twenty, thirty voices or more joining until the chorus filled the night.

'Is she…?'

'Dead? She always was,' Thorbad said. 'That is no longer a human child, only a shell for a thing of evil.'

Karla wasn't alone. More children shuffled barefoot through the muddy streets, their deathly procession ringing the Garden of Morr.

The priest had buried young Gren that evening. His corpse was still fresh.

'They are not children,' Thorbad stressed, pitching his voice above the ceaseless drum of the rain. 'They can't be allowed to live on after we dispose of the woman.'

'But look at them,' Meusmann said. 'How can we just—'

'The innocent souls they were are gone, priest.'

Another howl split the night, the mother calling to her children.

'I have no liking for this.'

'Good,' Thorbad said, 'let it stain your dreams and haunt you into madness. Just remember, what we do is salvation, not damnation, however vile it feels. We kill because we have to. We do not enjoy it.'

Skargrim and Kragar nodded.

Together they followed the girl through the storm and into the Garden of Morr.

It was no longer a place of peace.

The woman stood over the freshly turned grave. She was dressed in the rotten white of her burial gown, her raven-black hair streaked with dried peat and rain. Her skin was mottled and grey, her lips utterly without blood. Rot ate away at the softer parts of her flesh, leaving behind ragged hollows of bone and sinew.

A bell tolled in the spring night.

The noise drew her gaze. She turned and turned again. She saw the children flocking towards her with open arms and hungry faces, and beyond them, the dwarfs: Thorbad and Kragar clutching their hammers, Skargrim with his huge double-headed axe, and the priest.

Thorbad entered the heart of the garden side by side with the priest of Morr. He turned the hammer over and over in his huge hands and planted it in the soft ground no more than ten paces from the wild eyed dead girl and her sick children. His fingers caressed the lines of the rune carved into the weapon's head, releasing the magic held within it. The air crackled blue around the hammer, and then erupted into flame. The rain singed into steam around it.

Thorbad hurled the weapon end over end through the air, not at the woman in her burial rags, but at a mark carved into the weeping willow fifteen paces to her left. The hammer thundered into the trunk. All around the Garden of Morr the runepriest's carefully concealed sigils roared into life, triggered by the breaking of that first rune.

The thing that had been Kristyn Delain gathered up the trailing hem of her rotten skirts and charged at the dwarf, vile fury contorting her already ghastly face.

Thorbad raised his fist above his head, watching. He waited until she was two steps from him, claws out to rake his face, and then he brought his fist down.

The dead woman froze, trapped within the binding Thorbad had laid into the grass. The grey skin of her lips peeled back to expose the decay beneath.

'Quickly, the binding is weak!' Thorbad yelled into the storm.

Meusmann stepped forward, monstrous in the moonlight. A hammer and a pouch of silver nails hung beside a silver dagger on his belt. He splashed anointed water in the face of the dead woman and seared her mottled skin before uttering the first words of purification. The shade raged within the confines of the binding. She bucked and writhed, fighting the grip of the rune. The binding would fail, that was its nature. Meusmann fumbled the knife, dropping it in the dirt. The dead girl cackled her delight. It was the first sound she had made since Thorbad had triggered the runes. The power of the enchantment was failing.

The sky flashed silver with lightning.

Meusmann splashed the water again into her leering face. It scorched where it connected, searing through the skin and into the dead flesh beneath.

Words tumbled out of the priest's mouth, his tongue tripping over the contortions of the invocation, his voice rising to be heard above the crash and boom of the thunder and rain.

'Out beast! Be gone!'

Instead of collapsing, the shade's head twisted completely around to stare at her children. A smile spread slowly across the ruin of her face. 'Kill them, my little ones!'

And the children surged forward, tiny hands gnarled and twisted by sickness into talons. Their movements were awkward, slow and disjointed. They shuffled towards Meusmann and Thorbad, arms extended, moaning their sickening wail as they closed in on the living, teeth bared, hungry to rend flesh from bone, and feast.

'Kaufmann! Now!' The Runepriest bellowed.

There was no sign of the mage.

* * *

SKARGRIM CHARGED, HURLING himself at a small, stumbling corpse and burying his axe deep in the boy's skull. It crumbled beneath the blow. Skargrim yanked the axe-head free in a spray of blood and brain.

Meusmann stared in mute horror at the killing, unable to see anything but a child in the pouring rain.

Skargrim roared his anger as three more corpses clawed at him. Five more pressed in behind them. There wasn't enough room to swing the huge axe, so he butted the handle into the jaws and temples of the relentless dead. Any doubts Skargrim might have harboured were brutally vanquished, as rotten fingers worn down to jagged bone spars tore through his cheek, down his chin and into his neck.

He fell to his knees, borne down by the sheer mass of bodies.

Skargrim's fall snapped Meusmann out of his paralysis. He screamed, brandishing the silver hammer above his head and hurling himself into the fray. Before his first blow had landed squarely he felt his grip on the weapon fail as the shaft crumbled in his hands and blew away, dust on the storm. The remnants of the hammer's head snapped the neck of a monstrous girl. She didn't fall. She reached out for him, clawing at his face.

Meusmann turned to flee even as Kragar launched himself at the dead girl, smashing a powerful fist into her head.

THE SPELL BINDING Kristyn Delain's shell snapped and she was on them in a banshee fury.

Thorbad reacted first, lunging for the silver dagger the priest of Morr had dropped. He came up with it clenched in his fist and slammed it into the dead girl's chest, between the third and fourth ribs, deep into her rotten heart.

He thrust it in again and again, driving her back step by step. Her flesh buckled beneath the savagery of each silver blow. There was no blood, no screams.

Thorbad drove the dagger into her stomach, spilling her guts, opening her throat and giving her a second mouth. Still she did not scream.

The insidious righteousness of the blessed blade finally poisoned her dead flesh. With the silver dagger protruding from her raw breast, she fell back into the shallow pit of her own open grave.

Thorbad took the hammer and nails the priest had dropped and leapt into the wound in the earth. He drove the first silver nail into her skull, the second through her right eye, the third through her left. Her screams were terrible to hear.

The fourth pierced her tongue and jaw. He drove a fifth through her left wrist, deep into the wood of the coffin, and a sixth through her right. He hammered two through her open stomach. She fought him, desperately trying to be free. He shattered her ankles and pinned them to the base of the coffin.

The final nail was not a nail at all, but a huge silver spike, which he held over her ruptured heart. She stared at him through ruined eyes as he drove the spike through her chest and into the earth beneath. Two feet of metal protruded from the wound. All around it, the vile revenant spirit leaked out through the ragged hole and into the aethyr. The last vapours of unlife seeped out of her ruined lips, like ghostly giggles and the delights of children playing.

Beneath the sounds of joy were the faint screams of fear. And then there was only the sound of the rain.

She was gone.

Wiping the gore from his face, Thorbad soaked the dead girl's corpse in oil before he clambered back out of the funeral pit.

MEUSMANN WATCHED THE dwarf walk to the weeping willow where his hammer lay. He felt sick. There was nothing heroic in what they had done. For all the monstrosity that she had become, she had been a young woman once, troubled by death and guilt. This fate was not the one she deserved. He prayed that her soul would find peace.

Skargrim and Kragar stood among the small corpses. Meusmann wanted to believe the raindrops were tears streaking down their haggard faces, but he knew they weren't. A tongue of lightning split the sky, branding the harrowing sight of the garden on his mind's eye now and forever. There was nothing clean about this, nothing righteous.

Then he heard the scream and saw the shape come shrieking out of the shadows at him.

Even in his madness, Iago Kaufmann's power was awesome. His hands crackled with the deep purple veins of raw magical energy as he levelled them at the priest. Streamers of blistering force arced out from his fingers and slammed into Meusmann's chest, hurling him from his feet. The priest lay in a whorish sprawl, wreaths of steam rising up from his body. He twitched, his mind fighting for control of the muscles that no longer obeyed it.

Kaufmann stood over him, lips tight, the words of an incantation ready to spill out and end the priest's miserable existence.

'IT'S OVER, WIZARD,' Thorbad said. 'She's gone. You can't bring her back.' He didn't need to shout for his voice to carry. He stood between the open grave and the two men, hammer in hand, his finger tracing the outline of the fire rune carved into its head.

The hammer ignited in his hands, the hammer head consumed by bright blue flame. 'This time she stays dead.'

Thorbad threw the weapon into the grave.

The minutiae of the garden were locked in time for a moment, the fat rain frozen in the air, and the scream trapped on Iago Kaufmann's slack face. Then a low *crump* brought the world snapping back. Flames leapt out of the grave as the cleansing fire consumed all that remained of the mage's lost lover.

Kaufmann surged upwards, the priest forgotten. His scream was primal, full of rage, despair, guilt, failure, and, ultimately, agony. He stood over the grave, the rising flames contorting his face, conjuring elementals to reshape his pain. No words could voice his desperation, his need for love and absolution, or the depths of his guilt.

Kaufmann met Thorbad's gaze. He stepped forward, soundlessly falling into the fires of the grave.

The dwarf looked down into the flames. The wizard had impaled himself on the silver spike. His arms cradled the woman he had loved in life, and in death, forever joined. The angry fire fused their flesh into one form, before consuming them utterly.

Beside him, the priest struggled to stand. Thorbad reached out a hand to help him. Tears and rain mingled on the priest's ashen face.

Thorbad looked back at Skargrim and Kragar, death all around them. 'We should have seen it. We should have known. The fool turned his back on his beliefs because of some misguided love, and sacrificed his sanity to bring her back. The mirrors in his tower were hers. The chains on the doors kept her locked up. They were all part of the same thing. Even the ribcage on the floor was used for binding her soul. But as her flesh failed and decay set in, his hold on her weakened, if he had ever truly been in control. So she came into the village, drawn by the vitality of the children, leeching the life out of them to renew her beauty. The more she fed, the more she needed to feed. The stench in the air at night was her children on the prowl, their rotten corpses reeking. Beauty: the ultimate lie of the flesh. It made monsters of them all.'

PERILOUS VISIONS
by Mike Lee

IT WAS ONLY just midsummer, but the narrow, arched door at the top of the *Harath-uin* was sealed with an inch of grey ice. The door's heavy iron ring rattled agitatedly in its rusty socket, then heavy blows shook the dark, blooded oak panels until sprays of ice flew from the seams and the portal swung open on creaky hinges. A gust of sharp, freezing air stabbed into the arched doorway like a sword-thrust, drawing a curse from the young druchii standing upon the threshold.

Tethyr stepped gingerly onto the broad stones of the walkway, remembering the warnings of the guards they'd passed on the long climb up the tower. In the predawn gloom the flagstones looked dry and worn, but almost at once the young highborn skidded silently on an invisible coating of black ice. More than one sentry had fallen from the tip of the God-spear, the tower guards said, especially when the moon was down and the summer winds blew. Steadying himself with another muted curse, the young highborn could see why.

The tip of the *Harath-uin* was the tallest point in all of Naggaroth, a blade-like tower of black stone rising two hundred and fifty feet above the fortress of Karond Kar, which itself sat on a granite cliff more than four hundred feet above the sea. The walkway at the top of the tower was no more than four paces across, with a smooth stone parapet that rose to the middle of a druchii's chest.

Without warning the wind shifted direction, banging the heavy door against the side of the tower and buffeting the highborn from behind. Even with the harness of articulated plate armour and mail skirts Tethyr wore beneath his heavy bearskin cloak the young druchii staggered beneath the blow, his hands flailing out before him for support. For a dizzying instant it felt as though the wind was going to fling him right off the walkway, and on impulse the highborn staggered to the lip of the parapet so he would have something solid to hang on to.

He fetched up hard against the stone and found himself leaning out into empty air, nearly seven hundred feet above the restless sea. A thin rime of ice crunched beneath Tethyr's hands as he gripped the lip of the parapet. The slate rooftops of the slave markets and the merchant quarter looked as small as nauglir scales from where he stood.

'Good place to murder someone.'

At the sound of his master's rasping voice Tethyr took a deep breath and forced himself to stand upright. He even hazarded a weak grin as the wind clawed at his narrow face and thick, black hair. 'Indeed so, my lord,' the young druchii replied. 'Have I reason to be concerned?'

Tethyr was the image of a dashing, cold-hearted druchii knight: large, dark eyes as sharp as flint, deep-set over strong cheekbones and a hawk's bill nose. His teeth were white and even, filed expertly to sharp, fashionable points, and he smiled with the wolfish charm of a druchii just coming into his prime.

In contrast, the tall figure that limped slowly through the arched doorway bore the weight of years like the heavy cloak of dragonscale that hung from his shoulders. Lord Nuarc's enamelled plate armour was etched in gilt and marked with powerful wards of protection, buckled over a wide skirt of ithilmar mail that shone like frost in the weak light. The paired swords buckled at his waist were set with dark rubies the colour of cooling blood, resting in scabbards ornamented in ruddy gold. Armour and weapons together amounted to a drachau's ransom, and they had been hard earned on more than a hundred battlefields.

The old general's face was dreadful to behold. Years before on a raid into Ulthuan, a griffon's talons had drawn three jagged furrows across the left side of Nuarc's head, clawing away half of the general's ear and putting out his eye before leaving his sunken cheek and upper lip in tatters. The left side of Nuarc's face was misshapen, a broken ruin, and the scar tissue had pulled the corner of his upper lip into a permanent snarl. The bridge of his long nose was notched in two places by slashing sword strokes, and the side of his lean neck was dimpled by the scar of a spear thrust that had ravaged his once commanding voice.

The thick, golden hadrilkar, his collar of service, still bore the deep mark where it had turned aside the deadly blow. Wrought in the shape of a sinuous dragon, it marked him as one of the Witch King's personal retainers and by rights one of the most powerful nobles in all the Land of Chill. There was more iron grey than black in the general's dark hair, which was drawn back and bound with a band of gold to help cover the lines of hairless scar tissue that ran across the side of his head.

Tendrils of steam rose from a large, clay goblet in Nuarc's hand. He splashed a bit of the hot wine across the paving stones and studied its effects with his one good eye. 'If I'd wanted you dead, boy, I could think of a dozen ways to do it that don't involve climbing so many damned stairs,' he said with a grunt. 'Take out that glass of yours and let's see what's out there.'

From the top of the God-spear a sharp-eyed druchii could observe nearly the entire length of the Sea of Chill and watch the coastal Slavers' Road for more than a hundred leagues as it wound its way westward, past Har Ganeth and on to the black walls of Naggarond itself. South and east, less than twenty leagues away, stood the mouth of the Slavers' Straits, the twisting passage that druchii corsairs took on their raids to Ulthuan and the human lands beyond. Another passage to the sea lay only a dozen miles due north, beyond a set of narrow islands called the Witch's Knives. Not even the sea-wise druchii hazarded the Witch's Straits however; the narrow channel was rife with deadly ice floes even in the height of summer, and home to dreadful sea creatures born in the Chaos-tainted seas further north. A sole ferryboat crossed the mouth of the strait during daylight hours, carrying flesh traders from the Slavers' Road to the slave markets at the foot of Karond Kar.

The ferry's first run wouldn't begin for several hours yet. The coastline around Karond Kar and the twin straits was wreathed in shifting layers of pearlescent fog. South and west the sky was still deep indigo, scattered with the cold gleam of countless icy stars. Dawn was little more than a pale grey tinge on the eastern horizon, its wan light all but eclipsed by the shifting patterns of colour bruising the sky to the north above the Chaos Wastes.

Tethyr brushed the melting flakes of ice from his gauntlets and pulled a long, dark cylinder from his belt. The dwarf-wrought spyglass had been borrowed from Karond Kar's drachau.

Tethyr opened the spyglass and raised the cold, brass ocular to his eye. 'If I haven't said so before, my lord, I'm grateful you chose me for this task.'

Nuarc let out a snort. 'As it happens, you've got a number of qualities that made you a good choice for this little errand,' the general said. 'Two good eyes, for starters. Now tell me what you see.'

Tethyr frowned and swept the spyglass slowly from east to west. 'Darkness and fog,' he replied. 'What exactly am I looking for, my lord?'

'You'll know it when you see it,' Nuarc said, sipping noisily at his wine.

The young highborn swallowed his irritation. Secrets within secrets: that was the way of things at court. Malekith told no one, least of all his personal retainers, any more than they absolutely needed to know. He hadn't even known he was leaving Naggarond until Nuarc had arrived at his apartments, packed and ready for the journey to Karond Kar.

Tethyr swept the spyglass back from west to east, his young eyes straining to pierce the early morning darkness. They had been ordered to stand here, at this particular time and on this particular day, to watch for something, but what? 'Are we looking for a particular corsair?' the young highborn asked. 'Someone sneaking out of Clar Karond?'

'It's midsummer,' the general rasped, 'every ship that's seaworthy has already left port for the raiding season.'

'Someone sneaking back in, then?'

Nuarc didn't reply at first. 'Keep an eye on the straits,' he said carefully.

Aha, the young highborn thought triumphantly. He turned the glass on the Slavers' Straits. 'Thick fog,' he reported. 'Only a fool would be out sailing in it before sunrise.'

'Undoubtedly,' Nuarc agreed, 'but I think you're looking in the wrong direction.'

Tethyr glanced at the general. 'I don't understand.'

Nuarc jerked his scarred head to the north.

'The Witch's Straits?' the young highborn asked, incredulous.

The general nodded. 'Put it down to an old warrior's intuition,' he said.

Tethyr shifted position so he could cover the narrower approach. He swept the glass over the ferry dock and found the broad-beamed boat tied up where she was supposed to be. Scowling, he studied the length of the Witch's Knives, their wooded shorelines fading in and out through the fog. He was just about to lower the glass when he caught a tiny hint of movement out beyond the furthest island.

He focused on the spot, but the fog had closed in once more. Tethyr rested his elbows against the parapet, suddenly forgetting all about the height and the treacherous wind. After a moment he shifted the glass slowly to the west.

There, a glimpse of red and white!

'What is it?' Nuarc demanded.

The light was improving. The wind shifted again, and the fog parted.

Tethyr jerked his eye away from the ocular as though stung. 'Impossible!' he hissed.

'Tell me,' the old general said in a steely voice.

The young highborn glanced over his shoulder at Nuarc. 'Twin masts and race-cut sails,' he said in disbelief. 'A ship from Ulthuan!'

If the old general was surprised at all by the bizarre news his scarred face gave no sign of it. 'Just one?'

Tethyr turned back to the spyglass. After a few minutes he nodded. 'Just the one, my lord,' he said at last. 'She's clear of the straits and heading out into the middle of the sea.'

'They'll cross the Sea of Chill by mid-morning and then follow the southern coastline,' the general mused. 'If they followed the north coast they'd be in full view of the Slavers' Road the entire way.'

'The entire way where?'

Nuarc scowled at the young druchii. 'The west coast of the Sea of Malice,' he said gravely, 'within a few days' march of Naggarond. Where else?'

Tethyr gaped at the old general. 'Is this an invasion?'

'A single ship?' Nuarc sneered. 'Don't be stupid, boy. It's a raid.'

'Through the Witch's Straits and across the inner seas?' Tethyr shook his head in wonder. 'They're brave, I'll give them that.'

'They're fools,' Nuarc growled, 'but that doesn't make them any less dangerous.'

'What do we do now? Alert the harbour squadron?'

Nuarc stared into the depths of his cup. 'No,' he said. 'We tell no one. We're to secure a pair of neshuin from the aerie and fly immediately to Naggarond with the news.' Only couriers charged with the most crucial information were permitted to use the flying horses quartered at the kingdom's six great cities.

Tethyr's brow furrowed. 'But... that makes no sense.'

'It makes as much sense as it needs to, boy,' Nuarc said. 'Those are our orders.'

'But...' The young druchii looked out to sea. Without the aid of the spyglass the raider was invisible in the faint light. 'I mean... how did Malekith know?'

'His mother has some minor skill at divination,' Nuarc snapped. 'Name of Morathi, perhaps you've heard of her?'

Tethyr bristled at the rebuke. 'I just meant–'

The old general cut him off with a wave of his hand. 'I know what you meant, boy,' he said gravely. 'The raid is being led by Eltharion, the blind swordmaster. Malekith's had his eye on him ever since he took that wound at the

Dragon's Gate.' The old druchii sighed. 'Now his obsession has doomed us all.'

'Doomed?' Tethyr echoed. Something in Nuarc's voice sent a chill down the young highborn's spine. 'How can that be?'

Nuarc glared balefully into the darkness. 'Because Naggaroth is a cold and unforgiving place, and we have never been a numerous people,' he said, his ravaged lips twisting at the bitter taste of the words. 'The only way we have been able to survive here, to till the poor soil and draw iron from these ancient hills, is through the labour of tens of thousands of slaves.' He turned to the young highborn. 'At any given time there are a hundred slaves for every single druchii in Naggaroth, and that's still not enough. We spend four to five months out of every year at sea hunting for more.' Nuarc gave Tethyr a hard look. 'What do you think would happen if we had no flesh harvest one year?'

Tethyr frowned. 'It's happened before, or near enough. We survived.'

'It hasn't happened in your lifetime, boy,' Nuarc snarled. 'I remember the last one. The price for slaves soared. Flesh houses closed, and then the mines and forges went idle. Cities raided one another for slaves in the dead of winter. And that was *one* bad season,' the general said. 'Imagine what two seasons would cost us, or three.'

'But that would never happen,' Tethyr said.

'Oh, but it could,' Nuarc replied. 'It's been our secret nightmare for hundreds of years.' The general pointed, first to the Slavers' Strait, then the Witch's Strait. 'They are the choke points. Right now all of our ships are at sea on raiding cruises. Imagine what would happen if they returned and found an enemy fleet waiting for them in the straits, outnumbered, heavily laden, no room to manoeuvre...'

'They wouldn't stand a chance,' Tethyr said, his expression grim.

The general nodded. 'Exactly, and a blockading fleet would only have to stay in place for a few weeks to a month, right at the end of summer. Once the straits freeze over in early autumn they sail for home, leaving us without a flesh harvest. And they can do it again the next year, and the year after that.'

Tethyr's eyes widened as he realised the implications. 'Then why haven't our enemies ever attempted such a thing?'

'For the simple reason that Ulthuan hasn't known how vulnerable we are,' Nuarc said, 'until now.' He pointed out into the darkness. 'The elves in that boat have just seen with their own eyes how easy it would be to choke off our supply of slaves. If even one of those raiders make it back to Ulthuan with an accurate report of the straits our worst fears will one day come true.'

'Blessed Murderer,' Tethyr cursed. 'Is there nothing we can do?'

'There is,' Nuarc said quietly. 'We end the long war with our brethren. We make peace with Ulthuan.'

For several long moments Tethyr could only stare in shock at the old general. 'You're mad,' he finally said.

'Mind your tongue, boy,' Nuarc hissed. 'I was fighting against Ulthuan four hundred years before you were even born. I'm being *realistic*. We can either negotiate a peace that's favourable to us now or have one forced on us later. Which would you choose?'

Tethyr shook his head. 'This is treason. Malekith would never agree to such a thing.'

To the young druchii's surprise, the general only nodded. 'On this much at least we agree, which is why we must overthrow him.'

'*We*?' Tethyr exclaimed.

'I'm not the only one at court who can see the danger we are in,' Nuarc said. 'A number of us have been talking about this for some time. So long as Malekith remained strong we counted ourselves secure, but since he was wounded in Ulthuan it's clear that a change has come over him. He's not the ruler he once was.'

'But Malekith–'

'The Witch King is one man, Tethyr. With all his power and all the power of Morathi behind him he still cannot rule the druchii without the support of the nobility.' Nuarc edged closer to Tethyr, pointing out to sea. 'The Witch King has all but invited our foes to Naggaroth's shores. This obsession has made him reckless and weak. We can use this to our advantage, letting Eltharion and his elves give us the opportunity we need.'

Tethyr swallowed, his face grey with horror. 'What does any of this have to do with me?'

'Isn't it obvious? As the lowest ranking member of Malekith's retinue you're his Master of Horse and Gate. Naggarond's Dark Riders and the fortress guards are under your command. Eltharion and his pitiful band can only be here for one purpose: to finish what the swordmaster began during the duel at the Dragon Gate.' The general gave the young highborn a ghastly smile. 'Normally they wouldn't get within a mile of the Witch King's tower, but with your help…'

'No.' Tethyr said forcefully. 'You're not going to make a traitor out of me! I should report this to the Witch King at once–'

Swift as an arrow, Nuarc's left hand shot out and seized Tethyr by the front of his cloak, bending the young highborn backwards over the edge of the parapet. Gasping in terror, Tethyr grabbed Nuarc's wrist and tried to twist away from the general, but the old druchii's grip was like iron.

'You forget yourself, boy,' Nuarc rasped. 'Your oaths are to me, not Malekith. It was my patronage that got you where you are today. I'm a general with centuries of loyal service and countless battlefield honours, while you are nothing but a landless knight without a single ally at court. Your denunciations would come across as nothing more than a clumsy grab for power, and Malekith would have you vivisected for it.' Nuarc's gruesome smiled widened. 'At the same time, if my scheme fails, the Witch King will have you and your family crucified simply because of your association with me. You are a part of this plan, Tethyr; I've groomed you for your role for the past ten years. At this point your only hope of survival is to do exactly as I tell you. Do you understand?'

Tethyr glared at the old general. 'What would you have me do, my lord?' he asked through clenched teeth.

Nuarc nodded his approval. 'I knew you'd come around,' he said, drawing the young highborn back over the parapet. 'For now we only watch and wait,' he said. 'We follow orders as always. It will take the enemy two weeks to make the passage across the inner seas and reach the coast near Naggarond. I expect that Malekith will choose to meet them at the cliffs. Keep your eyes open,' the general cautioned. 'Judge the Witch King by his actions, and you will see why we must take matters into our own hands.'

Tethyr clenched his hands into fists to keep them from shaking. A glimmer of defiance still burned in his dark eyes. 'What if you're wrong?' he asked.

Once again, the general surprised him with a grating laugh. 'If I'm wrong, we're both dead men,' he said, 'so there's little use in worrying. Let's get out of this damned wind and find some more wine. It will be a cold flight back to Naggarond.'

With a humourless grin, the general limped for the doorway. Tethyr had little choice but to follow.

DACHLAN KEEP WAS a typical druchii watchtower, a single square citadel some three storeys high with a good view of the cliffs and the Sea of Malice to the south. Smoke rose from the blacksmith's forge, set in a low stone building close by the tower, and a trio of despatch horses whinnied nervously from a wooden corral nearby. Both moons shone just above the western horizon, limning the citadel in silver and throwing lanes of deep shadow between the clustered tents of the small army camped around the keep.

The retreat had been an orderly one, Nuarc observed, watching balefully as the battered columns of spearmen limped up the narrow road into the encampment. No one spoke as the ragged companies shuffled along. Only hours ago these same warriors had marched from camp singing the dire war songs of their people. Now many of them returned empty-handed, their spears broken in battle and their pale faces caked with dust and drying blood. An aura of defeat hung over the soldiers like a poisonous fog.

'Disgraceful,' Lord Saarha growled, studying the broken army over the rim of his wine cup. Orange light from the iron brazier outside Nuarc's campaign tent picked out the gilt scrollwork ornamenting his plate armour. The sullen glow cast deep shadows in the highborn's sunken cheeks and accentuated his sharply angled features. 'Better they had died defending our shores than slink back here like whipped curs!' Several of the knights in Saarha's company murmured in agreement as the highborn took another sip of Nuarc's wine.

'Had we been there, things would have gone differently,' Lord Ashrul hissed, his arms tightly folded over his ornamented breastplate. Unlike his companions, Ashrul was bald as an egg. A rival had employed a shade caster to kill him almost a century ago and the battle had turned his hair as white as a temple witch. He'd shaved his scalp ever since. 'One good charge, lances levelled, and we'd have thrown them all back into the sea,' Ashrul declared, his thin lips curling into a snarl.

'We had our orders,' Nuarc said flatly. Like the other members of Malekith's retinue, he was clad in his full panoply of war, awaiting a call to battle that had never come. Late in the day, when it had become apparent that they would take no part in the fighting, Nuarc had invited his fellow highborn to share some food and drink he'd brought with him from Naggarond. He studied the seven nobles and their attendants carefully as they stood around the brazier and watched the army's return. 'Clearly the Witch King felt we weren't needed.'

Saarha shook his head bitterly. 'Left to guard the camp-site like a bunch of conscripts,' he grumbled. 'If I didn't know better I'd say Malekith meant to insult us.'

Several of the highborn shifted uneasily, casting glances to the low hill several hundred yards away where the Witch King had put down his pavilion. The assembled lords could hear the rumbling hisses of the great dragon Seraphon as it was attended to by Naggarond's beast masters.

A whipcord lean druchii to Nuarc's right cleared his throat and spoke carefully. 'No doubt our lord saw no need for our strength in the face of such a pitiful force,' Lord Uran said. His gaze never rose from the shifting embers of the brazier.

A deep voice chuckled further to Uran's left. Lord Indir swirled the dregs of his wine and studied its shadowy depths. Spots of colour shone on the highborn's sharp cheekbones. 'Rumour has it that Eltharion is leading the enemy force. Perhaps our great lord intended to settle things himself and his courage failed him.'

An uneasy silence enfolded the assembled lords. Indir glanced up from his wine. 'It's the wound,' he explained. 'Am I the only one who's noticed the change?'

'No,' Nuarc said, casting his gaze around the circle and daring anyone to gainsay him. 'We've all seen it, whether we care to admit it or not. I've served Malekith longest of all of us, and I say he's different now. Eltharion's blade cut him more deeply than anyone suspected.'

Lord Ashrul eyed Nuarc warily. 'Are you claiming that Malekith is... unfit?'

'I claim nothing,' the old general replied. 'The facts, however, are hard to deny.'

'What facts?' Uran asked quietly.

Nuarc spread his hands. 'Look around you,' he said. 'Malekith knew Eltharion and his troops were coming more than two weeks ago. He could have called out ships from Clar Karond to intercept them at sea or ordered Lord Malus to march Hag Graef's army to meet the invaders at the shore. Instead, the Witch King summoned the executioners from Naggarond's temple, a single squadron of cavalry scouts and a few meagre companies of city guardsmen: no cold ones save our own, no crossbows, and no witches. He didn't give the order to march until well past dawn, giving the enemy plenty of time to disembark. I defy any of you to tell me you'd have done the same thing.'

Uran shrugged. 'I'm certain Malekith has a plan.'

'To do what? Humiliate us?' Nuarc shot back. 'This is the first time in the history of Naggaroth that invaders have trespassed on our soil, and Malekith has all but handed them a great victory. Eltharion and a handful of troops have driven us back from our own shores! It makes us look weak. What possible reason could Malekith have for such a thing?'

The nobles shifted uncomfortably, letting the question hang in the air. In the ensuing silence the faint cries of the wounded sounded across the druchii camp. On the south road the spearmen had given way to the ragged band of temple executioners, who marched to their own tents in grim, mournful silence. If anything they seemed to have suffered worse than the spearmen, having borne the brunt of the fighting with Eltharion's Swordmasters. A troop of Dark Riders brought up the rear, the heads of their mounts drooping from the exertions of covering the army's retreat. As the riders reached the outskirts of the camp their leader spurred his horse into a trot and wove his way through the camp towards Nuarc's tent.

Nuarc indicated the approaching rider with his wine cup. 'Here's Tethyr,' the old general said. 'Now we'll hear what happened.'

A pair of servants hurried from the general's tent to take the reins of Tethyr's mount and help the young lord to the ground. His armour was covered in dust and grime, but was otherwise unmarked. He approached Nuarc and bowed curtly.

'Report,' Nuarc commanded.

Tethyr straightened. The muscles of his jaw clenched as he struggled for the proper words. 'You were right,' he managed to say. 'It's Eltharion. He landed with a force of Swordmasters and Shadow Warriors, perhaps two hundred of them, all told.'

Murmurs of consternation rose from the assembled highborn. 'We outnumbered them almost four to one,' Ashul snarled, 'four to one! Your horsemen should have slaughtered their scouts and then ground the Swordmasters under your hooves!'

The young highborn glared hotly at Ashul. 'We were not permitted to do so, my lord,' he said tightly. 'Our orders were to harangue the enemy and keep them from manoeuvring around our flanks, nothing more.'

'Go on,' Nuarc commanded.

Tethyr took a deep breath. 'There's not much else to say,' he continued. 'Malekith ordered the infantry to advance with the executioners in the centre and the spear companies on the flanks. The executioners went right for the Swordmasters and kept the spearmen from using their weapons to any great effect. Eltharion and his men just stood their ground and killed any druchii that got close.'

'What of the Witch King?' Indir asked. 'Did he take no part in the battle?'

'No, dread lord,' Tethyr said bitterly. 'He kept his distance, circling overhead on his dragon.' His lips curled in disgust. 'We kept waiting for him to swoop down and hit the enemy from behind. One pass and he could have turned their ranks to ash, but he never did.' Tethyr looked Nuarc in the eye. 'It was almost as though he was afraid to fight.'

'What of Eltharion?' Nuarc asked.

'Struck down late in the day, Khaine be praised,' the young highborn replied. 'Malekith sent one of the temple assassins against him. The Swordmaster was poisoned, but just as it seemed that the tide might turn, a company of Sea Guard arrived from the shore and the Witch King ordered a retreat.'

'Did Eltharion survive?' Nuarc asked.

Tethyr shrugged. 'I can't say, my lord. The last I saw of him he was being carried off the field by a group of Shadow Warriors.'

'An assassin,' Indir spat. 'He sent an assassin after Eltharion rather than face him directly, even with Seraphon at his side.'

The scarred general nodded gravely. Then he asked Tethyr, 'Has the Witch King issued any orders or sent any despatches by your men? Has he summoned reinforcements from Naggarond or Hag Graef?'

'No, my lord,' the young highborn responded. 'The standing order is to enter camp and await further commands.'

The nobles eyed one another in the stunned silence. Saarha shook his head and tossed the dregs of his wine onto the brazier, making the coals hiss like an angry nauglir. 'It's madness,' he said. 'They'll hit us tonight, just after the moons set.'

Tethyr frowned. 'How can you be so certain, dread lord?'

'Because he is here,' Nuarc interjected, nodding in the direction of Malekith's pavilion. 'And because the only other major target within striking distance of here is Naggarond. Eltharion will have to deal with the keep before pressing further inland, and the best time to strike will be tonight. It's likely we'll be driven back to Naggarond if that happens.'

'What do we do?' the young highborn asked.

Nuarc shrugged. 'There's nothing we can do. Malekith remains in command.' The general turned to his peers. 'Thus, we must consider what happens afterwards.'

Ashul studied Nuarc warily. 'What do you propose?'

'Don't be coy,' the general snapped. 'It's clear we have to take action. Today's debacle proves that the Witch King is no longer the ruler he once was. He must be forced to cede his authority, one way or another.'

'This is Malekith you're talking about,' Indir hissed. 'We aren't any match for him!'

'We don't have to be,' Nuarc countered. 'Eltharion has wounded Malekith once before, and he's come here to finish the job. All we need do is ensure that the Swordmaster gets his chance. Once we're back at Naggarond we can make that happen.' He shrugged. 'Afterwards we can discuss how we'll divide the kingdom between us.'

Ashur nodded curtly, the hungry gleam in his eye belying his impassive expression. Saarha stared into the brazier's glowing depths, and then gave his assent as well.

Nuarc turned to Indir and Uran. 'We've talked of this for years and now the moment is upon us my lords,' he said. 'What say you?'

Indir met Nuarc's eyes and started to speak, but thought better of it. Finally he shook his head. 'I do not know, Nuarc,' he said softly. 'It's a terrible gamble you're contemplating. Let me think on it further.'

'He's right,' Uran blurted, suddenly very sober. 'We should think on this a bit more.'

Nuarc's composure never changed. 'Very well,' he said. 'You have until we return to the city before you must make your decision. After that things will have to happen very quickly.'

The two nobles nodded curtly and took their leave. 'Thank you for the wine,' Uran said, setting his goblet on the ground, before retreating into the darkness.

Nuarc turned and considered the three remaining noblemen, who had held their tongues while their betters spoke.
Lord Diaran, Lord Teruvel and Lord Myrthen were all young
nobles who owed their current wealth and power to
Nuarc's patronage. As one, they inclined their heads to the
old general and murmured their assent.

'Then the rest of us are agreed,' the old general rasped.
'Let's adjourn and make what preparations we can. I have
no doubt Lord Saarha's prediction is correct, so we have
only a few hours before Eltharion and his men launch their
attack.'

With curt bows the gathered nobles dispersed, stealing
quietly down the dark lanes between the campaign tents.
Tethyr waited until the last of the conspirators had disappeared from sight before addressing his master. 'You
haven't told them of your plans for Ulthuan,' he said.

Nuarc shrugged. 'First things first, boy,' he said, drawing a
poker from the brazier and stirring the coals. 'Once
Eltharion finishes with Malekith he'll make an ideal choice
for carrying our message back to the Phoenix Court, and
our compatriots will be in more of a position to listen to
reason,' he said. The general shrugged. 'Of course, it might
not have to come to that. It's possible that the threat of facing Eltharion will be enough to force Malekith to cede
much of his power to us. That would be the ideal outcome,
since the Witch King could reign as a figurehead and allow
the rest of us to govern the kingdom from the shadows.'

Tethyr looked out into the darkness. 'What of Indir and
Uran? Do you trust them?'

'I trust that they won't betray us immediately, if that's
what you mean,' the general replied. 'No, those two can be
as timid as mice sometimes. They have to think everything
through, forwards and backwards, before they'll commit to
anything.' With a snarl Nuarc thrust the poker deep into the
coals, sending up a cyclone of fiery sparks. 'Do what you
can for your troops and plan a retreat to Naggarond,' the

general said, 'then be back here before the moons have set. Once the attack begins there will be important work to be done.'

No SOONER HAD the bright moons disappeared over the horizon than the attack began.

Shouts and screams rose from three sides of the druchii encampment, and almost at once orange flames leapt from one tent to the next as the Ulthuan raiders tossed torches and knocked over lamps to sow chaos among their foes. Hoarse shouts and confused orders rang through the air as officers tried to rally the spear companies to resist the attack. Black-fletched arrows hummed lethally out of the darkness. Warriors fell, gasping their last breaths, while their comrades raced in panic down the camp lanes striking out at any shadowy figure in their path.

Tethyr leapt from Nuarc's tent into the cacophonous darkness with his long sword ready. From where he stood the fighting was still some way off, and the fires from the burning tents glowed in a ragged line from west to east. A druchii spearman ran past the general's tent, his eyes wide and his pale face streaked with blood. He shouted something unintelligible to the highborn and ran on into the night.

Nuarc slipped from the tent right after Tethyr, his heavy dragonscale cloak held tightly around his armoured body. The old general took stock of the situation with an experienced eye. 'The raiders are well within the camp,' he growled. 'They'll be at the keep in no time. We have to move quickly!'

Without waiting for a reply, the general limped off down the lane to the west. Despite his age and his injuries Nuarc moved with speed and purpose, navigating easily in the dim light. He knew the layout of the camp, and sped like an arrow to his objective.

There were no guards outside Lord Uran's tent; perhaps they'd been sent to fetch the highborn's mount or had been caught up in the confusion of the attack. Nuarc pushed the flap aside and entered. Inside, a pair of braziers filled the wide space with heat and ruddy light.

Uran sat on a stool while a pair of servants buckled on his ornate greaves and breastplate. The highborn had a half-drawn sword in his hands as Nuarc and Tethyr burst into the tent, but Uran relaxed at once when he saw who it was. 'Blessed Murderer, Nuarc!' the highborn shouted. 'I might have killed you!'

'I know,' Nuarc rasped. 'That's why I'm here.' Then he threw open his heavy cloak and levelled a small repeater crossbow at Uran's face. The heavy bowstring thumped and the bolt struck Uran just beneath his left eye, punching through the cheekbone and exiting the back of the highborn's skull with a sharp, wet crunch. As the highborn's lifeless body slid from the stool Tethyr dashed across the room and beheaded the first of the servants, spraying a fan of bright crimson across the back wall of the tent. The second servant screamed in terror and tried to flee, but the young highborn caught up with the druchii in three swift strides and drove his sword between his ribs.

Nuarc reloaded his crossbow. 'Well done,' he said. Then he put a boot against one of the braziers and kicked it over, spraying fiery coals across the tent. 'Now let's go catch our other mouse.'

Uran's tent was just starting to burn as the two nobles dashed back into the darkness. They passed half a dozen bodies strewn along the lane, slain by the arrows of the shadow warriors. A horse careened across their path, its empty saddle covered in blood. Shouts and the clash of steel rang through the air near the stone flanks of the keep, and the air was thick with smoke and the stench of burning flesh.

Indir wasn't in his tent. Even the servants had fled for their lives.

'What now?' Tethyr asked as they surveyed the wreckage strewn within the tent. It appeared the servants had helped themselves to Indir's valuables before taking flight.

Nuarc shook his head irritably, considering his options. Just then, a fierce war shout sounded nearby, followed by the ringing notes of swordplay and screams. 'That way!' the general ordered, and the two druchii dashed outside.

A fierce battle raged not twenty yards from Lord Indir's tent. At once, Tethyr and Nuarc saw the long, straight blades of a pair of Hoeth Swordmasters flashing and clanging against the shorter blades of Lord Indir and a pair of his retainers. Four spearmen of the Sea Guard hemmed in the druchii from either flank, cutting off their escape as the Swordmasters closed in for the kill. As Nuarc watched, one of the Swordmasters slid forward and slipped past his opponent's guard with fearsome speed, splitting the retainer's helmeted skull from crown to chin.

'At them!' Nuarc hissed, his one eye gleaming balefully. Tethyr dashed forward, and was upon the two closest spearmen before they realised their peril. The young high-born split the air with a savage war scream and swept his blade up in a vicious arc, severing a spearman's right arm at the shoulder. The raider collapsed with a horrid cry, blood pouring down his side.

Nuarc raised his crossbow and shot one of the Swordmasters in the chest. The Hoethi staggered, blood bursting from his lips as the armour piercing bolt punched through his breastplate. Then he fell to the ground. The second Swordmaster decapitated the last of Indir's retainers with a quicksilver stroke of his two-handed blade, and then rushed at Indir. Tethyr turned his attention to the second spearman as Nuarc tossed aside the crossbow and drew his twin swords with a savage war cry of his own.

The two remaining Sea Guard ran wide of the duel between Indir and the Swordmaster and charged at Nuarc with spears levelled. Nuarc let them come, grinning fiercely. Then, at the last moment, he sidestepped into the right-most spearman's path. His left-hand sword knocked the oncoming spearhead aside, letting it pass harmlessly by. Then Nuarc pivoted on his left foot and chopped his right-hand sword into the spearman's side. The enchanted steel cut through the spearman's mail hauberk as though it were rotted cloth, slicing below the ribcage and severing the war-rior's spine.

As the dying spearman collapsed his companion lunged in from the left, aiming for Nuarc's heart. The spear tip struck the general's breastplate and was turned aside, slip-ping between Nuarc's chest and left arm. Without thinking, the general clamped his arm tightly to his side, trapping the spear haft. Then he stabbed the spearman through the throat with his right-hand blade.

There was a ringing crack of steel against steel, then a hoarse, bubbling scream. Indir staggered backwards, his sword tumbling from his hands and his face twisted in agony. The Swordmaster's blade had rent him open like a slaughtered steer, the long blade shearing through his shoulder and down into his breastbone. The Hoethi put a boot against the noble's breastplate and dragged his blade free. Indir was dead before he hit the ground.

Nuarc advanced on the Swordmaster, smiling a hungry wolf's smile. 'You've done me a good turn,' he told the Hoethi. 'For that I'll do you one as well.'

The Swordmaster charged at Nuarc with his deadly blade held high. The old general met the charge with cold, calcu-lating skill, using both swords to block each powerful blow. Rather than give ground he drove himself against the Swordmaster, advancing inside the longer sword's reach. Realising he was in peril, the Swordmaster checked his for-ward momentum and began to back-pedal, but it was too late. Nuarc's right-hand sword stabbed deep into the elf's hip. As the Swordmaster staggered, the general pulled the blade free and struck his foe on the brow of his steel helm. Sparks flew and the helmet fell away in pieces as the Swordmaster plunged to the ground.

Tethyr pulled his sword free from the last spearman's chest and joined Nuarc beside the fallen Swordmaster. 'I don't think he's dead,' the young highborn warned, studying the elf's bloodstained face.

'He's not. I have a purpose in mind for this one,' Nuarc said. Suddenly a flare of orange light filled the sky to the south-east. Dachlan Keep was on fire. 'Bind him quickly, and then go and fetch my mount. He's coming with us back to Naggarond.'

THE TORTURE CHAMBER was silent, save for the soft clinking of barbed chains and the soft shuffle of boots as the torturers went about their labours. The Swordmaster's back was arched in agony, his arms and legs dangling off the narrow vivisection table. His jaws were clenched tight against the excruciating pain, and a trickle of blood seeped down his chin where he had bitten through his lips. Drops of crimson pattered steadily onto the dark slate tile, echoing softly in the vaulted chamber.

Tethyr slipped silently through the chamber door and joined Nuarc. The old general was sipping wine and studying the torturers' work with professional interest. He acknowledged the young highborn with a distracted nod. 'Impressive, is it not? They manipulate the nerves in such a way that the subject's body clenches in reaction to the pain, so that he cannot utter a single sound unless they permit it. Screaming is a release, you know. It's a way to expel the tension brought on by pain. Take that away and the subject breaks all the more quickly.'

The young highborn glanced at the torturers' efforts. They had clearly been working on the Swordmaster for hours, and had moved from gross physical injury to more delicate manipulations. Already they had peeled back the skin on the prisoner's forearms and were separating the muscles beneath with fine steel tools. Tethyr swallowed. 'Have we learned anything yet?'

Nuarc shrugged. 'No. That's why they're working on the arms. The longer he holds out the more harm they inflict. Soon they will damage the muscles so severely that he'll never wield a sword again. That's a far worse fate for one such as him. I expect it will be his undoing.' The old general took a few steps forward, peering intently at the open workings of the elf's forearms. 'What have you to report?' he commanded.

'I've finished inspecting the garrison and doubled the watches,' Tethyr said, 'and the officers on duty have been warned to expect an attack at any time. We also have mounted and foot patrols combing the foothills outside the fortress day and night. There's no way Eltharion can get inside Naggarond at this point.'

Nuarc chuckled. 'Never underestimate the power of hate, Tethyr. With hatred, all things are possible.' He nodded curtly. 'You've done well. The only vulnerable point is the sally port where the patrols enter and leave the fortress. Which port are you currently using?'

The highborn shifted uncomfortably. 'The brass portal, my lord, on the east side of the fortress.'

'Good. Order your men to keep a careful watch. When Eltharion strikes, it will be there.'

'Do you really think the raiders will get past the walls?' Tethyr asked.

'We have to assume they will. When the attack begins, the safety of the Witch King will be paramount. When the alarm is sounded we will meet Malekith in the throne room and defend him from there.'

A shudder wracked the Swordmaster's body and a terrible hiss slipped past his torn lips as his body went limp. The torturers put aside their tools and rose to their feet. Their leader turned to Nuarc and bowed regretfully. 'We can do no more for now,' the torturer said softly, 'his mind and body are spent, and he lies near death.'

'And he told us nothing?' Nuarc said.

The torturer shook his head. 'His will is strong, dread lord. He would rather live as a cripple than give us what we wish for.'

Nuarc grinned. 'Admirable. See to it that he gets his wish. For now though, bind him up and give him some hushalta. I don't want him dying on us too quickly.' The torturers bowed again, and Nuarc turned on his heel and headed for the door.

Tethyr followed the general from the room into an antechamber that connected to Nuarc's personal apartments. Armoured sentries stood before each of the eight doors leading from the marble floored room, and a pair of servants waited with a bowl of warm water and towels in the event that their master needed to cleanse himself.

Nuarc waved the servants away. 'What of my orders regarding the garrison?'

The young highborn took a deep breath, composing his thoughts. 'It is as you commanded, my lord. I've hand picked the watch officers and given them their instructions.'

'It is crucial that they understand their task,' Nuarc said, giving Tethyr a penetrating stare. 'They are to press the raiders closely and drive them in the direction of the throne room. Whittle down their numbers without rendering them powerless. It will require considerable finesse.'

'I understand, my lord,' Tethyr replied, clearly unhappy with the plan. 'I've put my best men in place. Do you believe the attack will come soon?'

Nuarc nodded. 'Of course, time is the one thing the raiders cannot spare. They will strike as soon as they are able, which I expect will be tonight.' He turned and levelled a finger at Tethyr's chest. 'Eltharion will be a dagger aimed

right for Malekith's heart,' he said, tapping the young highborn's breastplate for emphasis. 'And through his demise a
new age will dawn for Naggaroth.'

THE TORTURER'S EYES were wide with surprise, his thin lips
slack with wonder. Specks of fresh blood glistened on the
polished silver grip of the flensing knife buried in the
druchii's throat.

With a clatter of plate armour Tethyr burst through the
doorway into the torture chamber. 'My lord, word from
the brass portal – blessed Murderer! What's happened
here?'

Nuarc looked up from the body of the dead torturer.
The chamber, formerly kept scrupulously neat, had been
transformed into an abattoir. Streaks of blood cooled on
the dark walls and spread in viscous lakes across the slate
floor. The torturer and his four companions lay in a rough
semicircle around the vivisection table, their bodies punc-
tured and torn by expensive and delicate instruments.
There was no sign of the Hoethi Swordmaster, save for a
trail of bloody footprints leading towards the door.

'It would appear that our prisoner was not as helpless
as he'd led us to believe,' the old general rasped thoughtfully.

'He's escaped?' Tethyr cried.

The general nodded. 'About three hours ago. See how
the blood has cooled around the corpses?'

'But... he heard us talking this afternoon. He'll find
Eltharion and tell him everything!'

Nuarc rose to his feet with a grunt. 'Of course he will,
boy. Why do you think I dismissed the guards in the
antechamber?' The general surveyed his handiwork and
smiled coldly. 'Now he'll lead the blind zealot exactly
where we want him to go.'

The young highborn gaped at Nuarc. 'This... this was
part of your plan?'

'This is what it means to be a general, boy,' Nuarc hissed, 'thinking two steps ahead of your foe and making him dance to your tune.'

Tethyr eyed the dead men. 'And these...'

The general shrugged. 'An expensive bit of misdirection, but necessary. I couldn't make the escape seem too easy. Now, about the brass portal?'

With effort, the young highborn tore his gaze from the carnage. 'Eltharion and his men are in the fortress.'

'How long?' the general snapped.

'No more than half an hour. One of the roving patrols found the bodies of the gatekeepers just a few minutes ago. I've alerted the garrison. They're drawing the noose tight.'

'Excellent,' Nuarc replied. 'The time has come at last.'

The general crossed the room in half a dozen strides, leaving the startled Tethyr scrambling to keep up. Nuarc crossed the empty antechamber and pushed open a tall, oak door. A large, dimly-lit receiving room lay beyond. Witch lamps glowed from hanging fixtures suspended from the arched ceiling, casting pools of greenish light over tables set with bottles of wine and trays of rare meats. Armoured druchii rose from low-backed leather chairs as Nuarc entered the room; Saarha, Ashul, Diaran, Teruvel and Myrthen, along with almost a dozen trusted retainers accompanying the two older lords.

'Eltharion has entered the fortress,' Nuarc began without preamble, his voice strong and assured as the prospect of battle drew near. 'The garrison has been alerted, and word will have reached Malekith, who will be in his throne room awaiting our report.' The general laid a gauntleted hand on the pommel of one of his swords. 'For centuries Malekith has ruled us with an iron fist, treating us as little better than slaves. We have served him without question for too long! Tonight there will be a reckoning, and we shall become masters of our own fate!'

Ashul raised his goblet. 'Power and glory!' he cried.

Nuarc nodded. 'Power and glory.'

'And peace,' Thethyr shouted, his voice echoing from the stone walls. 'Tell them, Nuarc! Tell them about your plan for Ulthuan!'

Silence fell among the conspirators. Nuarc turned slowly, his one eye burning with rage as he stared at the young highborn.

Ashul frowned. 'What is he talking about, Nuarc?'

Before the general could speak, Tethyr lunged into the breach. 'He means to end the war with Ulthuan!' he cried, his face twisted with anguish. 'Damned, hateful peace! He would betray our righteous hate by seeking terms from the Phoenix Court.' The young highborn stood straight and tall, fixing Nuarc with a look of triumph. 'I've borne his secret for more than a fortnight, and I can bear it no longer. He wishes to overthrow Malekith and make cowards of us all!'

For the first time, the canny general was caught unprepared. His scarred lips trembled with rage, but permitted no reply.

The young Lord Myrthen turned to his erstwhile patron. 'Is this true, my lord?'

'What I do, I do in the name of all the druchii,' Nuarc growled, his face white with fury.

'You intend to ruin us!' Lord Diaran said.

'What do you know of ruin, stripling?' Nuarc roared, rocking the young druchii back on his heels. 'I've fought this war for longer than you've been alive. I can see where it is leading, and we must change our tack before it's too late.'

'Better death than surrender!' Diaran shot back. He drew his sword. 'You won't tarnish my honour with your weakness, Nuarc!'

'We don't have time for this!' Nuarc snarled. 'Eltharion is fighting his way to Malekith even now.'

'Let him,' Tethyr said, drawing his sword. 'He will die at the Witch King's hands and we will deliver his severed head to our debased cousins in Ulthuan. *That* is the way of war, Nuarc!'

The general turned to Saarha and Ashul. 'You know the truth as well as I do. Tell them!'

Saarha stared coldly at the old general. 'How long have you been planning this, Nuarc?'

'Seize him!' Teruven cried, and the young lords leapt at Nuarc like a pack of nauglir.

But the old general was not so easily overcome. With a bestial roar he drew his enchanted blades and met their charge head-on. A less experienced swordsman might have faltered before four attackers, but Nuarc let them come. At the last moment he dodged to the left, bringing his right-hand sword around in an arc from left to right that caught Lord Diaran's slashing blade and deflected it into Lord Myrthen's face. Myrthen fell with Diaran's sword buried in his forehead, and Nuarc used the opportunity to bring up his left-hand blade and thrust the sword into Diaran's neck. The young highborn faltered, choking on his own blood, and the return stroke of Nuarc's right-hand sword took off the top of Diaran's skull.

With a shouted curse, Tethyr swung wide of Nuarc, striking a ringing blow on the general's breastplate. Teruvel recovered at the same moment, lunging forward with a thrust that scored the side of Nuarc's head. The general swung both of his blades at the young lord, and his right-hand sword sliced through Teruvel's right pauldron and vambrace as if they were paper, slashing open the druchii's arm from shoulder to wrist. Teruvel's sword fell from nerveless fingers, moments before Nuarc thrust his enchanted sword deep into the young highborn's chest.

At that moment Tethyr seized his chance. With a furious cry he brought his sword down on Nuarc's right arm. The stroke was well aimed and should have severed the general's arm at the elbow, but the sorcerous runes crafted into the steel turned aside the blow. As it was, the violence of the blow knocked Nuarc backwards, causing him to lose his grip on his blade. Tethyr lunged forward, swinging for the general's exposed head, but Nuarc parried the blow with his left-hand sword.

'You're a fool, Tethyr,' Nuarc hissed. 'I showed you the truth and you shrank from it.'

'You're mad,' the young highborn shot back. 'I said so at Karond Kar! But now your plan is finished, your conspirators have deserted you. You're just one man,' he snarled. 'Not even you can overthrow the kingdom alone.'

Tethyr charged forwards, hammering Nuarc with a rain of razor edged blows that struck at head, shoulder, waist and hip. The general parried each stroke save the last. He raised his blade and let the young highborn's blow smash against his mail fauld, trusting the enchanted armour to turn the blade aside. Then he slashed his sword across Tethyr's face. At the last moment the young highborn saw the danger and attempted to leap out of the way. The sword raked across Tethyr's cheek, spinning the druchii around and knocking him into Saarha's arms.

Tethyr sagged against the highborn. His sword arm drooped. With a trembling hand, he pushed himself away from Saarha and stared down at the hilt of the dagger protruding from a seam in his breastplate. He swayed on his feet. Slowly, his gaze rose to Saarha's face.

Saarha's expression was bleak. 'You, too, are just one man,' he said to Tethyr.

The young highborn toppled to the floor.

Saarha and Ashul exchanged looks, and then turned to regard Nuarc with cold, predatory eyes. 'You have some explaining to do,' he said.

Nuarc pulled his sword free from Teruvel's body. 'None of that matters so long as Malekith still reigns,' he said. 'Let's seize power first, then worry about what to do with it afterwards.'

* * *

THE DOORS TO the Court of Dragons were forged from solid blocks of iron more than twenty feet high, etched with coiling drakes.

Malekith's guards raised their weapons in salute as Nuarc, Saarha and Ashul approached with their men. Nuarc laid his hands on the great doors, and the mighty portal swung open on silent hinges.

The Witch King's throne room was no place for multitudes. The entire octagonal chamber was barely thirty paces across, its walls set with broad niches where stone dragons bowed in obeisance before the high throne at the far end of the room. Tall iron stands arrayed along the gleaming marble floor held aloft large witch light lamps that bathed the chamber in greenish light, but all of them combined paled before the terrible white light that seethed from its iron cage above the centre of the room. The Ainur Tel – the Eye of Fate – was a roughly faceted crystal the size of a small boulder set in a framework of enchanted iron. Legend had it that the crystal had come with the druchii out of lost Nagarythe, and before that it had been quarried from a mountain deep in the Chaos Wastes many thousands of years ago. A druchii of surpassing willpower could look upon any spot in the world with it, no matter how far away. The Eye hung from the ceiling by four enormous iron chains, raised to a level whereby the druchii seated on the high throne could view its depths at his whim.

Malekith the Witch King, tyrant of Naggaroth and bane of Ulthuan, sat upon a throne fashioned of razor-edged barbs, on a high dais that loomed from the shadows above the gleaming witch lamps. Shrouded in darkness, the Witch King's form was discernible only by the furnace-like glow seeping from the joints in his ancient armour and the oculars of his horned helmet.

A lesser druchii would have quailed in terror at the sight, but the old general was unfazed. Leading the conspirators, he marched stiffly to the foot of the throne and raised his face to the king.

'Speak to me, Nuarc,' the Witch King said in a voice of ringing iron.

Nuarc took a deep breath, feeling his heart labouring in his chest. He could sense the forces of destiny swirling around him like an invisible storm, propelling him onward. 'Eltharion and his men have entered the fortress,' he said, feeling a surge of triumph. 'He has come to finish what he began at the Dragon Gate.'

A fearful hiss rose from the depths of the Witch King's helmet. 'You have failed, me, old one,' the Witch King said. It was tantamount to a sentence of death.

'No, Malekith, it is *you* who have failed,' the scarred general fought back. 'You have brought us to the edge of a precipice in your blind war with Ulthuan, and your obsession with Eltharion has brought defeat and humiliation upon our warriors.' Now that the words had been spoken he found his courage increasing as the last elements of his plan fell neatly into place. 'For too long we have allowed you to rule unquestioned over the Land of Chill,' he declared. 'Well, that time is over. After leading our forces to defeat on our very shores, you have proven that you are no longer worthy to rule over us.' Nuarc turned and gestured at his fellow conspirators. 'It is our wish that you continue to hold your place as our father and protector, Malekith, but your time of unquestioned authority must end. We have agreed that you may remain as king over Naggaroth, but you must swear an oath to Khaine, here and now, that you will relinquish your temporal authority to us as your royal council. Otherwise, when Eltharion arrives you will have to face your destiny alone.'

The echoes of Nuarc's voice fell away, leaving only silence. There was no bellow of rage or torrent of fiery curses from the armoured form high above, and the old general knew he'd won.

Then Malekith began to laugh. It was the most terrible sound Nuarc had ever heard.

'You fool,' Malekith said, his cruel mirth raking at the stone walls. 'The great general has succumbed to the most elementary gambit of all.'

Nuarc's hand drifted to the hilt of his sword. 'What are you talking about?'

'Feigning weakness to lure one's enemy into the open,' the Witch King said. 'I suspected you for some time, Nuarc, but I wondered how deeply your conspiracy ran. Once I learned of Eltharion's coming I knew he would make a fine stalking horse to lure out my true foes.'

The world seemed to tilt away from Nuarc. He staggered, struggling to come to grips with what he'd learned. With a savage cry he drew his swords and raised them to the throne. 'If that is so, then you've outsmarted yourself and welcomed your own doom into your hall!' he said. 'There is still Eltharion to reckon with, and if the Swordmaster wounded you once, he can do so again.' Even as he spoke, shouts and the clash of steel echoed in the hall outside the throne room. 'He comes even now, Witch King,' the general said, steel creeping back into his voice. 'My offer still stands.'

'I have no interest in fighting the Swordmaster, here or anywhere else,' Malekith said. There was a creak of ancient armour as the Witch King rose from his deadly throne. 'If you are so eager to be reunited with your Ulthuan cousins, however, you are welcome to it.'

Before Nuarc could reply there was a clap of thunder and a flash of blue light that enveloped Malekith. When the light faded, the Witch King was gone.

Then the iron doors to the Court of Dragons swung open on silent hinges and the old general turned to meet his doom.

* * *

THE ELF SHIPS were beating out to sea, riding the iron grey waves as the sun set against the jagged mountains to the west. With luck and two weeks' hard sailing they would reach the Witch's Strait and then the open sea.

Invisible against the storm clouds high overhead, Malekith watched the two ships begin their long journey home. He imagined the weary sailors climbing the cold, wet shroud lines and staggering numbly across the deck, exhausted by days of hard fighting in a bleak and foreign land. Later, perhaps, they would sing of their triumph, having made a daring raid into the very heart of Naggaroth and lived to tell the tale. For now though, he expected that the victory had the taste of ashes to it.

For a spiteful instant he considered giving the great black dragon its head and swooping down on the hapless elves, turning their boats, and their hopes, to ash and cinders. Yet he contained himself. Better by far that the blind Swordmaster return to court and fester there, fuelled by sweet hatred and tempted by the possibility of even greater triumphs to come.

Alone and safe from prying eyes and ears, the Witch King admitted to himself that he'd played the gambit a bit too close to the edge. He'd never imagined that Eltharion would know about the Eye of Fate, much less grasp how to use it. But for Alith Anar, the Swordmaster might have dealt the druchii people a mortal blow. The thought that he owed a debt to the Shadow Warrior curdled Malekith's insides. One day he would repay it in fountains of blood.

The elves of Ulthuan were worthy foes, Malekith thought. In fact, he'd counted upon it. He'd known all along that Nuarc had been right. Naggaroth was vulnerable, and once the Phoenix Court realised it, the elves would stir themselves and mount a real invasion. And that was something he dearly wished to see. He had learned to his bitter regret how costly such an effort could be. Instead of striking out at Ulthuan again and again, he would draw them to Naggaroth and let the elves bleed away their strength on his cold and lonely shores.

Malekith watched the two elf ships racing west into the welcoming darkness and laughed into the icy wind.

ABOUT THE AUTHORS

Jesse Cavazos V

Jesse Cavazos V was born and raised in the American South-West, where he has been repeatedly forced to endure the big hats for which the region is renowned for. In his free time he plays both Warhammer and Warhammer 40,000.

Steven Eden

Steven Eden was born in 1960 and grew up on airforce bases around the world. He has served in the US Army since 1982 and will be retiring this summer. His published work includes several non-fiction articles and two books of military history. This is his first work of published fiction.

Nick Kyme

Nick Kyme hails from Grimsby, a small town on the east coast of England. Nick moved to Nottingham in 2003 to work on White Dwarf magazine, then moved to the Black Library. His writing credits include several short stories and the Necromunda novel *Back From The Dead*.

Mike Lee

Over the last eight years Mike Lee has contributed to almost two-dozen role-playing games and supplements. Together with Dan Abnett, he has written five Darkblade novels. An avid wargamer and devoted fan of pulp adventure, Mike lives in the United States.

Nathan Long

Nathan Long was a screenwriter for fifteen years, during which time he had three movies made and a handful of live-action and animated TV episodes produced. He is now a freelance novelist. He has written three Blackhearts novels, and has taken over the Gotrek and Felix series. He lives in Hollywood.

Steven Savile
British author Steven Savile is an expert in cult fiction, having written a wide variety of sf, fantasy and horror stories, as well as a slew of editorial work on anthologies in the UK and USA. He won the L. Ron Hubbard Writers of the Future award in 2002, and has been nominated three times for the Bram Stoker award. He currently lives in Stockholm, Sweden.

Robert E. Vardeman
Robert E. Vardeman is the author of over a hundred novels, ranging from science fiction to fantasy, from westerns to action/adventure and mystery novels. Vardeman is a long-time resident of Albuquerque, NM, graduating from the University of New Mexico with a B.S. in physics and an M.S. in Materials Engineering.

Rick Wolf
Rick Wolf grew up in the late 80s reading Warhammer stories and is delighted to be able to contribute one of his own many years later. This is his first published story. He currently lives with an understanding cat.

Chris Wraight
Chris Wraight is a freelance writer and teacher currently living and working in Oxford. He is a long time fan of Games Workshop background art and fiction.

Bloody tales of heroism from the gothic world of Warhammer

By popular demand we've collected some of the
best fantasy short stories ever written for
the Black Library into one mighty tome. A great
introduction to the Warhammer world.

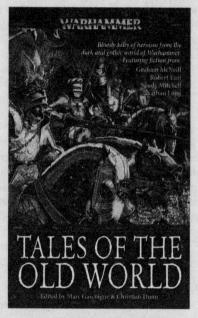

Tales of the Old World
ISBN 13: 978-1-84416-452-3
ISBN 10: 1-84416-452-7

*Read extracts from the book and buy it now
from www.blacklibrary.com
or by calling +44 (0)115 900 4144*